Trouble Out West

Six weeks surviving rattlesnakes, cowboy
pranks, the ghost of General Custer and
the girls on the corner.

Moynihan
2018

Written and Illustrated by
Kate Moynihan

Note from the Author

I lived in the wide-open spaces of Bismarck, North Dakota,
more than twenty years ago — and that's probably twice as
old as you are, young reader! Because of all the time that has
passed, you can imagine that many little things have changed
about that place. The public swimming pools I write about,
for instance, now offer splash pads to play on instead of the
mile-high diving boards they used to have. Also back then,
way long ago, video-game rentals were super-cheap at five for
five dollars. Not bad! Because the fun of this kind of fiction
is to mix the old memories with things from the present day,
some stories in this book have stayed true to how things used
to be, back when I lived in the Dakotas, while others have
been changed. Like all stories in fiction, many things in the
storytelling are made up a little bit to make them especially fun
for the reader.

A special thanks here to the Bismarck community for supporting my art business during those years. Governor George Sinner was in office at the time, and it was North Dakota First Lady Jane Sinner who gave my family the tour of their home. St. Alexius Medical Center published "Alex the Cat" and his coloring books. Med Center One, U.S. Healthcare, Kirkwood Medical Center, and the south-side Main Street McDonald's were just a few of the Bismarck-area businesses that purchased my artwork during those early years. Additionally, Bismarck Art and Gallery Association hosted a number of shows for me, along with the summer art fair on the Capitol Grounds, even when it was in the pouring rain.

I cannot begin to thank all the people who collected as many as four or five of my paintings in their home. My landlord, Marge Brandt, was never Mad Witch. She, too, was one of my biggest fans. Steve Tomac was the boys' rodeo hero. Finally, but in no particular order, I thank Dr. Michael Goebel and his wife, Karen, who lived next door with their four sons. Having best friends right in the neighborhood was a dream come true, and the license plate on their always-in-motion blue minivan summed up the memories of that happy time: SCORE4BOYS!

I did eventually move back to my birth state of Michigan, hanging my artist brush in a lovely space in downtown Holland, a city about the same size as Bismarck. I traded mud sliding at the Missouri River for riding the surf of Great Lake Michigan. I married "the big guy," Larry, and to this day he still calls both of the boys: "Son." We enjoy having family and grandkids nearby.

Table of Contents

Chapter 1

Jam-packed From the Start

A frightful squawk echoes around us as the airport luggage conveyor belt jerks along and then spits out my bulging black suitcase. The beast of a bag bowls its way down the chute, thumping end over end toward me. I grab the handle and heave "the beast" onto an airport luggage cart – but I've forgotten to lock the wheels! Instantly, the cart jets across the baggage-claim area.

"Watch out!" I yell as I chase after it, running full tilt, my feet pounding as loud as my heart.

Mom and my older brother, Brian, do a double mouth drop, too surprised to budge.

"Eeek!" I hear a scream in the crowd.

"Quick, move out of the way, Ruby-Mae!" It's a round little man shouting now. Hurriedly, his chubby arms scoop up an even shorter, gray-haired lady. The out-of-control cart misses them by inches.

Frantically catching up, I latch onto the cart handlebars, but the cart is still flying full throttle and I can't stop it. My shoes squeal, sliding on the smooth floor. The cart and I sail another five feet before I screech to a stop.

"Dang young whippersnappers," the round man remarks.

"I'm sorry," I say, feeling my face turn so red I think my ears are on fire. I keep my head down, knowing everyone is looking at me. Trouble just seems to find me.

Slow and steady this time, I steer the cart. My snail-like pace gives the gray-haired couple a chance to peacefully wander away. As for Mom, well let's just say she doesn't look happy at the moment.

"What's that awful scraping sound?" Mom asks, hearing the cart make a metal-on-metal, rattling racket as I bulldoze it across baggage claim.

"Adam's suitcase is dragging a bit," Brian is quick to point out. "He had to use the metal combination lock from his school locker just to get that thing shut."

Mom raises an eyebrow and gives me one of her silent stares. Her jaw is set tight and her lips draw into a straight severe line. This is the complete opposite of the sweet look she gave me only moments earlier, when Brian and I met up with her on our arrival. Spotting us, she had let out a crazy shout of glee and then hugged me so tight her shoulder-length brown hair tickled my face.

But now, after being on the ground for less than five minutes, I'm already in trouble.

"Uh ... Sorry about the monster suitcase, Mom. But ... um ... I couldn't decide what to pack," I stammer, still unsure if I had brought the right stuff for a six-week summer vacation to a place I've never been before – Bismarck, North Dakota. I'll be ten years old in three days, and I crave my stuff – so flying with a two-bag limit made for some tough choices: baseball mitt or swim fins, skateboard or walkie-talkies.

My name, by the way, is Adam Moynihan. I'm used to spending long summer vacations with Mom and Brian, but in previous years we've used Papa's camper and had our adventures at Muskegon State Park back in Michigan. The park is near Dad's house, where Brian and I live during the school year.

In the past, while camping, Mom has chewed me out numerous times about cramming too much stuff into the tiny camper drawers. Now, looking at her pinched face, I can imagine her same words scolding me for over-packing. The Beast sits on the cart in front of us, bulging as if the seams will give way any second.

Trying to stay out of trouble, I draw attention away from the jam-packed bag, saying, "The flight was awesome. I liked the fire-shooting flames from the roaring engines."

3

"Yeah," Brian says, "the lift-off torque rumbled so loud, it vibrated the entire cabin on takeoff!"

I roll my eyes. I've been blasted with big words like *turbine, torque, accelerate, and velocity* all afternoon. My brother has really been getting into this flying thing.

"Sounds like it was a great flight," Mom says. The look on her face clearly softens as she tosses an arm around my shoulder and pulls me close into a cuddly hug. I can tell she's forgotten about the runaway suitcase and is settling herself a little from waiting for our flight. I think she got nervous about this being the first vacation we traveled to her house all the way out to Bismarck – almost one thousand miles from Grand Rapids. I don't understand why she was worried. We were buckled in good and tight – and they served us root beer the entire flight.

Now we are on the lookout for Brian's suitcase, and the luggage carousel is a sea of checked items spinning round and round.

"Which bag is yours, Brian?" Mom asks.

"It's coming up next," Brian calls out as he snatches his bag, which is pint-size compared to mine, and tosses it one-handed on top of The Beast on the airport cart. The impact of his lightweight suitcase doesn't even cause the cart to budge.

I give a huff and push the clanging, two-ton cart toward the wide open space of the airport lobby.

"Look up," Brian says and points to the expansive ceiling. My eyes follow his hand up ... and up. Far above, the ceiling is painted all blue with marshmallow clouds to make it look like the sky.

"Sky's the limit," Mom almost sings the words as she refers to what the local folks call the terminal's ceiling. Leave it to the artist in Mom to get excited about a ceiling. I have to admit, though, it's pretty cool.

"Hey, Brian, I bet if I fired my slingshot, the acorn bullet wouldn't even come close to hitting this ceiling, it's so high," I say as my voice echoes up and across the gigantic space.

But my brother has wandered ahead. "The mural is 57 feet above our heads," he says, reading aloud from an information sign. I stroll over and he ad-libs, "That's half as tall as the Stratosphere in Las Vegas."

Brian is Mr. Fact Finder; put him on Jeopardy and he would win first place. Me? I'd be happy just to ride the Stratosphere's X-Scream rollercoaster, and I'm still wishing I had brought my slingshot to go for that ceiling.

Now, back at the cart, I nudge it toward the parking lot. Automatic doors slide open, and I wrestle the heavy cart over the rubber indoor/outdoor floor pads. Once outside, we gaze at miles of brilliant blue sky all around, just like the painting inside. And the sun, even though it's five o'clock, is high in the sky, making me squint.

Then, without warning, the wind whips up. A gust shakes the cart and swirls around me like a tornado cloud, spitting gritty sand in my face. I cough, choking on the brown dust.

"Did you bring your bandana?" Mom asks.

"A what?"

"Bandana, Adam, like the cowboys wear in old Westerns," Brian says.

"Are we robbing a bank?" I ask, scratching my head in confusion.

Suddenly Mom is laughing. And not a soft giggle. No, this is a full-bodied laugh that makes her blue eyes sparkle and her face light up.

"You don't need the bandana for a disguise," Brian says. "You need it to keep dust and dirt from going up your nose." His grin is so big it splits his face.

I may have missed Mom's joke, but her laugh and Brian's smile are catchy. I chuckle too.

Brian easily tosses his bag into Mom's van. I grab the handle of The Beast, give it a big jerk – and it whacks Brian in the knees.

"Ouch!" he moans. "Why'd you pack all seven books of your fantasy series?"

"I had to," I explain. "What if there aren't any kids to play with at Mom's house?"

Mom's house. The words stick in my throat. When Mom talks about Bismarck, her stories are ho-hum grown-up stuff like work or shopping. There's nothing about what kids do in North Dakota. Is it like when we go camping and hunt for night crawlers for fishing off a Lake Michigan pier?

Riding co-pilot now in the van, I watch a blur of brown fields rush by the window. The land is dead grass with a few rocks mixed in. It's flat as an empty roller rink. There's not even a rolling hill, which tells me we won't be dirt biking up sand dunes or anything. And without many trees anywhere here, I know there won't be rope swings or acorn ammo for any slingshot.

Restless, I squirm in my seat as we ride along. The thought of not having any lakes or ponds sends more than a hundred tingling pinpricks of worry to my already squeezed-in-the-airplane-seat numb butt.

"What's that white speck out there, Mom?" Brian asks. We both squint at the only dot on the brown horizon.

"It looks as tiny as a cargo barge way out on Lake Michigan," I say, mentioning the Great Lake and longing for the body surfing I usually do in the summer.

"That's the North Dakota State Capitol building," Mom tells us. "At 19 stories high, it's the tallest building around. I live near that skyscraper so keep your eyes on the white target and we'll find our way home."

It turns out Mom's right. All we do is look out across the flat land and watch as the white dot grows bigger with every mile. Along a two-lane highway, the van rolls closer to Mom's home. In the wide-open fields here, the only "trees" are the telephone poles. Occasionally a tumbleweed sails by. I wonder what I'll do in a place that looks like an empty bowling alley. My heart starts drumming: boom, boom, boom. Dread of my archenemy – boredom – creeps into my thinking.

Soon I rub my eyes and look closer ahead. It's not a mirage, it's real. Shapes appear ... a barn ... and a farmhouse. Shortly, I see clumps of buildings, traffic lights. Trees, too!

"This is downtown Bismarck, where I live," Mom says playing the travel-tour guide. "And over there is the library. You'll be able to walk to it from our house." It's a gray, no-frills building with L-I-B-R-A-R-Y in big chunky letters carved in stone across the entrance.

Then I spot a movie rental store. In my book that's a lot better than the library.

We turn into a neighborhood jam-packed with large, older-looking houses. They're shaded by tall trees so big their trunks force huge cracks in the sidewalk – which is not too good for skateboarding, I pause to think.

Mom pulls into the driveway of a boxy, two-story yellow house with fancy trim. With the houses standing so closely together, there are no side yards, meaning no room to play baseball. And the front yard is so small I wouldn't even earn two dollars mowing it. It makes me wonder what we will do at Mom's house. I brought as much stuff as I could, but my stomach tightens as I wonder if it'll be enough. I still haven't spotted any kids.

We park now. Glad to be free from all the sitting, I snag my backpack, dash out of the van and hustle up the front door steps, practically tap-dancing on a cement porch that is so small I barely fit. I wish Mom would hurry to let me in. I can't wait to see our new bedroom.

"Wrong door," Mom calls, "I live all the way around the back." This house is so big it has *two* apartments!

I scramble down the front steps, hustle along the driveway, turn a corner, fly over three small steps, and discover the rear entrance. I twist the knob and the door flies open. I freeze. Is this the right place?

From behind, Brian bumps into me, followed by Mom. Brian's mouth drops open, too, as we scan the beehive of action. It's Mom's art studio.

"Howdy, Brian. Evening, Adam," an older lady says. Her short white hair stands on end and reminds me of a bottle brush.

"Hey, you guys," says a gal with a yellow pencil tucked beside her ear. She waves us into the studio with a bright-white smile.

I grin, realizing Mom has told them we were coming. I've never shared a home with Mom's studio. And this one is bigger than the art room at school. I knew Mom earned her living as an artist, but this makes my head spin.

The buzz of activity continues as I step into the large room with Brian and Mom behind me. Swoosh. I turn toward the sound and see a long blade, like a small sword, being guided by Bottle Brush Lady. As she forces the heavy blade down, it slices paper into small pieces. The trimming machine is the size of a toaster oven and sits on a surface that is bigger than a Ping-Pong table. Clamp lights drape over it like octopus arms, providing light for a project.

Bottle Brush Lady finishes her cutting and looks up from her work.

"Boys," Mom says, "this is Laurie."

Laurie nods, giving us a wink.

"And this is Bobby-Jean," she says, turning toward the brown-haired gal at a different table. The pencil behind her ear bobs as Bobby-Jean raises her eyes to meet our glance.

"Well, yee-haw," she bellows. "Your mom has been chattering like a chipmunk for days about you boys coming to visit. It's mighty fine ... it's mighty fine indeed to have you boys here."

Bobby-Jean is clipping small papers to a funny-looking rack. The rack is like a large wooden cage with yards of kite string wrapped around it. Bobby-Jean carefully handles one of the small squares of paper by the edges. It's wet with paint. She clips one corner, and the paper square gently swings from the rack. There must be more than a hundred little papers clipped onto the rack to dry.

All during the introductions, Brian and I are stuck in place like we landed in cement. Now, Brian turns to Mom and asks, "Does everyone in North Dakota live like this?" I sense that even Brian, who can solve the most difficult puzzles, is wondering about our new home, too.

Mom smiles. "Keep going," she says, poking me to move forward.

I tote the backpack through the art studio maze, pressing forward into the long, narrow space. As I make my way to the kitchen, the windows become smaller, telling me we're deep into the basement of this big, old house. From here, I see what looks like Mom's bedroom, and across from it, a bathroom. My stomach does a flip-flop. I can't tell if there is a place for us.

"Hey, Adam, check this out," Brian says.

I follow the sound of his voice, creeping through a doorway that is tucked around a corner off the kitchen.

"It's the Nintendo player Mom brings when she visits us," Brian says, turning on the game console in the out-of-the-way room.

I drop the backpack, eyes zeroed-in on the video console. I grab the controller – a familiar favorite of mine. My fingers move like lightning across the buttons, making Mario leap, twirl, hop, and dance. "Hey, look ... my magic touch works in Bismarck, too," I snicker at Brian as I soar ahead.

After beating Level One of Mario, I take a minute to look around. It's a small room, fairly dark, tucked in the back corner of the basement. It's kind of mystical. What grabs my attention is a really cushy rug under my feet. Then, on the wall, I notice a huge Detroit Tigers baseball poster, my preferred team after the Chicago Cubs.

"Look at the best part, Adam," Brian says. "A hide-a-bed. It's a couch to play on during the day, and at night, it unfolds into a bed. Pretty cool."

"I found something better," I say, reaching out and giving it a push. A door swings shut completely sealing off the kitchen.

It's dead silent. We're completely separated from the buzz in the art studio. And, better yet ... we have privacy from the chatty grown-ups, including Mom.

In the hushed hidden room, I inch closer to Brian. "This is a secret place like Batman's bat cave," I whisper.

"We need a Keep Out sign for our hide-out," Brian says, and he quickly finds colored paper and markers from a drawer below the game console. Mom has stocked all the things we like.

"Yeah, we need rules for someone to follow before they can enter," I say.

Brian writes as I rattle off the rules:

* *No one 35 or older is allowed to enter without permission.*
* *You must know the secret password to enter.*
* *Never be polite.*
* *No bad gas.*

I tape the list of rules to the kitchen-side of the door. The isolated room is officially our wondrous Bat Cave; ten times better than a secret clubhouse.

Brian nudges me, "Earth to Adam," he says, snapping his fingers in front of my face. "It's time to get the suitcases from the van."

Jeepers, I think, shaking my head. My brother's promptness and attention to detail could earn him a merit badge in Boy

Scouts. But as Brian heads out the door, I stay to loaf a few minutes longer. I enjoy being tucked away inside the depths of this old house that comes with a game console, unlike my room at home. Wait until I tell my friends back home.

I'm so excited I hadn't even noticed the washer, dryer, furnace, and hot water heater in a corner. Until now. No big deal, I think. Having a bedroom as a secret cave that's secluded from adults is pretty swell, even if it is the apartment utility room.

* * *

When I finally wander out to the van, I snatch Brian's suitcase. Lucky for me, it's the one on top. That's when I feel a tug at my pant leg, causing me to look down. I can't believe it. Right at my feet is a small, very bouncy brown and white puppy with a pink collar. Releasing my pant leg, the pup yips and yaps, and her tail wags wildly the entire time.

"Hey, little gal," I say, reaching out my hand. She takes a quick sniff and then spins in a circle, chasing her tail. I mosey down the driveway with Brian's suitcase. The pup is eager to come along, trotting at my heels.

"I've made a friend, Mom," I say, opening the apartment door. Instantly, the puppy sprints through the studio, whizzing past Mom and the helpers. I hustle to catch up to her, finding her in our hideout – the Bat Cave – where she springs into my arms, knocking the suitcase and me to the floor. I squirm as the pup prances on my face and her tongue licks my ear. It tickles and makes me giggle. Her fur is soft and incredibly huggable.

"I can't wait to show you to my brother," I say to this new frisky friend. "Brian must be getting the last load from the van. Let's go find him." I scramble to my feet and head out of the room, passing through the kitchen-studio with the dog following my every move.

Once outside, I hear someone calling, "Annie! ... Annie!"

Rounding the corner of the driveway, I look up and see a boy about my age. Brown hair pokes out from a Minnesota Twins ball cap.

"Hi. My name's Zach Grunner. And that's my dog Annie," he says, pointing downward, as the pup is now weaving in and out between our legs, her tail wagging nonstop.

"I'm Adam Moynihan," I say while scanning the kid from his ball cap to his toes. Hmm ... I think, he has on some nifty shoes, with his right foot worn, meaning it's his kick-off foot for skateboarding, just like me.

Zach sees me looking at his roughed-up right shoe. He wiggles his foot and his toe almost pokes out of the ragged shoe. "I love to skateboard. Do you have a board?"

I am so glad he asked. I have a top-notch "anti-gravity" board, spring loaded for extra pop. The deck is fiberglass and light as air, and the graffiti-like graphics look as if they are part of the board, not a peel-and-stick decal. But it's at Dad's house. So I play it cool. "Yeah," I say, "I have a board, but it's back in Michigan."

It turns out Zach is as friendly as his dog. "I can't wait to have you meet my brother, Brian," I say. I let out a big sigh of relief because the worry of no kids in North Dakota is no more.

I wave good-bye for now and head to the van for my mammoth bag: The Beast. I push it out the van door, and it tumbles onto the driveway with a thud. Grabbing the handle, I walk backward to drag The Beast up the drive. The combination lock rattles as it scrapes on the cement, but I keep going, eager to find Brian to tell him about Zach and Annie. I roll the suitcase down the three steps, shove it through the doorway, and then push it across the studio carpet, gaining speed as I go. The suitcase is moving like an out-of-control freight train.

"I met the kid next door," I say to Brian as I plow The Beast into the Bat Cave.

"I met him too," he says.

"We can play with his dog Annie," I say.

"I didn't meet a dog yet," Brian says. "When I went outside to get the suitcases, a basketball bounced over, so I scooped it up. Then, a kid from next door came looking for it. He laughed when I told him we had the same brand. Next, he showed me the basketball hoop in his backyard. It's right behind the tall, wooden fence."

"I didn't see the basketball hoop," I say.

"Let's go see if we can find Joey," Brian says.

"His name isn't Joey," I say. "It's Zach."

"Does he have brown hair?"

"He sure does."

Brian scratches his head. I'm confused, too. Brian thinks I don't listen very well back in school, but I know the boy said his name was Zach. I'll bet my entire savings account on it – even though I've lost a few bets before.

Brian and I head out of the apartment, and just as we turn the corner, we bump into two boys. Joey and Zach! They're brothers, both with brown hair.

I think I'm going to like it here.

Chapter 2

Getting to Know Big Muddy

Trying to cool down, I wave a fan made out of glued-up Popsicle sticks. Yesterday I was a little embarrassed to use this preschool-looking craft project. Today I'm wilting in Mom's non-air conditioned basement apartment as I suck in air as hot as steaming soup. I now understand our new friend Joey's excitement about his Popsicle stick fan. The homemade gift was a welcoming present from Joey, our next-door neighbor, who is seven. "It's part of a North Dakota summer survival kit," he said, with a beaming smile as he presented the gift.

I'm furiously waving the fan now, but really, it only swishes hot air around. I fetch an ice cube from the freezer and pop it into my mouth. A cold trickle slides down my throat. I bite, and little icy chips swirl through my teeth, melting quickly in my hot mouth.

Wondering if it might be cooler outside, I wander through the art studio toward the back door. Unlike yesterday, when the studio was a hum of activity, today it's silent. Saturday is Mom's helpers' day off. Not a creature or contraption is stirring.

I step outside onto the cement pad that serves as a tiny entryway to the studio. Instantly I feel the heat from the concrete sizzling through my gym shoes. Lifting my foot, I see a semi-melted wad of gum stretching like pizza cheese from where it's stuck in the grooves on the sole of my shoe. It sure isn't any cooler out here.

With the blazing sun beating down on my head, I feel as dried up as the little patch of dead lawn that makes up the placemat-size backyard. An old garage barely fits inside the yard. With the houses wedged closely together – city living-style – there isn't a puff of a breeze between the houses to rescue me from the heat.

On tiptoes, and squinting against the sunlight, I stretch my neck trying to see over the fenced-in yards. Maybe I'll glimpse a swimming pool somewhere in the neighborhood. Nope. Frantically, I flutter the fan I'm still carrying. How will I ever cool off in this scorching city?

Then, like she was reading my mind or something, Mom pokes her head out the apartment door. "Let's go to the river," she says.

"What river?" I ask.

"The Missouri, of course," she says to this new kid in town.

Truth be told, the only thing I know about the Missouri River is that Lewis and Clark followed it centuries ago as they explored America and looked for the Northwest Passage. But what they mostly found was the killer smallpox disease. A wave of panic runs up my spine.

Mom tells me more about the Missouri, saying, "We'll have fun, Adam. Everyone goes to the river to swim and cool off."

Cool off! The magic words snap me out of my trance. I'm thinking clearly again, realizing the dreadful smallpox was more than 200 years ago. Then I notice that Mom is way ahead of us because she's already in a bathing suit, flip flops, and a sun hat. "Let's go to the beach!" I sing out while dashing into the apartment to look for Brian.

I find him playing a video game in the privacy of the Bat Cave; I spill the news about going to the river.

"Where do you keep the sand toys, Mom?" Brian asks. "I'll pack them up."

"We won't need any beach toys," Mom says.

"But how can I bury Brian in the sand without a pail and shovel?" I ask, thinking about a favorite Lake Michigan sport – which is burying Brian neck-deep so he can't budge. It's the only time he can't bug me.

"Adam, you can't bury Brian," Mom replies, crushing my fantasy.

"Why not?" I'm still hoping for a chance to get the upper hand on my brother.

"Because there isn't any sand," she says.

"Ah ... I get it," I say, forcing a chuckle. "This is another joke, like the bandana trick when I thought it was for bank robbers." Mom is a good sport about us boys clowning around. Sometimes, like now, she has a trick up her sleeve, too. She says it adds spice to our life.

"There's no trick, Adam," she says on her way out the door. "There just isn't any sand along the river; now hurry up and get your swimsuit on. I'll meet you outside at the van."

While trying to believe it's no joke about no sand along the Missouri, I hear the back door close behind Mom. I'm alone with my thoughts.

Cripes. No sand? Even Grandma Barb's Florida beach has crunchy sand made from crushed seashells. Maybe the Missouri River is full of rocks. My heart lifts as I imagine myself climbing huge boulders. Then I remember the hot sun. Ninety-three degrees will bake the rocks, making my bare feet sizzle like eggs frying in a pan. I wonder if Lewis and Clark were this disappointed, too.

Beep, beep! The van horn snaps me out of my daze. In a flash, I change into a bathing suit and dash out the door to pile into the co-pilot seat next to Mom. Brian rides in the back. We're off to the crazy, no-sand river.

Once we are beyond Mom's neighborhood, the city sidewalks end and the land unfolds into those endless, wide-open brown fields. Traveling on, the van starts climbing a small hill. Once at the top, we coast through a valley of small rolling hills.

Mom lowers her window and a rush of hot air sails inside. She raises her chin high into the breeze, and her dark sunglasses flash in the bright sun. She smiles like a homecoming queen sitting on a float in a parade. Then, she does a dippy hand wave out the window.

Suddenly, I hear a snicker. It's Brian, hand over mouth, hiding a laugh. "It's a good thing there's no one else on these country roads," Brian whispers.

I give him a nod. The only thing that could make Mom look sillier would be if the van was covered in tissue pom-pom flowers. Maybe the no-sand Missouri isn't a joke, but Mom has found another way to clown around.

The van cruises up a gradual slope until we reach the top of the rise. Unexpectedly, there is an enormous patch of blue stretching out before us. It's not the sky, but the Missouri River shining brilliantly blue. It shimmers brighter than the neon blue of the Chicago Cubs away-game jerseys. But not only does the river stretch miles long, it's super wide. The far riverbank is more than a football field away.

Mom parks along the shoreline, and I swing the door open, ready to race to the water to cool off. Stepping out, my feet hit the ground with a slap. Yikes. Wet mud squishes between my toes.

"Big Muddy," Mom says. "The Sioux Indians nicknamed the river."

"They certainly gave it a proper name," I say as my feet smack the wet ground, leaving a trail of footprints in the mushy mud as I race to the river.

Anxious to cool off, I don't hesitate to plunge into the water. Instantly the shock jolts to my eyeballs and I see stars. The water is freezing! In seconds I'm blue like a grape Popsicle. I dash out, teeth chattering. The only thing worse would be to walk barefoot in a blizzard. My excitement to cool off in this river quickly melts away. Yet it takes only seconds for the hot sun to begin to bake my bare shoulders. The contrast of the heat makes the river water seem even icier.

I look down the length and width of the river, and I see it's a sea of activity – a summer Saturday on The Big Muddy. Speedboats whiz up and down, jet skis buzz in circles, and fishing boats bob in place. Pontoon boats, too. Back home, I call them party boats because music floats across the lake as they putter along. That's my idea of cooling off, but sadly I don't know anyone with a boat in Bismarck.

Mom is now at my side as we stand along the riverbank. That's when we hear Brian call, "Adam! Over here ..."

My brother has wandered farther down the shoreline and away from the river bank. He is surrounded by the muddy beach but is standing knee-deep in a giant puddle of water. Mom and I give him a big wave.

"Brian's found one of the secrets of the Missouri River," she says. "The strong current keeps shifting parts of the shoreline and trapping small pools of water. They form little sandbar islands like this."

"It's like bathwater in here, Adam!" Brian shouts, splattering water over his head and having a splish-splashing good time cooling off.

Hearing the words "bath water" warms my heart. Fast as a racehorse, I dash toward Brian. Headfirst, I dive into the gigantic puddle. Water sprays as I slide across the shallow, silky bottom. I stand up; my belly is grizzly-bear brown as mud clings to me all over.

"This is better than sliding into home plate!" I squeal. "Come on! Let's see who can slide the farthest."

We dart out of the water and sprint ten yards for a running start. "On your mark ... Get set ... Go!" I holler.

We're off, eyes glued on the near edge of the long, narrow pool. At water's edge, we leap, fly through the air, and then hit the water like missiles skimming the surface. We glide a hundred feet as mud splats into every pore of our skin. Once landed, we roll like pigs in a muddy pen, and we don't even care who won the race.

Catching our breath, Brian and I sit at the edge of the shallow pool. I reach into the water and grab a handful of sludge. "Have you ever had a mudpack?" I ask my brother, slapping a handful of mud onto the top of his head. Mud drips down his cheeks and off his nose.

"No, I've never had a mudpack, Adam." He scoops a pile of mud and slaps it onto my back.

Smack. Slap. Splat. Within minutes we're totally covered in mud, looking like two brown river rats.

"Hey, Adam. I can only see the whites of your eyes," Brian chuckles.

"Watch this," I say, dropping back into the warmth of the pool water. One quick swish and I'm crystal-clean.

"Yeah, this is better than taking a bath. All without soap," Brian says, flopping back and rinsing off.

I make another mudpack and then throw my Moynihan straight-curve baseball pitch – the throw that never curves, no matter how hard I try. I'm famous for this curve that isn't really a curve. Just as the mud ball speeds through the air, Brian is sitting up – and it smacks him dead center on his chest.

Before I can blink, Brian zings a mud ball at me. I crouch low and duck out of the line of fire.

"You'll never hit me, Spaghetti Arm!" I holler, running away to get out of his range. Brian has a noodle arm when he throws long distances. It's why he plays second base in baseball, not the outfield.

But Brian whips the mud bullet at me before I can get too far. I'm a goner, I think. Luckily, the mud doesn't pack very well; it's too wet and soupy. His shot falls into pieces before it can zap me. Instead, I'm sprinkled in gooey buckshot. No cannonball from Brian this time. Laughing, I dip into the warm pool again.

It no longer matters that the sun is like a blow torch beating down on us because Big Muddy is North Dakota's secret to staying cool.

*　　*　　*

After a great Saturday afternoon of fun, the sun starts to hang lower in the sky. We grab the beach towels and start heading to the van. Out of the corner of my eye, I see a pontoon boat filled with people whooping and hollering from the river. Oddly, they seem to be waving at us.

"Are they your friends, Mom?" I ask, since I hardly know anyone in North Dakota.

The pontoon draws closer and we read the name on its side: Little Muddy. Oh, I get it; it goes with the Missouri's Big Muddy nickname.

"Yip, yip," a small dog barks from the boat, its stubby tail wagging so fast I think its butt might fall off. Then the frisky pup spins in circles, yapping all the while.

"Hey! Moynihans!" they yell, pumping their hands wildly in the air. It's our new friends we met yesterday – the boys who live next door to Mom's house, Zach and Joey, and Mr. Grunner, plus their pup, Annie.

I'm stunned our new friends have a boat, and even more stunned that they found us along the endless miles of the Missouri. My eyes fix on the boat, watching it putt-putt up to shore. Its engine gives a little cough, and exhaust fumes fill my nose with the smell of oil. This is so cool, I think, gurgling with excitement.

"We're having Boys' Night Out. Do you want to come along?" Zach asks Brian and me.

I've never ridden on a river before, so my heart practically leaps out of my chest. I can tell Zach is excited, too. His eyeglasses slip to the end of his nose, and they wiggle as his head nods up and down, signaling yes, yes, yes!

Without hesitating, I dash for the boat. As I hop on board, Annie springs into my arms. If I had a tail, it'd be wagging, too.

"Can we go on a boat ride?" Brian asks.

Uh-oh. Instantly, I realize I'm in the doghouse for forgetting to ask Mom's permission. I bury my face in Annie's fur. Maybe if Mom can't see me, she'll forget I wasn't polite enough to ask for the go-ahead.

I hold my breath, waiting for Brian's charm to win her over, but I can't take it any longer and peek with one eye to check on Mom. Her eyes are laser-locked on me.

"I'll have them home before dark," Zach's Dad says, glancing down at his shiny, all-metal watch. It's huge, like a car's silvery hubcap. Maybe it has special boating signals. But the fancy watch doesn't wow Mom.

Ignoring Zach's dad for the moment, her eyes stay fixed on me. I can tell she's waiting for me to remember my manners.

"Sorry, Mom, I got so excited I forgot to ask permission before I hopped in the boat," I say, backpedaling.

Annie, still in my arms, yips and wiggles her whole body in excitement. I don't know if Annie's silliness or my apology wins over Mom, but something softens her. A corner of her mouth tips into a smile. "Have fun!" she sings out to all of us.

I blow out a sigh of relief, which is strong enough to fluff Annie's fur. Then she yips, again. I swear she is smiling, too.

"We'll have a great time," Zach's dad says to Mom. For the first time I notice he's tall ... six feet at least. His square shoulders hang over me and I can see up his nose. It's a little scary. But then when he speaks, his voice is soft and smooth as syrup. It's so friendly, it warms me up inside.

"And don't forget to wear life jackets," Mom adds, always thinking about safety.

"Absolutely. I'm Captain Mike, and everyone wears a life jacket," Zach's dad says, locking a finger through a strap of his own life jacket and giving its buckle a hefty tug. "The mighty Missouri is a rapid flowing river," he says, having turned to talk to my brother and me.

Until now I hadn't noticed the water really is furiously flowing. These are not gentle ripples from a ruffling wind. The river is moving like a race car at full throttle. In fact, the current is so strong Captain Mike's arm muscles bulge as his hands clench the side of the boat to hold it steady waiting for my brother to climb aboard.

Brian grabs a handrail and hops on.

"Say goodbye to your sandbar pool," Zach says to Brian and me.

"Why?" I ask.

"The river current is so strong it shifts the sandbars almost every day," Zach says.

"You mean we won't be able to swim here tomorrow?" I ask, pointing to the pool Brian and I were sliding in.

"Negative," Zach says, using an army-like word. Since yesterday, I've learned Zach likes to toss in military terms. To me, it makes him sound important and makes me feel a bit more in awe of my new friend.

"But you'll find another sandbar, and it'll be just as fun!" Zach adds. "They're one of the surprises of the Missouri."

Mom calls goodbye from shore, waving her arm high above her head. I wave back as she turns toward the van to drive home.

"Let me help you into a life jacket." Zach drapes a jacket over my head and tugs at the straps, making them snug around my chest. It fits tighter than a necktie that Mom choke-holds around me for church. It's worth it, though, for a ride on the mighty Missouri.

With the life jacket secure I take a moment to look around the boat. It's loaded with a cooler of drinks, chilled in ice. Nearby, four fancy fishing rods are secured in a rack along the rear railing. Also tied down is a suitcase-size tackle box. Through its clear plastic lid, I see brightly colored fake-fish lures with crazy hooks poking every which way. The hooks look big enough to catch a man-eating shark. But a shark lives in the salt water, of course, so I wonder for a moment what kind of giant fish they're catching here on the mighty Missouri.

"Do you fish, Adam?" Zach asks me.

There are a number of smart ways I could answer the question ... but, they're not for me. Not Adam Moynihan. I choose the absolute worst answer. "I can catch anything," I blurt out, even though I've only used worms for bait and a marble-size bobber to catch small pan-size fish, like blue gill. My bold bragging might just get me in trouble.

"Yep, you'll be able to catch anything," Joey squeals, "because Dad just got polarized sunglasses! He can spot fish down in the water, and now everyone will be able to catch the big ones!"

Whew, Captain Mike's sunglasses saved the day. For a minute I thought I might have to throw myself overboard. Then I look closer at the dark sunglasses perched upon Captain Mike's flat nose. His eyes are hidden. His jaw set tight. His thoughts are unreadable. He doesn't speak for a long moment. This is as uncomfortable as getting called to the principal's office on the first day of school.

Then Captain Mike clears his throat, and speaks slowly: "With these magic sunglasses," he says, pausing to clear his throat again and tap his special glasses, "I see the fish a' swimmin' all right!" I don't know if Zach's Dad is just pretending about the powers of his new fishing glasses, but after my embarrassing boast, I'm ready to keep my mouth shut and follow the crowd.

With my eyes glued on Zach, I watch him grab a six-foot fishing pole and, with one smooth move, he arcs the pole and whips out the line.

"Rig your line and cast out," Zach says to me. "Then let the line settle."

Zach knows the ins and outs of fishing. He goes on with technical fishing talk and Brian eats it up. While they chatter about scientific mumble jumble, I focus on fishing.

With a tight grip on the pole, I whip it over my shoulder and snap it forward, letting the line fly. It sails out and, luckily, it lands close to Zach's. Not bad for a beginner, I think.

"Nice cast, Adam," Joey says.

I nod at Joey, not taking my eyes off the line. I'm too busy trying to remember what Zach said about letting the line settle before reeling it in. Before I can blink, it happens.

Zach's pole bends in half. "What a tug!" he hollers, snapping the rod skyward and then reeling like a mad man.

"Wait! You're letting the line farther out!" I yell at Zach, confused that he's unreeling line.

"I have to give this walleye some play!" Zach cries out, struggling with his rod.

Play? How is this playing? I gasp as a fin of the fish breaks the water and makes a mammoth splash.

"How long will it take to tire the fish out?" Brian asks, leaning over the railing of the boat, his eyes wide. It's hard to tell if they're reflecting excitement or fear.

"I don't know. Every fish is different," Zach says. He cranks in some of the line and brings the fish toward the boat. Once again, it leaps out of the water, sprays a ton of water and then dives again.

Zach hangs on. After a few more wild tugs, and a lot of time reeling, a walleye twice as big as a football sails out of the water and slaps onto the deck. Zach wears an ear-to-ear grin. Annie barks and prances around the flopping fish. Joey jumps up and down, too, his red cowboy boots clickity-clack, practically tap dancing as they hit the boat deck.

Captain Mike starts to give directions, "Settle down, Joey or –" But before he can finish his sentence, Joey's foot is tangled in the line. He stumbles, pulling the line tighter on the fish, which then jerks and jumps even more, freeing itself from the hook on the lure.

"Quick! Take the helm!" Captain Mike shouts to Zach.

But somehow in the trade off, the steering wheel is deserted and the boat spins wildly from the forceful current. Zach is knocked off his feet and rolls toward the edge of the boat, crashing into Brian and me. We tumble into a heap, causing Captain Mike and Joey to fall on top of us. We're slipping like a mud slide into the Missouri. And the fishing poles are rolling in every direction.

The boat shifts again, and I slide away from the group. I'm clawing at anything within my reach to stop from sliding overboard. Suddenly, someone catches my hand. An angel? In a way, it is. It's my brother. Brian grabs my wrist and hangs on tight.

Luckily, Captain Mike's long arms snag the steering wheel. He hoists himself up and rights the boat, and then we slow to a coast. The rest of us begin to unfold from the jumbled mix.

"Uh-oh," Zach says. "You're bleeding, Adam."

I look down; a plastic lure with an ugly hook is sticking out of my leg. I feel the painful bite from the buried hook. My heart pounds in my chest faster than Zach's walleye had danced on the deck. And I'm sure that my face is whiter than that fish's belly.

"Grab the Hail Mary box!" Captain Mike orders.

"The what?" I ask. My fear triples. I don't know what a Hail Mary box is, and my leg begins to burn like it's on fire.

"The first-aid kit," Brian says which reassures me.

Zach dashes to a boat seat and flings off the cushion. He lifts the lid and yanks out a bright red, Styrofoam tool-style box, and it squeaks on the boat deck as he slides it toward us.

"Don't worry, Adam," Zach says. "My dad is a dentist but he can work on your leg, too."

Captain Mike smoothly passes the helm to Zach this time. As the boat putters evenly along, Captain Mike has the hook out in seconds. Until now, I thought a magician only knew how to pull a rabbit out of a hat. It turns out Captain Mike is a magician, too.

"This is rubbing alcohol," Captain Mike says as he gets ready to pour the clear liquid on my wound. "It's all we have on board to disinfect the cut. It'll sting."

I pull up my leg an inch. Then Brian squeezes my hand. No words. That's what I love about my brother; one minute he's driving me crazy being a talking encyclopedia and then – without words – he's squeezing my hand and silently making me feel better.

Captain Mike begins to pour the liquid, and I bite my lip. The sting is like a hundred hornets, but at least it only lasts a second. Next, it's a dab of antibiotic gel and a slap from a waterproof Band-Aid. In minutes, with one last hand squeeze from Brian, I'm feeling good as new.

"Have you had a tetanus shot lately?" Captain Mike asks.

"Don't worry, Captain Mike, his tetanus shot is always up to date," Brian says. "Adam gets stiches *every* summer."

My brother is back to using words. I simply grin, because they're all the right words. I've had stitches on my forehead, my lip, and my knee.

"Yip, yip yip!" Annie barks. All our heads turn. She is strutting with her head held high, boasting the prized walleye between her teeth.

"Leave it to the only girl at Boys' Night Out to catch a fish," I say.

Everyone laughs.

I think that's enough fishing for one night," Captain Mike says. "Let's head to Point Marine. We still have time to stop for ice cream on the drive home."

Did I hear ice cream? Now I'm in my comfort zone.

*   *   *

Captain Mike powers the boat to the marina. We dock, store the gear, snap the boat cover in place, and then pile into Captain Mike's blue van. Joey and I buckle in the middle bench seat, behind Captain Mike, while Brian and Zach slide into the bench behind us. Annie rides co-pilot next to Captain Mike.

The van rolls away from Point Marine and heads east toward home. Not even five minutes later, traffic comes to a halt. Believe it or not, we're stuck behind an ice cream truck.

Unfortunately, it's not the fun, sing-songy, music-playing kind of truck that cruises up and down neighborhood streets selling ice cream bars. Otherwise we could get our ice cream treat right now.

Instead, the stuck truck is a two-ton freezer that is blocking both lanes. No one in the van is moving, except for Joey. Something in his cargo pocket pokes about.

"What's that?" I ask, pointing to the wiggle in his pocket. Joey shrugs, avoiding the question. He sits quietly, arms folded across his chest with a big grin spreading across his face.

Zach leans forward. "There's always something in Joey's pockets," he says. "Sometimes it's dead, but most of the time it's alive."

Then all at once something big and green and slimy shoots out and lands on me. I jump. Annie yaps. The frog leaps again, and when it's fully stretched out, I swear it's longer than a kangaroo – even though I've never seen a kangaroo. I've caught frogs in Michigan ponds for years. Stroking their bellies and listening to their croaks is one of my favorite pastimes. But I've never seen a frog this big.

The frog springs from one side of the van to the other. Brian and Zach reach out wildly, their arms stretching over the middle seat for the Great Green One. Annie is up on her front paws, trying to hop over the back of the seat. I swing an open palm, but barely brush the slippery fellow, sending it toward Annie. She yaps and catches it mid-flight.

Again, leave it to the only girl at Boys' Night Out to rescue a frog and a fish.

Joey takes the frog from Annie and slips it back in his pocket, keeping a hand in place to prevent another escape. Captain Mike glares at us in the rear-view mirror. "Everything under control back there?" he asks.

"Roger that," Zach says, using his military talk to make it sound like everything is A-OK.

Zach and Brian sit back in the rear seat and begin to chatter about fishing gear. Joey gives Annie a gentle pat on the head, and she settles down into the co-pilot seat again. For the moment, it's quiet sitting next to Joey. Then he starts muttering.

"Hang in there big fellow. We'll be home soon," Joey rambles on. He drops his head and bends forward so his ear is closer to his pocket. "What's that? Yes, I'll feed you an extra fly."

I realize Joey is not only talking to his frog ... he thinks the frog is listening and answering! This seems a little odd, but that is one giant frog the little kid has. My curiosity kicks in about Joey's "talking" frog. I know frogs can't talk, but what I wonder is how a frog can swim in the strong current of the mighty Missouri.

"Where did you get that frog?" I ask Joey.

Zach jumps in to answer for his brother: "He snatches them between the marina dock railings, where the water is quiet."

Yep, the Big Muddy is one mysterious river.

Luckily, there is a break in traffic and the van begins moving again. At the ice cream shop, we all order Superman flavor, except for Annie. She gets the strawberry shortcake.

The ice cream is melting quickly in the ninety-degree heat so my tongue spins around the cone to catch the constant drips. I gulp several bites and lick fast, with my mouth still half full, to keep up with the dripping.

I look over at Joey. His cone is oozing ice cream. He has melted goo all over his one hand, sacrificing speed as he cautiously keeps his other hand inside his pocket so the Great Green frog stays put. Meanwhile, Brian and Zach give up trying to lick the melting treat and instead plunk their cones into a bowl to eat them with spoons. I wink at Joey, 'cause we know that it's much more fun to eat like a slob.

When we're all happily full of ice cream, we climb back into the van for the trip back to town. Soon, we pull up next to Mom's apartment, we unload, and she is there to greet us.

"Did you have a good time at Boys' Night Out?" she asks.

I'm ready to answer when Annie jumps into my arms, giving my ice-cream sticky face a ton of licks. It makes me giggle. Through my laughter, I tell Mom that "It was a blast, even with a girl on board!"

Chapter 3

A Wild Wild West Celebration

Today is my birthday, but I'm not sure I even want to get out of bed. My stomach churns like the sudsy water swishing inside the washing machine only a few feet away from my head, here in the corner of the Bat Cave. It's unsettling celebrating a birthday in a new city.

This is only my third morning in Bismarck, and Mom has invited my two new friends, Zach and Joey, for lunch. But what kid has a birthday party in the middle of a busy art studio with paper cutters slicing and dicing? Don't get me wrong; I love birthday parties. Especially my own. In fact, I kick off every summer by putting on one of the best birthday celebrations a kid could imagine. Last year, for example, I took the entire Cub Scout troop to race go-carts. The year before, the soccer team knocked down bowling pins; we rocked the local bowling alley!

But this is a whole new North Dakota thing for me – and lunch for two new buddies is feeling kind of lame. Time to rise and shine, I guess. Slowly, I pull on shorts and a T-shirt, then slap on a ball cap and pull it low, hoping I can just hide under the brim for a little while. It doesn't work, though.

"Happy Birthday!" Mom sings out as she cracks open the Bat Cave bedroom door and lets the morning sun peek in. The secluded Bat Cave is on the north side of the house so its tiny basement window doesn't let in much light. Today I am just fine with being in the isolated, darkened room, but Mom opens the door wider and sings the whole thing now: *Happy Birthday to You …* and so on.

I do my best and give her a slight smile.

Suddenly, the door busts wide open. "Happy Birthday, dweeb," Brian says with a snicker, and then darts away. I reply to dear brother with a growl so deep that it plays like the lowest note on Brian's trombone. It's easy for Brian to fling zingers at me today, considering that a couple months ago he invited the entire sixth grade band to his birthday party. Mine is going to be pretty simple this year, I'm sure.

Flopping back onto the hide-a-bed, I stare kind of blankly at the ceiling. The chugging, washing-machine feeling in my stomach speeds up to the spin cycle now. I squeeze my eyes shut and make a secret, all-important, extra-special birthday wish. There's no time to waste – no time to wait until I'm blowing out birthday candles for this wish. This one is a now-or-never, do-or-die wish. A pretty-please-with-extra-sugar-on-top wish. I take a deep breath and wish this: That the birthday lunch will still be fun even though it will be in Mom's art studio with two friends I only met a few days ago.

The telephone rings in the art studio. I hear Mom answer and then call out to me. "Someone is asking for the Birthday Boy," she says from the kitchen.

Who would be calling me before breakfast?

Shuffling to the studio, I pick up the phone and mumble, "This is Adam."

I hear music playing, hands clapping and then voices singing, *"Happy Birthday to You, Happy Birthday to You; Happy Birthday, Dear Adam, Happy Birthday to You."*

The line goes dead. Puzzled, I hang up the phone, not noticing the quiet hush in the studio. I should have, because before I can blink, Mom's art friends, Bobby-Jean and Laurie, pop out from behind a supply cupboard, trapping me into a corner. "Happy Birthday!" they yell together.

Instantly, wild ribbons of red, yellow, and blue Silly String shoot everywhere, and in seconds, I'm covered from head to toe. The ladies are bent over with giggles, and I squeak out a small smile, too.

If there was ever a time for a leap-frog of faith, it would be now. I have my doubts whether my birthday wish will come true. Even if we play games at the party, there's a problem, because grown-ups think big prizes are winning a dictionary or money for college.

Covered in the Silly String, I walk like a wrapped mummy back to the privacy of the Bat Cave, peeling the strings off as I go. I know Mom and her workers are trying, but with only two friends coming for lunch this could be a long day, indeed.

Ding-dong, the doorbell rings. That seems odd. In three days we've never had company before breakfast.

"It's a package for Adam," calls Laurie.

I trot to the back door and find Laurie standing alone holding a gift bag with *ADAM MOYNIHAN* written in big letters on its side.

"Who brought it?" I ask.

"I don't know. They were gone before I opened the door," she says, passing me the bag.

I sprint to the studio shaking the package to see if it rattles. "Can I open it?" I ask Mom.

"Sure, Birthday Boy," she says, easing into a teasing grin.

It makes me wonder why she's not nervous about uninvited visitors. Mom's Mrs. Safety-type radar normally goes into overdrive when anything suspicious happens. But a gift is calling my name and distracts me from concern.

Ripping into it, I find McDonald's gift cards. Perfect! And, get this, super flat top sunglasses with mirror lenses. I slip on the dark shades and no one can see my eyes – very cool!

"I'll be on the Missouri River in style," I say as I study my groovy look in the hallway mirror.

Next I head to the kitchen to eat breakfast, but I never make it. Ding-dong, the doorbell rings again. And again,

41

no one's there. But this time a Thunder Storm Super Soaker water gun is sitting there on the doorstep.

Barely having shut the door, the bell rings once more. I open it once more.

"Delivery for Adam Moynihan," says a tall man – Robert I assume, since it reads *Robert's Floral* on his shirt. He stands holding a massive bunch of balloons. Solid red, orange, green, and blue balloons hover in the air all around his head. And, not one, but *two* Spider-Man balloons bounce around, too.

"I'm Adam," I say as he tries to hand me the floating cluster of helium-filled fun, but it won't fit through the door! I give the ribbons a mighty tug and the balloons finally squeak through the entry, spring free and bob about. Before leaving, Robert hands me a cardboard tube and then leaves. I squeeze my way through the studio with all the balloons, bumping into a clamp light once and then bounce off Laurie.

In the snug Bat Cave Brian steps out of the way and watches the balloons fill the room. I let go of the balloon cluster and it hovers up at the low ceiling.

"Fun balloons," Brian says. "What's in the tube?"

"I don't know. The end caps are stapled shut," I say. "Can you grab Mom's toolbox?"

Brian digs out the box and flips open the lid. "Just as I remember from camping," he says. "There's one hammer and two screwdrivers." This bare basics of a box is quite a contrast to Dad's handyman house with a workbench full of drills, pliers, wrenches, and other gadgets.

"You'll have to do your best with this," Brian says, handing me the flat-end screwdriver which I wedge under one of the staples.

With a little pressure the staple lets loose and the end cap rolls off. Bingo. I shove my hand into the tube and pull out the curled paper. Unrolling the giant-size poster, I see a nearly life-size black bull staring at me with glaring dark eyes, a huge ugly nose, and two wicked horns. With its head low, the bull kicks up dust as it chases a clown whose legs are bent like he's doing the fifty-yard dash. In the background hundreds of people are cheering the rodeo action. It's as if I can feel their shouts coming off the poster.

Looking over my shoulder, Brian gazes at the poster, too. "I've always wanted to go to a rodeo," he says, beaming with interest at the bull and clown.

In the lower corner of the poster, my finger traces the personalized message and autograph: *It's the way you ride the trails that counts. Happy Birthday, Adam. – Rodeo clown Steve.*

"We don't know a cowboy named Steve, do we?" Brian ponders.

"Who cares," I say. "It's a cool poster. Let's tack it on the wall." I grab a couple of push pins.

Once we get it hung, we stare at the poster and feel the power of the bull. The pull of the clown. The pulse of the crowd.

Suddenly, there's a tug on my arm. It's Mom. "Didn't you hear me calling? They want the Birthday Boy on the phone."

I come out of my trance and go to the kitchen for the phone. More birthday singing from a voice I don't know. How do so many people know it's my birthday? I go to find Mom for some answers.

No sooner do I hang up the phone than it rings again. I answer the business phone myself, saying, "Moynihan Art Studio; this is Adam."

"Happy Birthday to You ... Happy Birthday, Dear Adam. Happy Birthday to You." Click.

I suspect someone has done some pre-party planning. But before I set the phone down, it rings again. This is crazy. Sure, the art studio is a busy place, but usually the phone doesn't ring as much as it is right now.

"Hey, Mom," I say, "maybe instead of hello, I should just say, 'This is the Birthday Boy!'"

Mom flashes a smile and says, "You better not. I might get at least one business call, today."

Just then the doorbell rings, again. I don't have time to ask Mom more questions about all this activity. I let Mom answer the phone and dash to the door. When I open it, the smell of boot leather and grit reaches my nose. At least this time I know the visitor!

"Hey, Grandpa Joe!" I yell, reaching out and giving him a bear hug. Actually, Grandpa Joe isn't my real Papa. He's my Michigan campground friend, my pal Red's grandfather who I met last summer. He happens to be a retired farmer who lives on an acre of wheat in North Dakota.

"Well, howdy little fellow," he greets me in his deep Wild West twang. "I scooted down from the farm to wish you a happy birthday."

Leading Grandpa Joe into the apartment, I grab his king-size hand. Just as I recall from last year, his farmer hand is rough as lizard skin. He's also football-player big. With a side-to-side swagger, he knocks three things over as he steps down the hallway. I look up into his eyes and notice his face is bronze and wrinkled from the sun. It reminds me of a weathered baseball mitt. Grandpa Joe catches my gaze on his face. "I may have retired from farming, but I still spend a hefty amount of time checking the crops."

"So you're still living on that acre of wheat?" I ask.

"Sure enough, little fellow. And I brought you a birthday present," Grandpa Joe says, whipping out two green ball caps. "John Deere," he says, mentioning the logo on the hat. "One's for your brother. I couldn't forget your partner."

I stroke the yellow deer sewn onto the cap and admire the gift from Grandpa Joe.

A second later, Brian is at my side, and he is excited, too. "This is great! Do you have a John Deere plow, too?" Brian asks.

"Reckon I do," Grandpa Joe says with a deep, from-the-gut chuckle.

Brian turns to me, now sporting the flashy green cap and says, "John Deere was a blacksmith who invented the first steel farming plow." That's my brother – always sharpening his senses and focusing in like a microscope, dialing down to the minutest detail.

Mom is at the door now, too. "Can you stay for lunch?" she asks Grandpa Joe.

"Sorry, Ma'am, I've got to get back to the farm," Grandpa Joe says. "But rustle up these young fellows and scoot 'em down to the farm to me sometime soon if you will."

Then Grandpa Joe gives my hand a strong shake and squeeze that turns into a playful arm wrestle. I do my best, but Grandpa Joe wins.

"We'll come visit real soon," I say to Grandpa Joe as he heads out the door.

*   *   *

By now it is almost lunchtime. I never did get breakfast, but it's been too crazy to notice. There's another knock at the door, and this time it's Zach and Joey.

"I couldn't wait for the party to begin," Joey says, almost tap dancing in his red cowboy boots. "So we came a little early."

"I told him the party wasn't until twelve-hundred hours," Zach says, using military time.

"Come in, come in," I say, beaming. "I'm glad you didn't wait until noon."

Zach hands me a card, and I read the message out loud: "Wild Wishes from the Wild West." He has drawn a picture of Annie with a big fish in her mouth.

Ding-dong. I dash to answer the door. As soon as I whip it open, the aroma of pizza floats into the apartment. The pizza delivery guy sings "*Happy Birth*day" to me and then leaves.

As I bring the pizza to the kitchen, Mom is picking up the ringing telephone. "Another call for Adam," she says, waving the phone at me.

Zach and Joey stand still and their mouths gape open. They are a bit surprised by the birthday silliness, what with all the phone ringing, doorbell dinging, and balloons floating.

On the phone, there is more birthday singing and a click before I can ask who's calling.

"Who was that?" Zach asks.

I shrug. "I've been getting mysterious phone calls all morning wishing me a happy birthday, yet no one tells me their name."

I look quickly over to Mom. She stares back at me with a poker-face … and then her lips arch into a trace of a smile. But before I can ask more questions, Joey pipes up, "I'm hungry. Let's eat!" He flips the lid of the pizza box and heavenly scents waft up. Instantly, I'm lost in the aroma.

Zach, Brian, Joey, and I gather at the small kitchen table to have some pizza while wearing colorful party hats. Brian bites into a slice, and with his teeth clamped down, he slowly pulls the slice away from his mouth so stringy cheese can stretch as far as his arm can reach. "I can pull farthest," Brian boasts with a mouthful of pizza.

"Watch this," Zach says, biting and pulling. His stretch is almost as long as Brian's.

Wanting to one-up my brother, I stretch the cheesy pizza. I do my best, but something is wrong. The pepperoni comes along with the cheese and makes it too heavy. I'm doomed. The stretched pizza instantly sags and becomes a sinking blob that nosedives to the table. Instantly, I'm in last place. But not for long. Joey bites, and before he can even stretch the cheese, it drips down his chin and gives him a red-tomato-sauce beard. Brian and Zach let out a roar, and I laugh so hard that soda sprays out my nose.

The doorbell rings. Quickly, I wipe my nose, race to the door and swing it open.

There stands Batman!

His trademark yellow Batwing badge across his huge chest sparkles in the sun. While I tip my head higher to gaze into his black mask, he suddenly spins around once; the black cap cuts through the air like a black storm cloud passing over.

"Come in," I stutter, barely able to utter the words. My legs want to wobble and my pulse skyrockets. Batman spins again, sending his Dark Knight cape sailing over my head as a gush of wind brushes across my face. It feels like there are fireworks in my chest.

Brian, Joey, and Zach push against me, trying to get a closer look at this real-life, in-person superhero. I hope my rubbery legs hold me up where I stand, or these guys are going to roll right over me to get to Batman.

"Are you the Birthday Boy?" he bellows in a voice so deep it echoes through me, forcing me to take a step back and crush Zach where he stands.

I try to answer, but my words won't come out any louder than a whisper.

Batman extends his black glove. "I want to shake your hand," he says. This time his deep voice sucks me in like a power sweeper. I reach out; goose bumps pop up and down my arm even though the June day already is sizzling hot. Batman's soft leather glove gobbles up my hand, and then his grip tightens. "Happy Birthday," he says, squeezing so hard my fingers tingle.

His all-powerful grip relaxes and he lets go of my hand. Wide-eyed and wordless, Brian, Zach, and Joey shake Batman's hand.

"Are you the real Batman?" Brian asks, finally finding his voice.

"Of course, he is!" Joey shouts.

"No, I mean," Brian hesitates, "Batman is cool, but it's the difference between fantasy and real life."

I feel the blood flood my cheeks. Brian's right. We love comics and movies, but are superheroes make-believe? I've spent so many years in awe of the action, power, and suspense, I forget to question.

But Joey is not questioning anything. "Of course, he's Batman!" he hollers, stomping his foot, determined he's genuine.

Batman doesn't say a word. His eyes, like a deadly weapon, peer eerily through the mask.

"Can we see your Batmobile?" Brian asks. That's my older brother, always thinking of the details.

"Yeah, a real Batman would have a real Batmobile," Zach says, pushing against me so hard his wire-rimmed glasses shift crookedly. He adjusts the glasses but is too excited to square them properly.

I'm ready to fly out the door to find the Batmobile to prove fact or fiction. But suddenly a hand from behind tightens on my shoulder. It's Mom, who has come from the art studio.

"The pizza is getting cold, and I believe Batman needs to be on his way," she says firmly.

Towering over me with her hands still pressed on my shoulders, Mom turns me away from the door.

"Hustle inside everyone," her voice is a command as she points stiff-armed toward the kitchen. We all obey.

With one last 360-degree spin of his superhero cape, Batman whisks out the door, creating a whoosh of air so strong the door shuts on its own.

Missing the chance to see if Batman had a real Batmobile makes me feel like a birthday balloon with its air letting out and sinking fast. Yet, I'm not sure if I really want to know the answer. Joey's enthusiasm makes me want to believe in Batman.

With Joey anything is possible; he can convince a kid the piece of candy hidden in the bottom of your ice cream cone has magical power – or that polarized sunglasses will let you catch invisible fish. So I'm not sure if I'm mad at all at Mom for sending Batman on his way before we could check out his Batmobile.

But I don't have time to consider my uncertainty. The art studio clock strikes twelve.

"Turn on the TV for the mid-day news," Mom instructs. "Channel seven, please."

Brian turns on the TV. On the screen, an announcer points to a weather map that is colored bright red across the entire state of North Dakota. Hot. Humid. Hazy. That's how the weather has been. The camera leaves the weather map and zooms to a lady newscaster.

"High temperature today of ninety-six, and hot for the coming week," she says. "No rain in sight – just blazing blue prairie sky. Also," she says, then pauses, "I have a special announcement. I want to wish Happy Birthday to Adam Moynihan. He's visiting Bismarck on his birthday."

"Hey, how did that weather girl know it's your birthday?" Joey asks, spinning on the heels of his cowboy boots.

"Yeah, how did a TV announcer know it's your birthday?" Zach asks. "First balloons, then phone calls, then Batman! I've lived here all my life and I don't know this many people!"

I look Mom straight in the eye, suspiciously. She's standing off to the side, smiling with a soft chuckle that tells me she has something to do with all the surprises. She knew I was coming to visit and that I wouldn't know anyone at first, right during my birthday.

"All these phone calls and gifts are from your friends, aren't they?" I ask, making it sound more of a statement than a question.

She nods, smiling like the kid who got the whole rose frosting on the birthday cake.

Mom has a way of making my heart sing even when I'm the new kid in town.

She steps toward me, but before she can sweep me up and wrap me into a hug, embarrassing me in front of my friends, I switch the subject. "Is there still time for us boys to play our Mario tournament?"

Mom has been watching the video game scoreboard and knows what a close race it's become.

"Unless you want to blow out candles and make a birthday wish, first?" Mom asks.

"Cake! Let's have cake!" Joey shouts, breathless with excitement.

Mom brings out a cake in the shape of Spider-Man, my second favorite superhero after Batman. The flaming candles on the cake dazzle us.

"Make a wish, Adam," Zach says.

Four wide grins flash at me with eyes lit up.

But I don't move. I don't close my eyes. I don't go to that magical place where only wishes are made. The wish from this morning flashes through my mind. The wish to have a fun North Dakota birthday is already coming true.

"Just blow out the candles, Adam," my brother barks, interrupting my thoughts.

By now melted candle wax is flowing like lava across Spider-Man.

"Hurry, Adam, blow!" Joey cries, putting his face only inches from the cake, ready to blow out a blast of air if I don't act soon.

I draw in a deep breath, sucking in the sweet sugary smell of frosting. I blow a gale of wind so big the candles are snuffed out in seconds.

"Can we eat the cake in the Bat Cave?" Zach asks Mom.

As we each get a big slice of cake, we head to the deep and dark Bat Cave. We close the door and instantly block out the noisy studio. In the peaceful hush we sit quietly, eating heaping chunks of cake and letting our eyes study the nitty-gritty details of the Mario scorecard.

Except for Joey. Being just seven, he can only sit quietly for a moment. His feet tap a clickity-clack as his cowboy boots smack the floor. He mumbles to himself as he shovels in the cake. There is always a hum of fun when Joey is around.

Once the cake is consumed, we zip through the next level of Mario and record the results. The tournament remains neck-and-neck as Zach and Joey start to leave.

"Wait! I just remembered your present, Adam," Joey says as he shoves his hand into his pocket and tugs. Something is wedged inside.

"Is it dead or alive this time?" I ask, thinking about the crazy things I've seen come out of Joey's pocket.

"This is better than alive," Joey says.

"What's better than a slimy frog?" I ask, remembering the Great Green One from Boys' Night Out.

"Adam, you're going to like this." Joey gives one last tug and yanks out something in his closed fist. Slowly opening his hand, he reveals a rock.

I stare at the flat, pointed stone. "Hey, I found one just like that at the river," I say, racing to the dirty laundry basket and fishing out yesterday's shorts. "I picked it up because it reminded me of stones I collected in Michigan to make arrows for a Halloween costume."

Pulling out the rock I found, I compare it to Joey's. Both flat gray stones are sharpened into a center point with two ridges at the base.

"Look at that! We each got genuine Indian arrowheads," Joey says. "Hundreds of years old, carved by Native Americans for hunting."

The smooth rocks are the size of a silver half-dollar. I spin the stone on its axis between my thumb and finger. It's dull and weathered at the edges.

"If these rocks are more than a hundred years old, they must be worth a lot of money," I say, feeling giddy, tingling all over.

"How do you know they're the real deal and not from a souvenir shop?" Brian butts in, reaching for the arrowhead. I'm quick, and snap my fist closed. Not quick enough, though, and Brian's hand smacks my wrist hard enough to send the arrowhead flying. We lose sight of it as it sails into the corner near the water heater. The four of us get down on our hands and knees to hunt for the arrowhead, but then the doorbell rings again.

My heart races because I figure it's for the Birthday Boy once more. I dart to the door. It's another man in a uniform, but not Batman. This guy is wearing a gray suit, white shirt, and tie. He looks like he's ready for church, except for the cap. It isn't anything like a baseball cap. Its brim is short, like a policeman's hat, but there's no badge on it. Who is this guy? I slowly look him up and down. Something at his feet catches my eye, making me squint. It's his shiny black shoes. They're so slick they shoot their own rays like the sun.

"I'm here to pick up the Moynihan boys," he says as he tips his hat with a gloved white hand. Then he stands arrow-straight with his arms stiff at his side.

Mom comes up next to me. "This is the Governor's chauffeur to drive us to the Capitol building. We're invited to the residence mansion," she says.

I slip the party hat off my head and try to straighten my wrinkly T-shirt. My clothes seem simple compared with this formal man, whose double-row uniform buttons flash in the bright sky. He looks like he's an army general.

I completely forget about the arrowheads, and the other boys must have, too, because they're huddled right behind me. Joey opens and closes his mouth several times before blurting out, "We were just going home."

"Roger that," Zach mutters. His military talk sounds almost tongue-tied.

Joey and Zach shuffle out the door, amazed again at Mom's party plans.

All within about three minutes we have combed hair, clean shorts and shirts, and we're out the door. The chauffeur leads us along the driveway of Mom's apartment. A limousine, longer than two mini vans, sparkles in the sun. It is big, black, and beautiful. I've never ridden in such a fancy car before.

With his gloved hand the driver opens the door for us. He tips his hat as I climb inside. A circle of seats surround me. I sink into a soft, cushy chair. There are cup holders on each side of me. And ahead is a flat screen TV, bigger than the one at my friend Lucas' house.

"There are cold drinks in the refrigerator," the driver says as he slides the door closed. He walks around to the driver's side and buckles himself in. A glass wall separates us.

Brian opens the mini-fridge and sees that it's jam-packed with pop. We select root beer. Mom pours and hands us each a drink. The glasses are ice-cold, too. We raise the glasses and clink for a birthday toast. I feel like a millionaire.

Driving through downtown Bismarck, we can hardly hear the engine or even feel a bump. Shortly, the limousine pulls into a long driveway surrounded by miles of green grass so perfect it looks like the Super Dome. The Capitol building, a tall white skyscraper, is straight ahead, but we turn onto a tree-lined street. The driver steers toward the mansion where the Governor of the State of North Dakota lives.

After the limo rolls to a gentle stop, the driver ushers us to the front door, where we stand under a white arch. The turn-knob-style doorbell sounds a long bong, fine and formal. The huge, wooden door opens, and another man in uniform appears. "Master Adam, and family," he says in a deep voice, "the First Lady is expecting you."

How does everyone in this town know my name?

Inside the castle-like home of the Governor, everything gleams. A chandelier with at least a hundred diamond-shaped crystals hangs over our heads. We step onto a floor of colorful swirling tiles. I make a small sweep with my foot and my shoe glides across the floor. "Brian," I whisper to my brother, "this floor is smooth enough to play sock hockey."

"Yeah, too bad it's the governor's house," he quietly answers.

I hear a soft whistle slowly float from Mom's lips and I see she is staring at the floor, too. Then I realize the tiny tiles remind me of one of her art projects: a collage.

"The floor is lovely, isn't it," Mom says. "A masterpiece on its own."

I still have my nose to the floor when Brian nudges me. Looking up, I see someone beautiful. I think it's her eyes. They're emeralds – all green and sparkly. And her smile is rich and hypnotic. Her dress swishes like a queen as she slowly walks. I'm beginning to think my outfit of shorts and T-shirt isn't fancy enough for this place.

"I'm the governor's wife," the noble lady says. "I'm very pleased to meet you, Adam. Happy Birthday." She hands me an autographed picture of her and the governor.

The only sound that comes out of my mouth is a gush of air. No words. Luckily, the noble lady takes a few steps into a sitting room, or parlor, as I learned when we studied Abe Lincoln. The man in uniform has us follow her. My feet sink into a cushy carpet.

"This is your mother's painting," she says, pointing to a watercolor on the wall. "I thought you'd enjoy seeing her artwork in the governor's mansion."

I look up, proud, into Mom's eyes.

"You must be famous," I say.

"I'm just like you," Mom says, "I do my best, using the talent God gave me." Mom gives me a gentle squeeze on my shoulder, letting me know she is proud of me, too.

We say good-bye and the limo takes us home. I'm spilling over with pride, standing straighter than when we won the Little League play-offs. To think I began today wishing I could have a fun birthday in a place where I only had two friends. It's the end of the day now, and I have so many friends, I can't even count them! What a wild, Wild West birthday.

Chapter 4

Show No Fear

My whole life I have wanted a tree fort – a big one that has a ladder and ropes for hauling up stuff. Sadly, I know a tree fort is out of the question here in North Dakota, not because Mom fixes everything with duct tape, but because the backyard is Mom's business entrance to the art studio. Grass has to be cut, sidewalk swept, and sticky fingerprints wiped off doorknobs. An awesome, boys-only treehouse just wouldn't fit in, I guess.

Still, I can't stop thinking about the giant black walnut tree that overhangs the fence from the Grunners' yard. It's just begging for a fort. What harm could it do to ask? Today, I decide to give it a shot, so I take a deep breath and prepare to give Mom my power smile and full-throttle charm. Then the phone rings.

Mom says a ringing telephone means money, and to ignore a business phone call is to kill the cash. I'm afraid if I ask about a tree fort now, she'll kill me instead of the cash.

Mom answers. "Of course. How many more? ... When do you need them? ... Yes, we can do that," she says. Her claws – I mean fingernails – clutch the telephone. She is like a business bobcat, a careful and clever hunter with a fierce spirit. I can tell it's a sizable order and that the deadline is making Mom anxious.

"Yes, it'll be on time," Mom continues, all business-like, her bobcat smarts creeping in. "We appreciate the business ... thank you ... good-bye," Mom says into the phone, making her voice purr though she spits out the words between clenched teeth.

After a five-count Mom spins on her heels and stomps back to where she is working on her painting deadline. Mom is great at organizing projects and juggling time for Brian and me, but right now I think she'd snap a little at anyone nearby. I decide going outside is the best place for me. I cut through the studio and head to the back door. I tug it open – and hot summer air hits me like a fist. This is my fourth morning in Bismarck, and every day has been nearly a hundred degrees.

Through the thick, almost steamy heat, I catch a fat and furry flash of orange darting around the backside of the old wooden garage. What was that? Following the movement, I see the tip of his thick, bushy tail slip through a crack in the side door of the shabby garage.

Even in daylight this old garage gives me the creeps. It is worn and weathered with not a speck of paint left on it. Dirt and cobwebs are packed in the corners of every window.

Hearing a muffled meow echo from inside, I sneak up and try to peek inside, but rubbing my hand across the grime-covered window just smears the dirt.

Then I hear another meow – this one more of a cry. The sound softens my heart. I'm scared to go in, yet I push my fear aside and turn the knob. The door creaks open. The dim room is stale and smelly, like sweaty gym shoes. A rusty old lawn mower is parked nearby below a wall cluttered with shovels and rakes. There is also a mean-looking pitch fork with shark-teeth spikes, and a wicked-looking ax too.

Off in a corner is a huge, oven-looking contraption with a gauge the size of the school gym clock. Above it are rows of shelves cluttered with jugs, mugs, and bowls. They stare at me and cast creepy shadows. Below, on a table, buckets of paint and brushes are scattered.

Then out of nowhere, something sputters a little "heh, heh, heh" that makes me jump. My pulse pounds in my ears. At first I think the old lawn mower came to life and then ran out of gas, but then I realize it's an older woman hunched over a jug twice as big as her boney hands. Her face is wrinkled and her nose looks like someone grabbed it and then pulled and twisted it, like it was made out of Play-Doh, but forgot to shape it.

"Lookee, here," she barks. I'm pretty sure she doesn't welcome surprises. And I am one. She leans forward and her eyes fire at me like two gun barrels going off at once. "What ya up to half-pint?" she asks, wagging her long, crooked, finger.

62

It's more of a warning than a friendly wave to come closer. I stand right where I am.

The Goliath-size cat I saw earlier is wrapped around her feet now. Even curled up, the thing comes up to her knees. Then he stretches. His hair bristles, his back arches, and his tail lashes back and forth like a ragged orange whip. The cat strikes out, his paw showing three-inch claws. All the while he hisses at me. One look at his vampire teeth and I think he could eat the metal pitchfork for breakfast.

"Heh. Heh. Heh," the lady again sputters the lawn mower cough. "You must be one of the Moynihan lads. I heard you were coming. I'm Marge Witt, your Mom's landlord. I live on the floor above your apartment." Her teeth are like corn on the cob; perfectly straight and just as yellow. "The house and this old shed came to me after my husband died. Got rid of all his old junk out here and turned this into a pottery studio."

I look around the shed again and take in all the old "junk." She must not have gotten rid of much. In the jungle of cobwebs are rows of old car license plates, loops of garden hoses, and farm-like tools hanging from the wooden rafters.

"Nice ... uh ... nice to meet you," I say, taking one step forward as my heart pounds. I try to paste on a smile.

"Humph," she says. This look comes over her face like the sun disappeared and wasn't going to shine again until Christmas. That's when I decide she doesn't like me.

"I keep this here shed locked when I'm not around so no funny business. Remember we do business around here," she adds. Her pointy finger now shakes and her teeth snap at me. Positively, this is a warning.

Marge Witt gives a new meaning to a prickly cactus. Her dark eyes drill into me with an intensity that makes the hair on my skin spike. I nod to her about "no funny business" and flee out the door.

It's hard to believe that only yesterday we had so much birthday-party fun and then today everything is just back to business. Business with a big, bad bite. Maybe there is a pair of bobcats in Bismarck. And Mom is the tamer of the two.

In my quick retreat from the shed, I don't look where I'm going and ram smack-dab into Zach, bouncing off him and landing on my butt.

"What's the rush?" Zach asks as he recovers from the collision and stares down at me.

I can only shrug, though, not knowing where to begin about the cranky old lady. I reach out my hand. He latches on and lifts me up.

"Wanna play Mario?" I ask, deciding it's best to skip sharing my uncertainty about the wicked widow.

"Roger that," Zach says.

We slide into the Bat Cave to find Brian quietly tucked away with his nose buried in a Nintendo magazine. Zach and I pick up the video controllers. Brian is happy to play the role of navigator. He reads from the magazine, giving us advice and short-cut tips to hidden passages. In minutes, Zach and I sail to the next level. Maybe there is something to say for reading instead of relying on my usual approach of luck and blind determination to become a game-playing master.

Mom opens our private door to the Bat Cave and pokes her head inside to give us an update: "The girls are finished with work for the day, and I'm going out front to help count and load a shipment for UPS pick up."

We nod; not taking our eyes off Mario's on-screen jumping, bumping, and block-breaking. Actually, I think Zach and I jump more than Mario. With every punch we shift in our seats, twisting and turning with right jabs and left hooks.

"Whew! It's hot in here," Zach says, pushing his wire-rimmed eyeglasses up his sweaty nose.

"Yeah, too bad that little window up there doesn't open," I say, referring to a small basement window tucked high above our heads in a far off corner.

"If we had a fan we could blow some air around to cool off," Zach suggests.

"That's a great idea," I say, "Mom has one in the studio."

Dashing out, I find Mom's large fan for drying paint and haul it back to the Bat Cave. I plug it in, but the fan simply blows the hot air around the small room. Our sweaty fingers slip and slide across the controllers.

"I wish that fan was air conditioning," Zach says. "I'd give anything to have cool air blowing."

"Me too," Brian says. "I feel like we're trapped inside a pizza oven."

"Hey! I know how we can get cool air," I say, darting to the kitchen. I pull out two glass bowls and set them on the counter. From the freezer I grab ice cube trays and give them a twist. The ice cracks and the glass tinkles as the cubes drop into the bowls.

Next I grab a hair dryer and bring all the gear back to the Bat Cave. I put one bowl of ice in front of the fan. Air blows across the ice. Zach stretches his hand in front of the ice bowl. "Hey, it does feel a little cooler," he says.

"Awesome," I say, setting the other bowl in front of the hair dryer. I switch the setting to "cool" and the other setting to "high-power." I plug the hair dryer into the last empty wall socket in the room. Zap! Suddenly it's completely dark and the fans shut down!

"What happened?" Zach asks.

"The power went out," Brian explains matter-of-factly. "When Adam plugged in the hair dryer he blew a fuse."

"What's a fuse?" Zach asks.

"It's a safety device for when you use too much electricity. The power in old houses hooks up to fuses," Brian says.

"So now what?" Zach asks. I can barely see his outline in the dim room. The small window high above doesn't let in much light.

"We should be able to replace a fuse and get the power back," Brian adds.

"So where are fuses kept?" I ask.

"Inside an electrical box," Brian says.

"No kidding, big brother," I snap, feeling my cheeks turn red. I'm getting hot – and it's not from the heat. It's my Irish Moynihan temper. Brian makes me want to blow just like an electrical fuse. But I need to focus; Mom will be back any minute and this black-out will turn her bad day into an even worse day. All because of me.

"We need to hurry," I say, trying to stay calm.

"Well, the electrical box must be somewhere in this room," Brian says. "After all, the hot water heater and furnace are in here. Usually, all the mechanical workings of the house are together."

We feel our way in the dark, our hands thumping walls around the washer, dryer, and utility equipment.

"I don't feel a box of any shape," I say, reaching and padding high and low.

"Maybe it's not in this room," Brian says, finding the door and opening it so light from two kitchen windows can help with our search.

"Where else would it be?" Zach asks.

"The electricity could be fed into the house from another building, like a garage," Brian says.

My stomach tightens. "Or inside a shed?" I ask, thinking about the jam-packed wooden shed with creepy cobwebs ... and the landlord, Mad Witch; I mean Marge Witt.

"Yes, the fuse box could be in a shed if it's near the house," Brian says.

"Oh no!" I can hear Zach gasp for a breath. "Not Custer's shed."

"What's Custer's shed?" Brian asks.

"Uh ... well ... it's the wood shed out back," Zach stutters. "Except there's a legend."

"What legend?" Brian asks.

"The famous General Custer was born nearby, and it's believed his spirit returns to the place he was happiest. You know, like where he played as a kid," Zach says.

"And he played in the shed behind this house?" I ask as my breath catches in my chest.

Zach shrugs. "He played around here somewhere. Custer left for the Battle of Little Big Horn not far from here – near Fort Lincoln, out by the Missouri river. Joey swears he's heard Custer's ghost calling from that shed."

I'm not too concerned about Joey thinking a ghost talks to him. After all, the little guy thinks his frog talks to him! But, jeepers, a legend is something passed down for generations. What if the shed is haunted with the ghost of Custer?

"Come on, Adam," Brian says, giving me a shove out of the Bat Cave.

"Hey, what are you doing?" I plant my feet firm, not being fond of the idea of meeting Custer's ghost.

"We need to fix this blackout before Mom gets back," Brian says, giving me another push toward the shed.

"Wait, wait; just one minute," I say. The talk about Custer's ghost has me so shaken I've forgotten about the landlady, Mad Witch. What if she's inside? I tell the guys about Marge Witt. We stand stock-still, but then the bong of the grandfather clock jerks us back to attention.

"Mom's going to be back any minute," Brian says. "We need to fix that fuse. Move it, Adam." My brother gives me another shove.

"Hey! You go first," I say. "You're the oldest."

"No way. It was your big idea to plug in the fan *and* the hair dryer at the same time," my brother snaps.

"Besides, Adam, it's only an old lady and a silly legend," Zach says. "You aren't afraid, are you?"

I can't believe Zach is daring me. And if I don't act fast, it could become a dreaded double-dare. I'll just have to do it quickly, like that first dive in May back home when Lake Michigan is still nearly freezing. Just rush ahead. No toe testing. No baby steps – just do it.

"Let's go." I bolt out of the Bat Cave and scamper to the shed. Brian and Zach are trailing behind. The opened padlock swings loosely from the door latch. Since it's unlocked, I figure Mad Witch must be inside. Using both hands, I yank the old wooden door of the shed. "Hello. Is anybody in here?" I squawk.

No one answers. Mad Witch must be at lunch or else she would have locked the door. She said she keeps the shed locked so there's no funny business. But the quiver in my stomach doesn't feel so funny.

Brian and Zach are now at my heels. I tug the heavy door open a bit farther. The hinges groan and let out a slow, eerie moan.

"Is that the ghost Joey heard?" I ask, hoping the creaking door is the answer to solving the mystery of Custer's ghost.

"Negative," Zach says. "Joey said he heard footsteps like Custer was leading his troops."

"Well, Joey's only seven; maybe he's just superstitious," I say, trying to make this ghost-thing disappear.

"He swears he's heard noises," Zach adds.

"Adam, move along," Brian grumbles and gives me a shove. "You're wasting time."

I stumble inside. The shed is darker than the apartment. No power in here, either. A wedge of light from outside shines a path across the dirt floor and casts an eerie beam onto the ax and the pitchfork. From behind, Brian thrusts a flashlight into my hand.

"Where did you get that?" I ask, fumbling to hold the flashlight between my shaky fingers.

"I grabbed it from Mom's first aid kit in the kitchen," Brian says.

Guiding the flashlight beam through the cobwebs, I search for a black or silver box. In fact, right now I'd take any kind of box with a bunch of wires leading to it.

Bang! Suddenly the heavy wooden door slams shut. We're surrounded by blackness, except for the narrow beam from the flashlight. I get a punched-in-the-gut, ready-to-puke feeling. Fighting the nausea, I coach myself to take a deep breath and exhale. I have to keep going, knowing it won't take Mom long to count and load the packages for shipping. I wave the flashlight. It barely casts a shadow across miles of cobwebs and dusty shelves.

"Hold on! Shine the light back that way," Brian says.

I swing the light and we see two big black boxes mounted on the rough wood. I inch closer and yank the door on the lower box, unleashing a cloud of old dust in my face.

"Front porch, side door, outside lights, upstairs apartment," Brian says, reading labels in the box over my shoulder. "Reach higher, pull the other door," he says.

On tiptoes, I pull the upper door.

"Furnace, dishwasher, side porch; nothing about laundry or hot water heater." It's Zach reading this time.

"There must be another fuse box somewhere in this shed," Brian says.

Cripes. Either Business Bobcat Mom or Mad Witch Marge could be back at any moment. Let alone the ghost of Custer! I shine the light across the old wood beams, looking for another electrical box of fuses.

Suddenly, from a far corner of the shed, we hear an eerie, scraping sound of some kind.

"What was that?" Brian asks.

"Custer?" I mutter under my breath.

"Roger that," Zach says, his voice quivering. I shine the flashlight on his face. Zach's eyeglasses are slipping as he nervously nods his head up and down.

More clatter. We all jump, and the flashlight flies out of my hand.

The movement is coming closer!

Brian bends to snag the rolling flashlight and aims it toward the sound. Two green eyes glare at us; it's the beastly orange cat.

"It's just that cat, Adam. The one you said belongs to the creepy lady upstairs," Brian says. Well, my brother didn't hear "that cat" hiss and snarl and bare his vampire-like teeth, like I did, otherwise Brian's voice would be ten notes higher and he'd be darting for the door.

My stomach does a crazy lurch. I can't get sick, not now, not in front of my brother and Zach! Besides, we've got to find the other box before Mom comes back.

Brian scours the shed with the flashlight beam. "Look up, there it is." High above is another big black box.

"We'll never reach it," I say.

"Adam, hop on my shoulders," Zach says.

"Why me?"

"Because you're the lightest," Zach says. Jeepers. Zach is right. Brian is a year older than me and Zach is my age, but they are both bigger than me. Climbing onto Zach's shoulders, I yank open the door of the fuse box, closing my eyes and holding my breath because I know a thick cloud of dust is coming. The door springs open, and I feel the soot dump onto my skin.

"That's it! Hot water heater, washer, dryer, utility room, shed," Brian reads as he shines the flashlight into the box. "Adam, you need to replace the fuses."

"With what?" I ask.

"There, on the ledge, are some. Those round knobs," Brian says.

I sift through the soot. Generally, dirt and I are like best friends, but somehow this grime feels coated in the spirit of Custer's ghostly cooties. Finally, I grasp a cold glass bulb.

"Pull out the pink one. And make sure the new one is black before you push it in," Brian says.

"But I can't even tell what color this new one is," I say, rubbing the dusty, knobby thing between my hands trying to brush off eerie cooties.

"Give it a little spit," Zach says. "But work fast. You're heavy, Adam."

My hand shakes as I spit and rub the glass knob with my T-shirt, trying to work quickly and yet not wiggle on Zach's shoulders.

"Oh no! It's pink!" I yell, finally seeing the color of the glass fuse.

"Look for another one," Brian says.

Mad Witch had said she threw away all her husband's old things, but I guess she forgot about the dead fuses because I find more pink fuses. I pat around some more. Nothing. I stretch my arm as far as I can reach. At last, my fingers grasp one last bulb.

"This is the last fuse up here," I call down, knowing Zach can't hold me much longer. I spit and rub one more time on the glass bulb. "It's black!"

"Quick! Pull out the pink and pop in the black," Brian says.

I pry out the dead fuse and push in the black one. The lights flash on!

Whew! Mad Witch didn't throw away all of her dead husband's stuff after all.

Tumbling off Zach's shoulders, I dash for the door. I'm not shy about being the first one out of the spooky shed. Back in the quiet corners of the Bat Cave, I keep the fan off. If my imagination can make believe I heard a ghost, I can easily make myself think it's not hot in here. In the comfort of the secret cave, my racing pulse begins to settle. Then Mom returns and, thank goodness, she doesn't notice a thing.

*   *   *

Just a short time later, I hear Brian, Zach, and Mom in the kitchen. With the door to the Bat Cave left open, like it is now, I can easily hear conversations.

"Zach invited us to walk to the Elks swimming pool," Brian says.

That's all I need to hear; I race to meet them in the kitchen. Trying to pretend it's not hot inside the apartment isn't working that well. In fact, my T-shirt clings to me with sweat.

"Bismarck has a swimming pool?" I ask, anxious to find a way to cool off.

"The Elks is the best outdoor pool in town," Zach boasts.

"Why is it the best?" Brian asks.

"Because it has the highest diving boards!"

Diving boards! "Can we go, Mom, please?" I ask, trying my best to mind my manners and not go sprinting to the pool at Olympic speed without permission.

Mom agrees, but reminds us about pool safety rules and the buddy system.

"But, there's one catch," Zach says, looking down at his shoes.

Oh no. The last time Zach paused like this he told us about Custer's ghost. Every muscle in my body tenses.

"We have to take Joey," Zach says.

Is that all? Sometimes the little guy is a bit hard to handle, but what seven-year-old isn't?

"The more the merrier!" I holler, pumping my fist in the air. "Let's go!"

After changing into swimsuits and meeting up with Zach and Joey, we walk down Second Street and cross Avenue C. We continue past Avenue B and then Avenue A, where we turn right, walking to First street. In this city, it's easy to find our way. We simply follow the right letters or numbers. Two more blocks and we're at the Elks pool. Brian and I pay a few bucks to get inside; Zach and Joey have a season-pass patch sewn right onto their swimsuits.

Making our way out onto the pool deck, the four of us stop and gaze up at the three diving boards. The lowest board is a foot above the water. The mid-height one is twice as high as I am tall. The third diving board is way, way up there. It is so high the diver at the top looks like an ant. I can't help but call it the Capitol Building diving board because it seems as tall as the 19-story skyscraper state capitol.

"I like the lowest board," Joey says, marching like he's the grand marshal of a three-ring circus. Joey struts up to the board, takes four stiff steps and then springs off, splashing into the pool.

"I jump off that one," Zach says, pointing to the middle board.

"Adam, which diving board are you going on?" Brian asks me.

Roller coasters are my life. I love the speed, the curves and most of all, the height. Today, however, after the fear of Custer's ghost and trying to keep the power-outage a secret from Mom, my stomach already feels like it's been on a roller coaster ride. There is no reason to risk the height of the Capitol Building diving board.

"I'm staying with Zach," I say, and turn to follow him to the medium board. "Are you coming with us?"

Brian stays put as he stares back and forth at the three boards. One time, my brother actually got sick on a roller coaster, so now he stays on the ground at amusement parks. That's fine with me, 'cause it's really gross and smelly when a kid gets sick.

Joey is out of the water already and heads over to Brian now to ask him, "Which board, Brian?"

"I'll watch you jump a few more times," Brian replies.

Joey darts back toward the low board, and Zach and I are getting ready for some fun at the medium board. Over and over, we twirl, whirl, flip, and flop off the board.

Waiting in line with Zach for our next dive, some kind of a black bullet speeds by.

"Catch it!" Zach shouts.

"What is it?" I ask as my eyes try to keep up with the mysterious brown dart.

"A grasshopper," Zach says.

"That big and that fast?"

"Roger that; this is North Dakota. They love the hot, dry heat."

We dart after the grasshopper, following it to the tall grass growing along the fence surrounding the pool. The stiff, dry grass pricks my bare feet, and the tall weeds scratch my legs, but for the sake of catching grasshoppers, I hardly even notice.

Zach and I each snag a giant hopper. "Let's do a science experiment and see if grasshoppers can swim," Zach says.

As we take the insects back to the pool deck, I hear Brian say, "I'm going to the top" and see him start climbing up to the Capitol Building board.

My mouth gaps open. Zach pushes my chin up to snap it shut. "You don't want a grasshopper hopping inside," he explains.

Brian calmly walks to the edge of the board, no bounce. At the edge he simply steps off with his arms at his side. His body stays pencil-straight, and he lands in the water without much of a splash.

"That was cool," Joey says to Brian after he swims to the edge. "Can you do a Spread Eagle?"

Brian promptly hikes back up the ladder of the high board and walks to the edge again. This time, though, he bounces once and jumps off spreading his legs and touching his toes with his hands. Then quickly, he slaps his hands flat at his side again and does another Pencil into the water.

"That's so great!" Zach says, clapping his hands and cheering my brother on. "But isn't Brian afraid of heights?" Zach asks me as he watches Brian climb the ladder yet again.

All I can do is drop my jaw. Zach snaps it shut with his hand, not bothering to repeat the grasshopper warning.

"Do a cannonball," Joey shouts, egging Brian on.

Brian launches off the board, pulls his knees to his chest, wraps his arms around them and cannonballs into the water below. Whoosh! Water gushes in all directions. What a splash! There's a hush across the pool as people look up to see who the super-soaker is.

"Over here, over here!" Zach and I yell, our arms flying above our heads like excited cheerleaders with pom-poms. The grasshoppers are no longer the most interesting thing at the pool.

Brian swims to the edge, to where we are standing in awe of the awesome jumper.

"Are you going to get sick?" I ask, wondering how Brian is brave enough to take on the tallest board.

"Nope; I feel fine!" Brian reports with a smile – not even a twitch or twitter. "When I had swimming last year, we took a bus to the high school pool where there's a tall board, and I learned how easy it was," he adds, casually kicking the water at the side of the pool.

Zach and I look each other with wonder. Brian is only one year older – and he's mastered the Capitol Building diving board!

"Remember the rodeo clown poster?" I ask Zach.

"Yeah, it's the way you ride the trails that counts!" he shouts.

We dash up the Capitol Building board and learn to jump off too. No one got sick that day. Not from the fear of heights, and not from the fear of Custer's ghost.

Chapter 5

The Right Side of Your Brain

I could hear him prowling around up there, creeping across the ceiling tiles, mewing. It's the big orange cat that belongs to Mad Witch, the landlord of this huge old house. At least I recognize the noise as the cat scratching, unlike Joey who swears any odd sound is Custer's ghost seeping out of the shed out back.

Meow ...

"There he goes again," I say to Brian.

The cat's purrs and scratching are directly above my head, interrupting my Nintendo concentration. Until now the out-of-the-way Bat Cave seemed to be the perfect spot, hidden away from the busy-ness and noise of Mom's business. But then this cat came along!

Me-Oww ... !

"What's he doing up there?" I ask, staring up at the ceiling. Meanwhile, on the videogame screen, I'm crashing my Mario racer.

"He's up there because cats are hunters," Brian says. "They're always searching for something to catch."

"What's he going to catch up there?" I ask, eye still glued on the ceiling tiles.

"Mice, maybe."

"Mice? Why would mice come inside the house?"

"They like to build nests in the insulation."

Mee-yeow! The cat wails louder than ever.

"That doesn't sound like he caught a mouse. I think he's stuck. What if he's hurt?" I ask with concern.

Despite being snarled at in the shed, I now have a soft spot for this cat. It happened when I saw the cat sleeping peacefully on the sunny window seat of the upstairs apartment. I pitched a pebble at the window, and the ping made the cat blink at me. The cat let out a gentle purr instead of displaying his angry vampire teeth.

Mee-Yeow ... Yeow! The screech grows louder.

"He needs help!" I cry. "I'm going up there."

I put one couch cushion on top of another – and another. The pile is sky high when I climb on top. "Come on! Help me!" I call to my brother. "Hold my legs steady."

Brian jumps at my request and grabs my ankles as I sway from side to side trying to balance myself. I punch at the ceiling tile, but it stays put.

"Punch harder," Brian coaches from his ankle-holding spot.

Bouncing on the cushions to gain a bit of height, I punch again. A tile lifts an inch – but quickly snaps shut again.

"Again," Brian encourages.

I jump harder, bending my knees for extra spring, and give the tile a mighty sock. It pops up all right, and out tumbles the big orange cat, his wad of fur exploding in my face. Now I can't see. I can't breathe, and his three-inch claws are hooking into my scalp.

"Yeow!" This time it's me making the loud cry for help, but all I get is a mouthful of fur and cat hair crammed up my nose. Brian still clutches my ankles, but I'm top-heavy with the cat clawing around my head. I wobble blindly from side to side, then cough a big, fat, fur-ball cough.

My whole body is swaying now, and I completely lose my balance. The cat launches off my head in a flash and lands safely on all fours to slip away into the studio. I should be so lucky. I'm left spinning, arms swinging, trying to grab anything to catch my balance as I slowly fall off the couch-cushion stack.

Wait! A long brown strip hangs from the ceiling so I grab for it, but it's no support at all. It's only paper, and it instantly crumbles in my grip. I crash to the floor, roll head over heels, and land in a heap.

Uncurling myself from the accidental somersault, I reach for where the cat had been ... and my hand sticks to the top of my head! Huh? I tug my hand and it pulls out a clump of my hair. Ouch! Why did my hand stick to my head?

Then Brian starts to laugh. Not a chuckle. Not a giggle. It is a roll-on-the-floor, hold-your-stomach, tears-streaming-down-your-face kind of laugh.

I look in the mirror. A wad of sticky brown paper is tangled in my hair and on my hand. Then I notice many small black dots on the paper. I peer closer into the mirror. Ick! Hundreds of dead black flies are stuck to the paper, plastered into my blond hair and scattered on my hand, too. It's a black fly graveyard!

"Adam, ha – ha – ha ... you're trapped in flypaper!" Brian manages to say between gasps for air.

I shake my head but the paper stays stuck; only a dead fly drops off the wad. This is awful.

"Hee-hee," Brian continues to snicker. "Remember, any minute now, Mom will be looking for us for Family Time."

Family Time! Mom works hard to juggle business and play time with us when we visit. If Mom sees this mess and I'm not ready for Family Time, she'll be warrior mad. The armor, the helmet, and the shield, will all come out.

Thinking about Mom walking in any second is all it takes for me to start shaking, for the walls to cave in, the ceiling to start falling, and my heart to start drilling through my chest.

"Quick! Do something!" I beg.

Brian steps up to the yucky fly-graveyard plastered all over my hand and head. "I'm afraid your hair is really tangled," he says as he pulls on the sticky paper.

"Tell me something I don't know!" I snap, picturing Mom's hawk-like eyes preying on me. I'll be grounded for the rest of this six-week vacation.

"Well, let's start with your hand," Brian says as he tries to pry a corner of the super-sticky paper off my fingertips. Ouch! It's worse than ripping off an extra-tough, waterproof Band-Aid.

"Just give it a good yank," I say, biting my lips and closing my eyes. I need this over quickly, but I can't bear to watch.

"Okay, here goes!" Brian says, taking my hand and jerking it hard. Yikes! My hand is free, but now the skin is pink and raw where the paper was stuck to it. As I open one eye and squint into the mirror, I realize my hand is nothing to worry about compared to my hair. The dead-fly graveyard is smashed onto one side of my head, and clumps of hair cling to the paper.

"What about my hair?" I stammer, looking at the clock. Tick. Tick. Tick. Time is flying by. Any minute now, Mom will be here to take us to "The Wave" swimming pool, whatever that is. All I know is it's the special trip Mom has planned for Family Time today. A trip I'll be missing if we don't figure out something quickly!

"Scissors. That's the only answer," Brian says.

Can I trust my brother with cutting my hair? Earlier today, Mom said, "We'll go to 'The Wave' pool right after I get back from dropping off these final ideas for the coloring book."

Before she left for the meeting, she handed Brian and me a copy of her coloring book. On the cover was a cartoon drawing of a cat and a doctor. St. Alexius Hospital in Bismarck had ordered drawings for a coloring book for patients, and Mom had created the whole thing.

"Hey! This cat looks like Brian," I said when she showed us the book. I tapped the cover of the cartoon cat with a big smile of braces. "He has a metal mouth of train-tracks."

"But look, Adam, the cat acts more like you," my brother was quick to snap back. "He's causing trouble for the doctor."

I studied the cover more closely and noticed the doctor was dressed for the operating room. He was wearing a mask over his face. And, yes, the cat was causing trouble – drawing a mouthful of metal braces on the doctor's facemask.

But Brian wasn't done with the razzing. "Mom must have used you for her idea. Adam Moynihan, the mischief man," he teased me.

Before I could shout a come-back, Mom stepped between us, arms outstretched like a school crossing guard. "Stop!" she snapped. "You boys know I get my ideas from both of you." Her blue eyes, now stormy, locked on each of us.

The room went silent. I turned my back on Brian and walked away not letting him ruffle my feathers any further.

But now with Mom at her meeting, I'm out of options except to let my brother clip my wings. Or actually, cut my hair. Mom usually grins at my embarrassing moments, but this is bigger, more troublesome. I glance back to the mirror and catch a glimpse of the wadded up flypaper jammed into my hair. This is more like trouble with a capital "T" because I can't go swimming at the Wave pool with black-fly-graveyard gunk stuck to my head. Mom has every detailed planned for this outing and, believe me, you don't want to mess with Mom when she has Family Time scheduled.

"Okay; cut my hair, but only a Buzz Four," I say to Brian, trying to suck in some air through my nervous, tight throat.

"Adam, this will be a Buzz One," Brian says, referring to an even shorter haircut. "Probably with razor tracks."

"Is it that bad?" I ask. Razor tracks would be row after row of hair cut so short you'd see my scalp. "Can you manage to do a line instead?" I beg.

"I don't think so," Brian says. "Maybe there's enough hair to leave a tail."

Oh no! Not a tail! That'd be too much like a girl's ponytail, but I can't let my brother know this secret. He has the scissors, after all. "Mom will hate a tail," I squeak out, trying to catch some air through the wheeze in my throat.

Cripes. Before this flypaper trouble, I was sporting a bowl – longer hair on the top of my head. Now I'm headed for the shortest buzz cut: a Buzz One. And the razor track will be the bare spot on my head once this wad of flypaper is gone.

The clock is ticking, and we both know it. "Start trimming," I say, barely choking out the words.

Brian tugs at the stuck paper, pulls my hair taut and begins the operation. Snip. Snip. Snip. Locks of golden-brown hair fall in clumps to the floor. I want to leap out of the chair and curl up into a ball. Or run screaming down the streets of Bismarck. I want to be anyone but me.

"One last snip," Brian says. The flypaper mess falls to the floor.

I'm afraid to look. The clock ticks, forcing me to find the courage to take a peek. I hold my breath and I look through squinting eyes. Yikes! It's worse than I thought. It's worse than anybody could have thought.

"Boys! Are you ready?" It's Mom calling from the art studio. "Put on your swimsuits and I'll meet you in the van."

My mind is swirling with worry. What am I going to do? I can only imagine the buzz-cut ideas she'll get for her next coloring book! Kids in the hospital will never be afraid. They'll be too busy laughing at me. Luckily, I spot my ball cap and slap it on my head.

In the meantime, Brian has thought of all the details. As I step into the kitchen, he has swept up all the trimmed hair and shoved it into an empty box of cereal. He folds the lid closed and dumps the box into the bottom of the wastepaper basket.

"Ready, Mom!" I tug the brim of the ball cap, silently wish myself good-luck and march out of the Bat Cave.

I am almost out the door when Mom calls from outside, "Adam, can you grab my canvas shoes? They're by the computer. Not the ones next to the dresser, and not the pink pair or the tennis shoes. And don't mix them up with the sandals."

I dart back to the computer room. No shoes of any kind. "Mom, could they be in the closet?" I call out through the window screen.

"Hmm ... maybe. But I don't need sneakers or flip flops. Remember they're white canvas – not the cream-colored with bows," Mom commands, her voice sailing in through the screen.

I begin to open the bi-fold closet door. Its hinges squeak as the panels press together, but then the track sticks. I bend down to get a closer look. The ball cap tumbles off my head.

Uh-oh. I'm going to have to be more careful if I want to fool Mom.

Quickly I slap the cap back on my head. I pull an overhanging shoelace out of the track. The door easily opens. A truckload of shoes stare at me. Why can't I be looking for football cleats or baseball spikes?

"Are they shiny?" I ask, not certain what canvas shoes are.

"No, they're not shiny. The shiny shoes are the black patent leather ones with kitten heels. I need the plain canvas. White."

Jeepers. I see furry winter boots and red high heels. Nothing plain and white.

"Wait, Adam, here they are! Inside the beach bag."

Only Mom. I mean, I misplace my shoes, too. But at least it's only one pair. And if I ask Brian if he knows where my sneakers are, he tells me to take a whiff. The funny thing is my brother is right. I can usually smell them nearby. It's so easy being a boy. I wonder why girls want more than one pair of shoes.

* * *

We pile into the van, and Mom soon drives us past the diving-board pool where we swam a couple days ago. We roll over a set of railroad tracks and then hit a few stop lights before swinging into a parking lot with a sign that reads Wachter Park and Aquatic Center.

Off to one side is a giant-size sandbox with a sprawling playground. There are tall slides, a maze of tunnels, and tractor-size tire swings. For the wee-little kids, there's a make-believe train. Mom parks the van in front of a small, one-story brick building. This must be the entrance to the swimming pool. A chain link fence wraps behind the building, and cement is everywhere. We get out of the van.

"Ten minutes to go." I hear a booming, echoing voice through speakers high above our heads, toward the back of the building.

"What's ten minutes away?" I ask.

But Mom is busy paying the entry fee for each swimmer, so she doesn't hear me. Brian and I go through the boys' locker room and soon meet Mom poolside.

"It looks just like an ordinary pool," Brian says, looking at the big rectangle of water.

I shake my head wondering why Mom was so excited about this pool for Family Time. Under my breath, I mutter to Brian, "This must be another one of Mom's silly ideas."

The sun bakes the top of my head. I tug at the cap. Instantly I remember about my short hair. Maybe Mom isn't the silly one, after all.

I glance over at Mom. Thank goodness she has settled in a chair and has her nose in a book. She doesn't notice me slip off the cap.

The hot cement makes my feet sizzle. I drop my towel, stepping on it to comfort my toasted toes. I let out a sigh;

at least it will be cool. Not "cool" like fun, great, awesome. "Cool" like in cold water.

"Five minutes to go," the loud-speaker voice blasts and bounces off the mechanical shed next to me. I'm startled by the announcement and jump. None of the other kids seem to notice the bossy, loud voice; they just splash or spray water at friends. Others dive, dip, and dunk.

I head over to the short, two-step side ladder. Suddenly I hear a roar. The water starts to whip and whirl. The sound groans like thunder as the water swirls and swells.

"What's going on?" I yell to Mom.

"You swim in waves for ten minutes, and then the pool will get quiet for fifteen minutes of free play," she says, not looking up from her book. "This is Wave Time!"

She's right. Big waves form, one after another.

"Let's body surf, Adam!" Brian shouts over the roar of the walls of water.

Soon I am standing waist-high in the mega-pool with my back toward the oncoming waves. When the top of the wave turns white, or crests, I hop on. Stretching my arms straight in front of me, I hold my breath and glide like crazy with the rushing crest.

"It's like swimming back home in Lake Michigan," I yell to Brian nearby.

"This is even better, no seaweed or sand in your swimsuit," Brian says, riding a wave.

I catch another wave and sail forward once again. It feels like I'm floating in wet clouds. Each time my head is fully under water, I hear a roar like the sound of a lawn mower. And when I pop back up for air, I'm ready to coast on another wave.

Then like the flip of a switch, it's instantly quiet. What's happening? My eyes scan the pool area, and I see the wave action is fading fast. The water settles and calms, becoming mirror-smooth. Then I remember what Mom told us: It's free time, now, between the wave sessions.

"Let's play catch," I say to Brian.

It's easy to enjoy the quick change from wave action to calm water. Lake Michigan sure doesn't change this quickly. Wind direction and strength determine if there will be waves or calm water, and we sure don't get both in the same day, let alone the same hour.

We stay in the water the entire four-hour swim session, coming out puckered and pruned. And my hair, well ... it's wrinkled in a different kind of wave.

"Adam, what happened to your hair?" Mom asks, staring at my lop-sided haircut.

"What?" I ask, trying to delay my answer and calm my instant nerves. The waves in the pool are no match to the tidal wave in my stomach.

"I asked about your hair." Her eyes drill into mine.

With our stares fixed, I search for a reply, and wonder if a good fib might be the way to go. Then Mom closes her eyes and gets real quiet. When Mom gets mad, she gets silent and serious. I decide to skip the fib and go with a twist Mom might like. "Ah, well. I know short hair is your favorite. It's a buzz cut! Brian gave it to me this morning. Doesn't it look great?"

My heart pounds out dozens of beats before Mom opens her eyes and says very simply: "Adam Michael."

Using my middle name is never a good sign. I gulp and break away from her glaring eyes.

"Lost shoes!" booms the official voice through the pool loudspeakers. "The owner of white canvas shoes can pick them up at Lost and Found."

"Mom, those must be your shoes," I say, pointing to her bare feet.

"Oh my! Yes, my shoes! I'll be right back," Mom says, darting to the Lost and Found. What luck! Mom's forgetfulness saves me. I slap the ball cap on my head. This cap will be glued to my head for a least a week until my hair can grow a little. I figure if my hair is out of Mom's sight, maybe it'll be out of her mind, too.

But I'm not that lucky. When Mom gets back she tugs the cap. "So, why did your brother give you a haircut?"

Yep; Mom's radar is up again.

Gazing into her eyes, I see a look of concern. It's a look I'm used to. It shows up on Mom's face whenever she doesn't know what is coming next, which happens a lot when I'm around. I know it's time to confess. I keep it short. Mom doesn't like me to sugarcoat the truth.

"Um ... I fell into some flypaper," I say.

Mom stops walking, standing more still than the "quiet time" of the wave pool. Her arms are folded across her chest, and I hear a huffing sound. This is not good. I can tell she is waiting for more.

"Well ... somehow the neighbor's cat got stuck in our room. When Brian and I were saving the cat, I landed in a wad of flypaper. We knew you wanted us ready for the wave pool so Brian took a few snips out of my hair to clean up the mess."

Mom's stern look doesn't budge. Finally she says, "I know you were trying to help the cat, but next time make sure to ask Marge Witt for help. I get worried about you boys alone downstairs, and she's just upstairs if you need her."

I give a silent nod. This is not the time to tell Mom that Mad Witch spits at us when she speaks. Maybe Mom hasn't gotten close enough to Mad Witch to notice this.

Then I figure a little humor can't hurt to soften Mom. I tug on my ball cap and say, "At least it's summer vacation and a ball cap is part of my uniform."

The corners of Mom's mouth rise up into an itty-bitty smile. "It is your favorite thing to wear," she says.

"And in this hot, humid weather, any haircut would give a guy silly hat hair," I add, slipping my hand into Mom's. She gives it a tender squeeze, and her smile gets a bit bigger.

"Besides, my hair will grow," I say. It feels good to be laughing with Mom again.

On the way home from the wave pool, I'm beginning to feel like I know the city of Bismarck a little, now that I've been to all three city pools.

"Which pool is your favorite?" I ask Brian.

"Hillside," he says, naming the park with the towering roller coaster slide we visited yesterday.

"Yeah, it was worth waiting for the pool to open," I add, remembering how Mom forgot to check the pool opening schedule. We stood melting in the heat, gazing at more than a hundred steps that lead to the tip top of the water slide ride. It was like a King Kong thrill ride waiting to be tamed.

"At least Mom had a great Plan B when we couldn't swim," Brian says.

"Yeah, we played catch on the lawn while we waited," I add.

"Now, boys. We were just a tad bit early for the water park," Mom says. "Besides, my forgetfulness is part of my creative nature – the right side of my brain."

"Speaking of forgetfulness, Mom," I teasingly say. "Remember this: 'lost sho-o-o-es ... would the owner of lost canvas sho-o-o-es come to the Lost and Found.'" I have my hands cupped around my mouth so my voice echoes like it's bouncing from the loudspeakers at the wave pool.

Brian starts to giggle and I do, too.

"Well, forgetfulness is part of the right side of your brain," Mom repeats. She doesn't exactly smile, but her mouth twitches at one corner, showing a hint of a grin to come.

Seeing Mom's eyes sparkle a bit, I joke around some more. "Remember the time you painted that big canvas? When we went to deliver the completed piece, it wouldn't fit through the customer's door."

"Now, Adam, I knew their garage door was big enough, I just forgot about their inside door." Mom flashes a full smile now.

Sometimes I think her creative right brain gets a bit harebrained. I call it her "crazy side."

"And remember the rest of the story," Mom says, her smile beaming.

"Yeah, Mom was a hero," Brian adds. "She simply popped the staples from that giant-size frame, rolled up the canvas and brought it through the door into the customer's home. Then she put it back in place inside the house. Ta Da!"

"Yeah, yeah," I rally, having to admit Mom is great at rolling with punches and finding creative solutions under pressure, like what to do at Hillside Park the other day.

Now as the van pulls into the driveway at our apartment, I hear a voice from next door.

"Hey, Moynihans!" calls out my buddy Zach. "Dad is taking Joey and me to the Mandan pool."

"What's a Mandan pool?" I ask, knowing mom said there were only three city pools. I scratch my head, not understanding.

"Mandan is the city on the other side of the Missouri River," Zach says. "The name comes from the Native American tribe who once lived on the prairie there."

Oh, Mandan is another city. No wonder there's another pool.

"Want to come along?" Zach asks Brian and me.

I hide my wrinkled, water-soaked fingers when we ask Mom if we can go to another pool. And she says yes!

We're off again. Outside of Bismarck, Captain Mike points their blue van west. We cruise across a wide metal bridge with steel girders crisscrossing above, below, and on all sides of us. The bridge rattles as the van wheels pound against the metal crossbars.

"Way down below shifts the mighty Missouri River," Captain Mike says with a smooth chuckle in the back of his throat. It's soft and rich, like he's humming a melody. Then he taps the smoky lenses of his dark sunglasses. They're the polarized glasses from the pontoon boat.

I nudge Zach: "Does he think he can see fish from this high up?"

Before Zach can answer Captain Mike flips his sunglasses onto the top of his head. His bright eyes flash in the rear-view mirror at me. "There's a walleye on the left!" he says, pointing out the window.

I lean over, gazing down at the fast flowing river.

Captain Mike merrily slaps his thigh and lets out a bark of laughter.

"Dad's just joking us," Zach says. "Having four sons, he likes to tease."

Now everyone is cracking up. Captain Mike's belly laugh can make you do that.

We pull into the parking lot of the Mandan Community Center. No pool in sight, just a big box of a building sitting on a wide open space.

"It's an indoor pool," Zach says after seeing me stare at a lawn of green grass. As soon as we're parked, Zach and Joey race ahead, swinging towels like lassos high above their heads.

Brian and I hustle up, following a few steps behind. But once inside, nothing is happening. And I couldn't be happier. No kids pushing and shoving. No waiting in line.

Then I stop. Could we be too early, like when Mom took us to Hillside and we had to wait for swim time to start? My heart sinks.

"Come on, Adam," Zach calls. "All the kids swim outside in the summer. This inside pool is our secret."

I rush to catch up. The pool is bigger than a football field. At each corner is a twisty-turny tunnel slide. The four slides – red, blue, yellow, green – all meet in the middle of the pool. This is quadruple the fun compared to one super Hillside slide.

A brilliant idea comes to me, "I'll take red. Brian you pick yellow, Zach green, Joey blue. Let's race."

We dart to our targets and scale up the ladders. At the top of the red ladder, I wave my arms high above my head to signal the others. From the yellow deck, Brian arches his arm in one smooth swoop. Zach smiles from the green platform as Joey tap dances his way up the blue stairs. He's almost in position.

"On the count of three," I yell. My voice bounces off the empty swim center. I can't believe we have this giant pool to ourselves.

"Roger that," Zach shouts back.

"On your mark, get set," Brian starts calling out.

Joey hustles up the last three steps. "Go!" he yells, hurling himself into the tunnel slide.

I fling myself into the red tunnel and fly through the first curve at lightning speed. Like a rocket, I soar, gaining speed as I whiz along. Wind rushes around me, and the sloping tunnel tosses me from side to side. Whoosh! Water explodes when I'm dumped into the pool.

Poosh! Poosh! Poosh! Brian, Zach and Joey hit the water, too. We whoop and holler and splash water at each other.

This is better than a carnival ride. I just had to come to the city of Mandan.

* * *

On the ride home Joey wiggles in his seat trying to snatch something out of his pocket. With Joey, you never know what might shoot out of his pocket.

"I brought bubble gum, but for some reason, something is stuck." Joey shifts about, struggling with his jam-packed left-front pocket.

"Did you shove chewed-up gum in your pocket? Is that why it's stuck?" I ask, choking back a laugh.

"Nah. It's a brand new pack. I figured we could have a bubble-blowing contest," Joey says.

Well, at least his heart is in the right place. Suddenly Joey's hand yanks free and out comes an explosion of M&Ms, stubby pencils and wadded-up gum wrappers. Two Indian arrowheads tumble to the floor mat, too.

Joey scoops up the arrowheads, holding them tightly in his fist. The M&Ms and other stuff are left to roll around in the van. The gum wrappers make me think Joey already chewed the gum, so there won't be any bubble-blowing contest.

Then with his other hand, the seven-year-old tugs his right-front pocket. Something brown and crusty plops on my lap. It rattles and I jump. Yikes! The thing looks like it'll bite. But then I realize it's a snake without a head – just a rattlesnake tail.

Joey whisks the tail off my lap.

"You have some real treasures there, Joey," I say.

"You bet I do. This here is a ten-ring rattle." He cradles the tail in his right hand.

"Which means?" I ask.

"The snake that grew it was ten years old," he explains.

"Not quite," Brian says. "It's true rattlesnakes grow another rattle every time they shed their skin, but the tail becomes brittle and can break off at any time."

"Oh," Joey says, looking a little disappointed. "But the arrowheads are from General Custer." He barely opens his fist of his left hand as he protects his treasures.

"Are those the rocks from the birthday party?" I ask.

Joey nods, proudly. He must have scooped up the arrowhead I found along the Missouri, plus his own arrowhead, when they fell to the floor during the birthday celebration. Until now, I had forgotten all about the arrowheads.

Joey's eyes catch mine as he cradles the arrowheads in his hands.

"So you think the rocks are valuable?" I ask the little guy, giving Brian a jab with my elbow. Earlier, Brian had searched the Internet and learned arrowheads can sell for as much as two hundred dollars – if they aren't fakes. But it takes a museum master and an official handbook to prove if an arrowhead is real. More than likely, they are just plaster souvenirs.

"Yeah, they're real, all right," Joey says, eyes growing wide as quarters. "Did you know that long ago General Custer traded rifles for arrowheads?"

Zach pokes me from the backseat. I give him a sideways glance. He winks at me, which makes his eyeglasses dance on his nose. I nod to Zach and then play along with Joey. "I knew Custer traded with the Native Americans."

"But we need to be cautious, Adam," Joey says almost in a whisper, like he's trying to be mysterious. "Late at night, I've heard Custer's ghost rattling around."

"Do you think Custer's ghost wants the arrowheads back?" I ask with a touch of mystery in my voice.

"Well, the ghost said I should keep them." Joey carefully slips his treasures back into his pocket and gives them a gentle pat. "Is that okay with you, Adam, that I keep them?" he asks. I watch Joey cross his fingers for good luck, hoping I'll say yes.

And I do. "You keep them, Joey. We don't want to upset Custer's ghost."

If Joey weren't such a cute kid, I'd laugh out loud. This little guy can sure spin a ghost tale. It must be his creative right side of the brain. The crazy side.

Chapter 6

King-size Craziness

There is nothing funny about a lawn sprinkler spitting water on dead grass. Nothing funny, that is, until you watch a big brown dog bounding into the misty spray, barking and biting at the sprinkler while spinning in silly circles. His mammoth paws splash mud almost as far as the sprinkler shoots water in Mad Witch's front yard.

From nearby, I watch, giggling, at this huge and hilarious mutt I've never seen before. Suddenly, in one giant leap, he bounces toward me and tackles me to the ground. He licks his huge tongue all over my face, and his soggy fur tickles my skin. I can't tell if I'm mostly wet from his dripping coat or his crazy dog kisses. My laughs are muffled in his mounds of mushy fur as I try to push him away.

"Settle down, boy," I say, turning my head back and forth to dodge his huge tongue. His muddy, catcher's mitt-size paws cover me in muck. I bet I stink like wet dog now, too.

"King! Come here, King!" I hear Zach, his voice coming from next door. "Come here, King!" Zach hollers louder.

With a name like King, this dog must be waiting for a royal salute because he is not responding to Zach's call in the least. Instead, he slobbers me with spit and drool. Seconds later, Zach's frisky small pup, Annie, sprints over to yap at us. The yip, yip, yip of Annie spinning in circles gets King to lift his monster-size head up off my face. Annie dances on her hind legs; King must like the show, because in one giant leap, he is at Annie's side.

"Who does the big dog belong to?" I ask Zach, pushing myself off the ground and trying to brush off the mud.

"King is my Aunt Sara's dog. He's still a puppy so he gets a bit excited," Zach says, while grabbing hold of King's collar. "My family is dog-sitting, but tonight we need to drive to Fargo and stay overnight there. Do you think you could dog-sit King and Annie while we're gone?"

King looks at me with his eager, chocolate-cookie eyes. He's so big that it's like having a bodyguard at your side. Then he lets out a powerful "Ruff!" On second thought, it's like having your own nuclear weapon.

Now the king-size puppy rolls onto his back. "Looks like King's ready for belly rubs," Zach says, squatting down to rub the fun-loving fur-ball. The mutt almost starts to sing as Zach rubs his tummy. Even wet and soggy, I'm falling in love with this big guy.

"I can't wait to dog sit," I blurt out. Then I bite my lip as I remember to add, "I'll need to check with Mom." Then King wiggles as he blinks his walnut-colored eyes at me. Instantly, I know we've got to sit for this big guy. "She'll think it's a great idea; she's got to! I'll be right back," I say, and dash off to find Mom.

Yikes! Who am I kidding? Mom is always business first. Pint-size Annie won't be any trouble bringing in the back-door studio entrance. But super-size King? He will stand eye-level to Mom's work table. One swish of his whale-size tail and I can imagine a paint pail spilling over and splattering wet paint everywhere. We'll have to keep King out of the art studio, for sure. But first, I have to get on Mom's good side.

"Hey, Mom. What are the plans for Family Time?" I ask when I find Mom in the apartment. I know family activities are Mom's favorite time of day with Brian and me.

"I promised Marge Witt we'd pick gooseberries for her. We can go during my lunch hour. It'll be fun," Mom says.

Oh no. Not only will I have to keep King and Annie from the studio, but now I'll have to hide the dogs from Mad Witch. I remember how the old lady landlord shook her crooked finger at me and squawked about her dead husband's treasures in the haunted shed. My heart races like a rabbit, knowing it will be impossible to sneak bear-size King and yappy pint-size Annie past Mad Witch. But when I picture King poking his wet nose into my chest and staring me down with his Hershey-bar eyes, I just blurt it out: "Mom, can I dog-sit King and Annie?"

"Sure. It'll teach you responsibility, and you can use the side entrance off your room," Mom says.

"What side entrance?" I ask as my ears perk up.

"The side door at the top of the stairs in the laundry room."

I give Mom a puzzled look.

"Oh, I mean the 'Bat Cave,'" Mom says, reminding me that the laundry room and our hideaway are the same room. But this still doesn't help me understand about the side entrance.

"Where is the side door?" I repeat.

Mom leads me into the Bat Cave and points. Behind the storage closet is a set of seven steps leading up to a side entrance. I've been so busy playing Nintendo tucked away inside the secretive Bat Cave that I've never explored further. The only door that has been important to me is the one that seals off our room from grown-ups in the studio. That is until now. Finding this side door is luckier than a two-for-one videogame sale.

"Remember though, you can't use the back studio business entrance," Mom says. "You'll have to use the side door only. And don't forget that you share that entrance with Marge Witt so we better pick her extra gooseberries."

I swallow hard. At the top of *those* stairs is where Mad Witch lives. What if she casts her piercing evil eye down on us? I'd better have Zach pack a heavy-duty leash to hold onto King; I doubt Mad Witch will like his frolicking nature.

"Where do we go to pick the gooseberries?" I ask Mom as she gathers containers for collecting the berries.

"Just out back, behind the shed," Mom says. "Marge told me that when she was young this land was used for farming. She used to pick gooseberries right in the backyard."

"The shed out back?" I ask, dropping the plastic picking container. It plunks and rolls on the floor. I'm remembering that Joey thinks he hears Custer's ghost mumbling and moaning back in that gloomy shed. I had my doubts about Joey's crazy claims until the other night, when I woke up and wanted a drink of water.

I crawled out of bed, half asleep, and as I headed to the bathroom, I glimpsed a light flickering in the shed. Then a rapidly blinking glow lit up the entire apartment, yet everything was dead silent. Before I could blink, it was pitch black again. Of course, I scampered back to bed and hid under the covers until I fell back to sleep.

Snapping out of my daydream about the shed, I realize Mom is talking to me: "That's right. The berries are just behind the shed. It'll be fun like when we pick blueberries in Michigan. We'll get started in half an hour. In the meantime, Adam, go ahead and gather the dog supplies you'll need for the weekend. I'm pleased to see you being responsible."

I head next door to Zach's house. He gives me dog food, water dishes, and a hefty leash for King. "Annie should stay right nearby for you," Zach says. "Well, on second thought,

Annie likes to chase squirrels, rabbits, wood chucks, and moles ... so here." He hands me a leash for Annie, too.

With both dogs on leashes now, I head for the side entrance to Mom's place. King is his usual unruly self, turning around and licking my hand as I hold the leash. His slobber is covering my arm, and the tickling of his big tongue takes my mind off the possibility of meeting Mad Witch at the side door to the apartment.

Out of the corner of my eye, I see Brian pulling mail out of the box from the front of the house. Suddenly, King darts the opposite way, his leash tightening and yanking me with a jerk. Annie runs in circles, causing her leash to wrap around my feet.

"Whoa, whoa! Wait a minute!" I cry. Annie's leash tightens now and instantly – plunk – I'm on the ground. The water bowls sail out of my arms and the dog-food bag spills, spraying some of its contents like shotgun pellets. "Stop! Stay! Heel!" I yell as I'm dragged behind King.

"Great start to dog-sitting!" Brian roars with side-splitting laughter as King tugs me along.

Finally, King stops for a moment and I untangle my legs from Annie's twisted leash.

"Mom told me you were dog-sitting. It looks like you're in over your head," Brian smirks between hearty laughs as he catches up to me. "Or, maybe the rug was pulled out from under your feet – without the rug, of course!" he adds, throwing another zinger my way.

"You're just jealous—" I cut my snide remark short because right then Mom steps out of the back studio door. Too late. I can tell she's heard everything.

"That's enough," she snaps. "No more squabbling. Got it?" she warns us.

I try to hide a snicker. It's not that I don't take Mom seriously; it's just that *squabbling* is a funny word, especially when Mom's face is red and her cheeks are puffed so the syllables drag out.

"Do you think this is funny?" Mom asks, jaw grinding.

I stand paralyzed under her heated gaze.

Mom's scolding isn't over. "I want you to say three nice things to each other. Go ahead, start now, I'm waiting," she says.

"Um ..." I lower my head.

"Ah," Brian stammers, too.

Just then King strolls up to Brian and gives his bare leg several gigantic licks just below the hem of his shorts. It makes me laugh on the inside and I can tell Brian is trying to hold back a giggle from the tickle too. Brian bends down, wraps his arms around the big guy, and nuzzles his neck into King's fur. I swear King is smiling. My heart softens, but not Mom's.

Towering over us with her hands firmly planted on her hips, foot tapping, she waits for us to say nice things to each other. I figure there is only one way to fix this mess and it's not with a fib or half-truth that I can sometimes get away with. I take Mom's warning seriously.

"Ah, Brian," I say. "Thanks for helping me dog-sit. I can tell King likes you scratching between his ears."

Mom holds up two fingers. It tells me I've got another nice thing to say. Somehow I untie my tongue and come up with a third answer. It turns out it wasn't as hard as I thought. Brian says three nice things and then even helps me gather the spilled dog food and water dishes.

"Now, one more step," Mom says. "I want you to say three nice things about each other every night before bed."

I want to groan and moan but know better than to cross Mom. Besides, after saying three nice things about Brian, I end up feeling better about my brother. Maybe Mom's warning isn't such a bad thing. I give her a no-nonsense nod.

Mom's face breaks into a slow smile. Then she snatches Brian and me into shoulder hugs. We yelp in surprise and laugh together. Something about her touch always feels good.

"Okay, so let's go pick some gooseberries," Mom says, her eyes dancing with delight. "The patch is on the far side of the shed."

Mom leads the way. A few steps behind her, I pass the spooky shed and notice the door is padlocked shut. That means Mad Witch must not be around – which is fine by me. And there are no flickering lights coming through the grimy windows, thank goodness. I hustle past the eerie building and turn my gaze down to the ground rather than peer any longer into the shed. Better safe than sorry, I figure.

The backyard is tiny with the shed taking up most of the space. The grass is unmowed and the tall grass and weeds there scratch my legs. Wedged along the back fence is a skinny apple tree which has one – no, two – fruits on it, both with an obvious worm problem. It looks like this spot hasn't been an orchard since old Mad Witch was a kid. The gooseberry patch isn't much, either: two skimpy bushes with only a few thick branches here and there.

All in all, it's pretty quiet back here. Not even grasshoppers hopping about in the hot sun. I figure King and Annie will stay nearby while we pick a bucket of berries.

I drop their leashes and reach into the berry bush. "Ouch! It bit me!" I yell, quickly putting my finger in my mouth to nurse the wound.

"Be careful," Mom says, cautioning me too late. "Gooseberries have sharp spines."

"More like spikes with stickers," Brian says, sucking on his own pricked finger.

"Hey, Mom, are you sure these berries are ripe? Every berry is green," I say.

"Gooseberries are green when they're ripe and usually pretty tart–"

She's too late again with her comment, because I've already popped a berry into my mouth. "Yuck! It's really sour." My mouth puckers, my eyes water, and I spit out the bitter fruit.

Jeepers. This isn't anything like blueberry picking where we pick one, eat two, pick one, eat three more.

Even nastier than the taste is the attack of the prickly gooseberries. With every reach I get pricked and poked as branches chew at my skin. It's painful, but fighting this bush is important to keep Mad Witch happy, especially since we're using her side entrance for dog-sitting. I just hope we don't run into her.

The plastic picking container is almost half full when King begins to wander through the tall dead grass. Annie stays still, panting in the shade as she lies in the cool shadow alongside the shed. Suddenly, King lets out a big "Ruff!" and rushes through the grass. Some kind of black and white fur ball scurries ahead of him. And then I notice the horrible smell!

"Pee-yeeuw!" I choke on the words because sour skunk stink spreads through the hot, humid air in seconds.

King doesn't stay put, though. Instantly he's chasing the critter into a hole at the base of the shed. Just in time, I snag King's leash before he can jam his snout into the hole and scare the skunk again. One dose of ghastly skunk spray is enough, I decide, as my eyes water from the nasty smell.

Now Annie starts yapping, too. She's up, and she's ready to bound over to the skunk's hole. Zach says that Annie is a bird dog and that she loves to swim in the Missouri River. But now I realize she hunts more than birds. This awful, skunky smell is not stopping her at all!

"Brian, quick, grab Annie's leash," I shout. The last thing I need is Annie getting sprayed with dreadful skunk stink, too.

With only seconds to spare, Brian snags Annie's leash. That leaves King with his king-size stench. The smell is worse than burning sulfur in science class.

Mom isn't saying a word because her hands are glued over her nose and mouth. It's a good thing Mom hates smells, or she'd have more than a few words to say.

"We'll have to give King a tomato-juice bath," Brian says.

"What?" I ask, unsure of what I heard Brian say.

"Zach gave me a Farmer's Almanac; it's filled with local customs and home remedies. Apparently, the acid in tomato juice balances the odor," Brian says. Wow. My brother is like a walking textbook. A big one. Without pictures. Just lots of really smart words.

Now, still holding onto King as the rank smell oozes from every pore, I ask, "Mom, do you have any tomato juice?"

Mom shakes her head yes, still holding her nose. It's lucky she believes in history. If the Farmer's Almanac is like a North Dakota bible, Mom will be okay. I say a silent prayer that the tomato-juice cure isn't just folk lore or fairy tale. But right when I think Brian and I have a plan, Mom finds her voice and it doesn't sound happy.

"This is a huge mess to clean up," she squawks through her pinched nose.

I turn to Mom. Her nose is running, and her eyes are red and watery. "Oh no!" she says, rubbing her eyes. "This smell is getting worse and making my eyes burn and itch! I need to step away. Go ahead and try the tomato juice and fast!"

"Don't worry, Mom" I say. "We'll be responsible. We'll fix King up good as new."

Mom nods as her tearing eyes force her to scoot away from the nasty odor.

Jeepers, sometimes I don't look for trouble – it finds me.

"Here, Adam, take Annie," Brian says, handing me her dog leash. "I'll go to the Bat Cave and start the tomato-juice bath in the laundry tub." Having Brian on my team is like having a bulldozer ready to flatten any mass.

"I'll sneak the dogs into the side entrance. We'll have to work fast so Mad Witch doesn't hear us," I whisper, but don't know why. Trying to keep this stinky skunk smell a secret seems impossible. I'm afraid the foul odor will creep up the stairwell right into Mad Witch's house no matter how fast I whisk the dogs downstairs into the Bat Cave.

"I'll tap Morse code on the window when I'm ready," Brian says, referring to his Boy Scout knowledge. "Then I'll watch for your legs to walk by and I can meet you at the side door."

The Bat Cave really is like a dark cave wedged in the back of the apartment. It has only one narrow, teeny window that is high above our heads. We use it to spy on people who are coming to the house. Brown shoes are UPS delivery. Nike gym shoes are Zach. Ugly chunky black shoes are Mad Witch.

Tap. Tap. Tappity-tap. Two long taps, one short tap for the letter G. Followed by tap, tap, tap. Three long taps? That's the letter O. It's Brian's "go" message on the window.

Quickly, I slip King and Annie through the side door and Brian helps me quietly guide them down the steps. Uh-oh. A horrible haze of skunk stink hangs around us as the gross odor becomes stronger inside the house. I can only hope Mad Witch's funny shaped, Play-Doh-looking nose doesn't smell scents well.

I hustle the dogs as fast as I can and make it into the Bat Cave without the door to Mad Witch's house upstairs opening. The smell is so strong I figure she's either not home or she's way up on the second floor in one of those rooms I've seen from outside. The windows are as high as the tree tops.

I make sure the door to the kitchen is closed tightly. We have to control the stinky smell as much as possible.

Brian has the laundry tub brimming full of tomato-juicy water and a lot of soap bubbles. Oh no. Why didn't I remember this? The laundry-tub sink is smaller than giant-size King.

"Here. Let's use these storage totes as steps to get King into the sink," Brian says, while quickly sliding and stacking the plastic totes.

I stare at my brother.

"Come on, Adam!" Brian tries to hurry me and tugs on King's leash.

"Uhh, Brian," I sputter, thinking this is really strange. "King is never going to fit."

"I know," he replies, putting his hand on my shoulder. "We'll have to wash him in two parts. Just put King's front end into the tub first."

I simply nod. My brother can do this to me: calm me down and scramble my brain all at the same time.

Meanwhile, Annie snuggles onto the hide-a-bed. At least one dog is under control. But not King. He immediately jumps onto the highest plastic tote and spins in a circle, causing his butt and tail to flop in the water. One swish with his giant tail and I'm soaking wet.

Yikes! Thank goodness Mom can't see the enormous puddle forming at my feet. Only we boys know the secrets that go on behind the Bat Cave closed doors. Right now I'm extra thankful for this hide-out.

King wiggles. I find it hard to breath with his butt in my face. The foul smell is more powerful with his fur dripping wet. I figure Mad Witch isn't home because if odor rises like hot air, she'd be racing down from the treetop room and stomping down the side staircase.

"Hurry!" I say. "Start scrubbing."

We suds King up using a mix of tomato juice and Mom's lavender soap. I didn't even ask my brother the reason for the lavender. He could rattle off the reasons, but I'd rather pretend lavender is magical and can get me out of this mess.

King shakes and shimmies during the entire bath. Once he's scrubbed, the red-colored water looks gray, and all the soap bubbles are used up and have disappeared. I just hope the rancid smell is gone too. It's hard to tell right now because I've been sucking in the stink for so long.

Brian lets the water out of the laundry tub and we dry King off with beach towels.

"Now change out of your stinky clothes, Adam," Brian says.

"What?"

"We need to wash our clothes and these towels or the smell will hang around."

My brother is right. We quickly change into clean clothes and Brian loads the washing machine. I sneak King outside, unsure if he smells like Mom's lavender bubble bath, tomato juice, or the skunk.

I take Annie and King for a walk around the block, figuring the fresh air can't hurt. There isn't much of a breeze to fluff King's fur, but the hot summer air dries his coat by the time we get back to the house.

Brian meets us by the side entrance. He pokes his nose deep into King's shaggy fur. "He smells like a rotten vegetable."

"That's better than skunk, so it's good enough for me," I say, sighing in relief.

"Well, now I guess we have to get rid of the skunk," Brian declares.

"What do you mean?" I ask, thinking we had all our problems solved.

"We can't let the skunk build a nest under Mrs. Witt's shed," Brian says.

Jeepers. Brian's right. I promised Mom we'd be responsible. I wish I could tell Brian to simply let Custer's ghost scare the skunk to solve the problem, but I'm not sure if Brian is a believer in Joey's tale. As for the strange flickering lights coming from the creepy old shed, I haven't told anyone about that, so I listen to my brother's plan.

"We'll make a Hansel-and-Gretel trail and lure the skunk out," he says. "Come on. We'll sneak into the kitchen for supplies."

Quietly Brian hands me a jar of peanut butter and a banana. "If this is a Hansel-and-Gretel trail, why aren't we using bread crumbs?" I whisper.

"We need food with a strong odor," Brian says.

I nod. It's hard to disagree with my brother's wisdom. In the privacy of the Bat Cave we smother banana chunks with peanut butter.

"The skunk will follow the scent, but not until it gets dark. Skunks are nocturnal," Brian says.

After dropping a trail of bananas leading away from the shed, I relax in the Bat Cave, hoping the skunk is hungry and we'll be out of this mess.

*   *   *

Early the next morning with the sun shining low in the sky, Brian and I creep back behind the shed. "The bananas are gone!" I jump and cheer.

"But not the skunk," Brian says.

"What?"

"Look." Brian points at the hole.

I squat down and peek inside. Two shiny black eyes sparkle at me. "He must have grabbed that food and crept back inside. Now what?"

"Mothballs."

"You mean those stinky things Mom uses to store winter clothes?" I ask, wondering if my brother has lost his mind. We just got rid of one horrible smell.

"The skunk will hate the smell and leave," Brian says. "And I know a trick for easily putting them in the hole."

I shrug my shoulders. Being around Brian is like living with a crazy chemist. At home he makes delicious foaming fizz pops – a treat like ice cream floats. I wonder what his secret weapon will be this time.

We go back inside to the apartment, passing Mom as she works at her desk in the studio. Her eyes are no longer red and swollen. In fact they twinkle, making me smile wide. I give Mom a wink. She laughs. She has a really nice laugh. It is soft and full of fun. It makes me want to get rid of the skunk once and for all. Brian and I head to the Bat Cave.

"We'll stuff the mothballs in this laundry bag," Brian says, snagging a mesh bag off a hook above the washing machine. It looks like a mini fishing net. "The holes in it will let out the scent of the mothballs. But the beauty of the bag is it'll take only one toss to get the mothballs into the skunk's tunnel. Then, after the skunk leaves, we can snag the mothball bag with Mom's golf ball retriever. Marge Witt will never know she had a skunk or mothballs under her shed."

What a great plan. And to think all these tools are stashed in the Bat Cave. Who needs real Batman gadgets like a Bat-a-rang boomerang or a grappling gun when we have our very own utility room filled with secret weapons?

I grab the telescoping ball retriever from Mom's golf bag tucked in the corner closet. The retriever is what Mom uses when she smacks her golf ball into a pond instead of staying on the fairway. I've had to fish out more than a few golf balls for her. Brian stays busy stuffing and tying up the mothball bag.

"Now we need to de-scent ourselves," Brian says.

"What?"

"Get rid of all human scent on our bodies so the mothball scent is as powerful as possible."

Brian's ability to recall details always makes my eyes glaze over, but I have learned to trust his knowledge – even crazy ideas – because they get me out of trouble. "So how do we get rid of our human scent?" I ask.

"First gargle with mouthwash," he directs.

Brian and I quietly slip into the bathroom not wanting to disturb Mom working. I swish and rinse my mouth with blue mouthwash.

"Now wash your hands and arms with the mouthwash, too," Brian adds.

I shoot Brian a look. Our eyes meet green to green. "Come on," he says. "We need to de-scent. This is our last chance to get rid of the skunk before Mrs. Witt finds out."

Mad Witch. The sound of her name gets me to rub and scrub with minty fresh mouthwash with whitening power.

"Now we need to slip into rubber boots," Brian commands. "I saw some tucked under the laundry room stairs in the Bat Cave," Brian says.

"What?" I ask.

"I saw winter boots when I was getting the mothballs, which were next to the winter clothes closet. The rubber boots will hide the scent of our footsteps," he explains.

Brian reaches the stairwell before me. He snatches a pair of chunky green knee-highs just like Dad's snow boots. Brian slips his feet into the He-Man-like boots.

That leaves me with a pair of fancy white snow boots that look like moccasins with fringe on top. Worse yet, white fur pokes out. "I can't wear these," I say, staring at the frilly boots.

"Adam, come on. It's just from here to the backyard," Brian says, stomping in his oversize rubber boots. His heavy footsteps sound like the boots weigh ten pounds each.

Grumbling, I slip on the white boots. Click. Click. Click. The hard heels tap the floor and sound like a pair of high heel shoes. "This better be quick," I say, trying to walk quietly in the boots, but with every step I hear more clickity-click, click.

"Don't worry, it'll be quick," my brother says.

"Yeah, right. You've got Army boots and I've got Eskimo princess boots," I gripe.

Brian turns away so he thinks I can't see him cracking up. But I hear him. How do I get myself into such embarrassing situations?

"I just need to grab one more thing," Brian says between laughs.

"What else could you possibly need?" I ask, restlessly standing in the white princess boots.

"Flour."

"Flour?!"

"Yes, flour. To be sure the skunk leaves, we need to sprinkle flour outside the hole so we can see his tracks," Brian says.

All I can do is shake my head. I'm in this far with my brother's plan; I may as well finish.

Brian brings back the flour. His boots clomp and mine click-click as we hike up the stairs of the side entrance. I peek outside. It looks reasonably safe. Nobody to the left, nobody to the right.

Once outside, I try to hustle Brian to the back yard before anyone sees me in the white fancy boots, but he can only slowly waddle in his chunky boots.

"Wait, we need one more thing," Brian says, halfway to the shed.

"What now?" I bark, putting my hands on my hips and leaning in close to Brian's nose. I'm so close I'm sure he can smell my minty mouthwash breath. "What else could you possibly need, big brother?"

"Walnuts. We need black walnuts," he says with certainty. "The scent of the nut will distract from our human scent. Besides, the tree is right here."

We stomp and click to the tree that overhangs from the Grunners' yard. A handful of walnuts have fallen from the tree and lie on the ground. But there's a problem.

Fresh walnuts from a tree drop in autumn. This is June. The ones on the ground look like wrinkled golf balls instead of prickly tennis balls. They're left-overs from last winter.

Without hesitating, Brian picks up a dried-up nut. "Just rub the husk on the cement and the scent of the walnut inside will seep through."

Before I can blink my brother scoops up a handful of shriveled nuts, clomps to the sidewalk and starts scraping the green ball. It roughs up into a fuzzy pod.

I shuffle over. He pitches me a couple walnuts.

"Shove them in your boots," he orders.

If I wasn't so eager to get out of these silly white boots before someone sees me, I'd tell my brother I think the skunk would be happy to keep living under the shed. Besides, what's wrong with a little odor leaking from Mad Witch's shed? Then I remember Mom's business entrance. Quickly, I shove the fuzzy balls into the boots. Believe it or not, a pine-walnut scent seeps from the pods. Brian's rubbing really did work.

The hot sun beats on my head and makes my feet sweat in the fur-lined frilly boots. I smell like a Christmas tree with foot odor! Tip-toeing, because the pointy heels on these boots are poking into the dirt causing me to trip, I shuffle to the shed. With each step I take, the walnuts drop deeper into the boots, now pinching my toes with each sweaty stride.

Gee whiz. The phrase "harebrained idea" spins 'round and 'round in my mind. And it's my own fault for offering to dog-sit and telling Mom I could be responsible. And I thought taking care of King and Annie would be fun.

Brian clomps next to me. Finally, we reach the skunk hole. Brian gently places the mothball bag into the opening.

"The skunk should be sleeping in the daytime," Brian whispers, not wanting to disturb the critter.

I silently agree and take a soft step backward. Brian treads lightly, sprinkling a trail of flour as he backs away, too. I lay the golf ball fetcher next to the shed to use later.

I sure hope this scheme works. I'm hot and my feet hurt more than the gooseberry cuts on my hands. Now, a few feet away from the skunk hole, I say, "Let's get out of these boots." I give my brother's arm a tug to hurry him along.

When we finally tromp back to the Bat Cave, King and Annie are waiting for us. I kick off the boots and flop onto the couch, pleased that no one caught sight of me in those silly white boots.

Annie jumps in my lap and her tail thumpity-thumps, double-time against my chest. Instantly, I giggle. Annie melts away all the troubles of the day. Then she lies on her back, sticks her four paws up, and looks at me, waiting for tummy rubs.

King sees Annie getting all the attention so he wanders over, too. No need to hop on the couch, his bear-like size already puts him at petting height. I reach out and stroke King with my other hand.

*   *   *

"Hey! What's this?" I pull a black crusty ball off King's fur.

"A tick," Brian says.

"A what?"

"A wood tick. A bug. He probably got them in the gooseberry patch," Brian says. "We'll need to check his coat and make sure they're all off. They'll suck his blood."

"Like a vampire?" I ask, feeling a rush of panic.

"Not that bad, but the bug can carry disease," Brian says. "We'll have to pull the head of the tick out, too."

"King isn't going to like this," I say.

125

"Especially since it'll pinch when we pull them," Brian says.

"I'll hold him steady while you yank." I wrap my arms around King and squeeze my eyes shut as Brian pulls the first tick.

Just then I hear the Bat Cave side entrance door swing open above us. Uh-oh. Because my eyes were closed, I missed spying the shoe signal at the little basement window.

Letting go of King, I creep a few steps toward the bottom of the staircase. I crane my neck and catch a glimpse of the top of the stairs. I see ugly, chunky shoes. Mad Witch is home! And that orange furry cat is slipping inside the door.

King smells the cat. Instantly, he leaps around me and sails up the seven steps in one jump. The cat darts out the door with King on its tail.

"Stop! Stop! My precious Butterscotch!" Mad Witch wails, her lawnmower voice almost spitting out smoke.

"We'll get your cat back," I call out to Mad Witch. If we don't, Mad Witch is sure to cast her evil eye on us. Already I feel her dark eyes target me with an intensity that makes my skin prickle.

Brian and I fly out the door chasing after King. He's already to the corner of Avenue B and heading south. We jog after him. King leaps like a horse while the cat runs like a jack rabbit. On Rosser Avenue, they flee left, flashing past Third Street. We race as fast as we can, but when we catch up, it's too late.

We're standing in front of an automatic car wash. Butterscotch weaves through the robotic arms of the car wash.

Brian scoops up the cat. But King is scared, frozen in place, smack dab on the conveyor belt, moving down the car wash line.

"I don't think he'll have one tick left after this ride," I say.

King is getting rubbed by fluffy spinning rollers and then sprayed with jets of water. Next, he moves along to the big flapping straps of cloth that swish back and forth. They scrub him down and the suds go flying. Soon he's in the rinse cycle, where water mists from every angle. Once out of the powerful blow dryers, his fur is fluffed straight out. I grab King by his collar, ducking my head away from the car wash attendant to avoid being scolded for the trouble we've caused. Instead, though, the attendant throws his head back and laughs until his eyes water. "That mutt just enjoyed the 'Ultimate Shine treatment,'" he says through a big grin.

When we get home, Mad Witch is so happy to see Butterscotch that she cradles the cat in her arms and snuggles her egg-shaped nose into its fur. The rough sputter of Mad Witch's lawnmower laugh is gone. Instead, the heh-heh-heh purrs right along with her Butterscotch. She tenderly rubs the cat with her boney fingers and carries him upstairs. Mad Witch doesn't even seem to notice King, which is fine by me. We quietly slip downstairs before anything else can go wrong.

That night, nestled in the Bat Cave with Annie on my lap, I play Mario with Brian. King is lying quietly at my feet. I hear a meow at the top of the stairs, but King doesn't budge.

Butterscotch meows again. King stays put. Puzzled, I look at Brian.

"I buttered the paws on King and Butterscotch," Brian says.

"What?"

"I rubbed butter on all four of their paws. By the time they lick off all that butter, they're happy to stay home."

My brother is like one of those displays at a museum: Push the speaker button, and out comes the most unusual information.

I don't doubt that Brian's facts are correct, because King and Butterscotch stay put. But I wonder if half a container of gooseberries will keep Mad Witch happy.

My fear lessens the next morning when we discover little white footprints leading away from the shed and then see that the skunk hole is empty. Nice work, Brian! You know, Brian's so smart, he could write a book of his own.

Chapter 7

Camouflage

On Zach's skateboard this morning, I sailed by a girl. Now two hours later, there she is again, standing on the same corner. This time she is staring at us, and she is not alone. She huddles with another girl, and they're giggling as they look our way. I feel my cheeks flaming bright red even though she is half a block away.

In general, I prefer frogs, snakes, and spiders to girls, so having them give me a slow, long look-over is troublesome, especially since I'm standing with my brother and two best friends, Zach and Joey. We have plans this morning.

Captain Mike gave us a handful of wood planks left over from a backyard deck he built, and our major mission this morning is to build an awesome skateboard jump. Problem is we're building it on the very sidewalk the girls are blocking.

"Who's that?" I ask, nudging Zach while glancing in the girls' direction. Their eyes are still glued on us, making my heart pound.

"New neighbors," he says. "They moved in on the corner."

"Have you met them, yet?" Brian asks.

"Negative," Zach says.

The girls don't budge. They're about my height, so I figure they're about our age. And with all their giggling they seem to be a lot like the girls I know in Michigan. Back home I keep a safe distance from the hush-hush of girls telling secrets.

"Maybe we should play basketball out back in your yard for a while," Brian suggests.

There's no hesitation from any of us. We nod as one. Together we hightail it to the backyard, behind the wooden fence. Our safe zone.

"Hey, I have an idea," I say. "Let's spy on them."

"Roger that," Zach says. "We need to make sure there aren't any more girls in their family."

"Yeah, maybe they've got more sisters, like Zach and I have two more brothers," Joey says.

Thinking about even more girls on the block, my knees turn to rubber bands. Two down on the corner are bad enough, but the possibility of more is simply alarming.

"Remember about Emma, Adam," my brother says, naming a girl from back at school. "She has seven sisters."

My knees give way and I start to slip to the ground. Fortunately, at the same time, Zach says, "Huddle up, everyone." He puts his arm around my shoulder and pulls the four of us into a tight circle. "We'll spy as a troop," he adds.

"Yes!" Joey shouts, clicking his red cowboy boots together. "We'll be soldiers on a top-secret assignment." He squats low, shifting his eyes quickly back and forth. The little guy is already play-acting he's a spy.

"Step one, we need camouflage," Zach says.

"Yeah, like GI Joe, so we fade into the background," I say. "The girls won't be able to see us coming."

"There's one problem," Zach says, giving his eyeglasses a nudge up his nose. "How do we hide our faces?"

He's right. Even with some summer tan, our faces glow white.

Around the huddle, eight eyes stare in thought. No one blinks. No one breathes. We take our spying seriously. Well, except maybe Joey, who starts shifting and squirming in the huddle. It's hard for a seven-year-old to hold still.

"I've got it!" Joey says. "Let's splash dirt on our faces like this." Instantly, the little guy is down on all fours, clawing at the dirt like a dog and flinging it into his face. Dust flies, and in seconds we're all spitting gritty brown wads.

"Joey, stop! Stop! You're just making a mess," Zach snaps at his brother.

Joey looks at Zach with eyes starting to tear up. If he was a dog, his tail would be between his legs about now.

"Hey, Joey, it was a good idea, but the dirt is just too dry to stick to you," I say, trying to comfort him. I know what it's like to have an older brother stomp on your idea.

The little tyke nods, but his lower lip sure hangs low.

I spin my next comment with some humor. "Joey, for the dirt to stick we'll need to smother you in butter, like an ear of corn," I tease, tickling him in the ribs. "Then, when you're slick all over, we'll toss you into the dirt, or maybe roll you in coffee grounds first. That'll get you covered!"

Joey squirms and says, "Yuck, I don't want to be greased and smeared!"

"Okay, guys, very funny; as you were," Zach says. He's really getting into his Army lingo. Talking about spying and camouflage will do that to a guy. "Think hard," Zach orders, returning to the battle plan. What can we use to hide our faces?"

We huddle up.

"We could make masks like we wear at Halloween," Joey says.

"Negative. It's too hot to hang a mask over our faces," Zach says.

Joey's head drops, again.

"Masks are a good idea, Joey," I say, proud of the little guy for coming up with another idea, even though it's not a great one. "Remember, it's colder at Halloween. Wearing a mask in this heat would make us scratch and itch and twitch. We need to be still and spy in silence." I put a finger to my lips, giving Joey a teeny "shh."

Joey grins and nods, twisting an invisible key over his lips.

Still huddled toe-to-toe, we stare at one another. How can sneaking up on girls be so difficult?

"I got it!" Brian says. "Face make-up. Mom does face painting at the summer art fair. We can paint our faces brown and green to look like the outdoors."

Leave it to "Brian the Brain" to come up with a brilliant idea. If I were as smart as my brother I could rule a small country.

"To the art studio," I say, waving for The Troop to follow.

"Wait." Brian snags my elbow, holding me back. "We need to ask Mom's permission."

"But she's gone to a meeting ... for an hour!" I say. Knowing an hour is way too long to wait for spying, my brain buzzes. In seconds I've got a plan to change Brian's mind.

I give Brian a quick nod of agreement. "You're right, we should ask Mom. But face paint is for kids, after all," I say, and then toss in another fact – because my brother likes facts. "Besides, face paint easily scrubs off with soap. Clean-up is easy-peasy. Mom won't mind if we use it."

"Ah, I don't know, Adam," Brian says with caution in his voice. "Maybe we should wait."

My stubbornness kicks in. "Mom has painted you and me dozens of times; she won't mind," I plea. "Remember, she's already crammed the Bat Cave with paper, pencils, scissors, and other art stuff for us to use anytime we want."

Brian stays silent so I take the lead. "To the art studio," I command, waving The Troop once more. Zach and Joey are at my heels. Brian brings up the rear, but at least he's following.

In Mom's art supply cupboard I find the box of face paint and whip open the lid. Oh no! The colors are blinding bright: fire engine red, bonfire orange and blazing sun yellow. We'll never hide from the girls with these paint sticks.

"Pull off the top layer, Adam," Brian says.

I peel back the paper. Black, brown, and green are hidden underneath! It sure is handy having a quick-witted brother.

"I'm first," Zach says, marching up. "I can't wait to be a soldier." He slips off his eyeglasses and sticks his chin high in the air.

Taking out the brown waxy crayon first, I start drawing on Zach's face. I use dark green next and then finish with a touch of black. Zach rushes to the mirror, rises on tiptoes, and beams. "It looks like real camouflage!" he reports.

"I'm next, Adam," Joey says, leaning his head back, closing his eyes. He wiggles as I stroke the face-paint crayon across his forehead.

"Quit squirming," I say as Joey jiggles this way and that.

"But it tickles," Joey says. I snatch his chuckling chin making him a wiggling, giggling prisoner. With the crayon I aim at the moving target. The brown and green marks smear. By chance it adds to the camouflage effect.

Brian's next. He holds rock steady, so I finish in a flash. Then, Brian paints me. Shortly my face is completely earth-colored.

All the while Joey bounces about like the non-stop battery bunny on TV. No matter what, he just keeps going and going. "Hey," I call out to the Energizer kid. "Time to focus. Time to spy on the girls."

"Wait, wait. We're not quite ready, Adam," Brian says.

"We're not?" I ask, puzzled.

"You look like a big red tomato," my brother says to me. I look down at my chest. I'm wearing a Chicago Bulls' T-shirt. I could be spotted from a satellite!

I rush over to my dresser, rifle through it and quickly slip on a green Oakland A's T-shirt. "This color is perfect," I say.

"Except for the big white A on the front," Zach gasps, pointing at my chest.

Ugh; I'll still stand out like a billboard. But wait. I turn the shirt inside out – there – now it's solid green! A perfect color for camouflage.

"I've got two black baseball caps. We can use those to cover our blond hair," Zach says. He runs home to grab the hats.

"Wait for me," Joey says, darting after Zach. "I've got to get something important, too.

"I'm in trouble," Brian says.

"Why?" I ask, wondering how he can be in trouble. My brother never messes up.

"I only have my Cowboy's ball cap," Brian says, holding a light blue Little League cap. "I'll stick out like a giant blue jay."

"Can you turn it inside out?" I ask.

He flips the cap, but now it's day-glow green, and that's no better at all! Brian's shoulders slump; his head hangs low. Then slow as a turtle, he nods his head up and down several times in thought. He stares out the kitchen window, still in thought. Thick green shrubs brush against the window, giving the basement apartment a treehouse effect. I've seen this blank yet thoughtful look on Brian's face before. My brother is using his Science Fair brain.

"I can wrap leaves around the cap," Brian says.

"And better yet, wrap them around this!" I say, reaching high and snatching his almost-new John Deere hat off a high shelf.

"That's brilliant, Adam," Brian says. "I forgot we left the hats to dry after King soaked us during his tomato bath."

It is rare for Brian to forget anything. Before I can tease my brother though, he is sprinting out the back door. Through the window I see him tugging at some green ivy. A long vine loosens. He twists it around the cap and then slaps it on his head. The vine-covered cap matches his painted face, perfectly.

Zach comes back. We slap on the black caps and cheer, "We're ready to spy!"

"Where's Joey?" I ask.

"Here he comes," Zach says.

"What's he wearing on his face?" I ask, squinting at his bug-eyed swim goggles.

Joey hustles over. "These are my Wild Planet Spy Gear Night Goggles so I can see in the dark," he says, flicking on twin beams of light. "I can see up to twenty-five feet in the dark."

"Yeah, but Joey, it's not d –" I start to say, about it not being dark, but then I remember the little guy is trying to help. "Gosh, Joey, you look like a super cool soldier," I say and let it go at that.

We creep toward the girls' house. Ah, spying: the mystery, the uncertainty, the goose bumps and heart-thumps. Could a boy's life get any better?

"Halt," Zach says, and The Troop grinds to a stop. "What if we need to protect ourselves?" he asks.

Visions of the girls' silent stare-down flash through my mind. Their sharp eyes can bore right through me, like Mad Witch's. On impulse, I raise one eyebrow and squint with the other eye. Through locked lips, I let out a slow hiss.

"Adam, you look like one of the snickering girls," Brian says.

"What if the girls are like Wonder Woman? One was wearing a sparkly crown. That's a deadly boomerang!" Joey squeals.

"I think we'll need to defend ourselves," Zach says.

"Yeah, we need weapons," Joey says.

"We've got those rubber-band shooters Papa made us," I say. "Mom's saved them in the toy box."

We rush back to the studio, zip through the kitchen, and launch into the Bat Cave – the room with all the treasures.

I search the toy box for the rubber-band guns that Grandpa made us. "Here they are," I say, then hand everyone their own rubber-band shooter.

I holster the weapon in my waistband. My face is painted and I'm wearing an inside-out T-shirt and two Band-Aids on a nasty gooseberry cut. Yep. I am a typical All-American boy ready to spy.

"Wait. We better test the shooters," Brian says once we're outside. "It's been a long time since we fired one."

"I'll go first," I say, pulling the big wide rubber band back over the butt of the gun, making it ready to fire. My trigger finger lets go. Plop. Instead of the rubber band sailing like a speeding bullet, it flops like a dead fish. The old rubber band has lost its stretch.

"Back inside," I command The Troop.

We dig through Mom's art supply cupboard looking for rubber bands that still have spring in them.

"How about these," Zach says, holding up rubber bands half the size of the ones we need.

"Too whimpy," I say.

"What about these?" Joey asks.

"Nah. Those are strings for lace-up cards. No stretch," I say.

"Hey! Look what I found!" Zach says, finding heavy-duty straws. The straws catch my attention.

"Who needs rubber band guns when we can fire with pea shooters," I cry out.

"But, Adam," Brian says. "Mom doesn't have any dried peas.

Details never slow me down. "That's okay. We can use raisins," I say, heading to the kitchen pantry. We pass the raisin box around and shove almost the entire box into our pants pockets. Joey's pockets are already brimming-full with other stuff, so he jams his raisins into his cowboy boots.

Armed with pea shooters, we creep away, ready to spy.

Luckily, the front yards of the houses along North Second Street are lined with plenty of hiding-space, shade trees and bushes.

"Adam, duck behind the pergola," Brian says.

"The what?"

"The arbor."

I look at him cross-eyed.

"The trellis," my brother says.

"This thing? With the vines?" I ask.

He nods. Why didn't he say so in the beginning? I sneak behind the clump of vines. No sign of the girls. I slither forward. Hiding behind tree trunks and bushes, we cautiously pinball to the corner house. All except Joey. He sits down. Shifts right. Shifts left. Shakes his right boot. Shakes his left boot. The raisins must be giving him trouble. Next, he scrambles off the ground, climbing a tree, and then drops down like Spider-Man. Finally, he makes it to the corner.

But the corner house is quiet. In fact, it is scary silent. Where are the girls?

A neighbor comes out. "Oh, hi boys. The girls left for a day-trip," the lady says.

We stop dead in our tracks. The enemy has disappeared. I fall back onto the lawn and spread my arms and legs.

"What are you doing?" Zach asks.

"Celebrating! I'm so happy the girls are gone; I'm making a snow angel. And I don't even need snow," I say, swishing my arms and legs. The dried-up grass rustles and kicks up dust, blending perfectly with my camouflage outfit. Zach plops down on his back too, swinging his arms.

"Wait for me," Joey says as he copies the snow angel swish.

While Zach, Joey and I are playing around like happy goofs, Brian's eyes are zeroed in like a laser beam. It's that frozen stare that tells me he's in the zone, again. Any minute he'll say something important.

"We need a secret hiding spot to store our weapons and head gear," Brian says. "When the girls get back, we'll need to be ready."

"Our house isn't safe with two younger brothers at home," Zach says.

"Yeah, and Mom will be back soon, along with her helpers," I say, thinking about the busy studio.

"How about the shed?" Brian asks. Yikes. Not the shed! Cold fear crawls through my chest. I saw flickering lights coming from that shed. What if it's the ghost of General Custer swinging a lantern and getting ready to attack? And if spooky Custer isn't scary enough, Mad Witch could be inside, hunched over her pottery wheel, carving her bony fingers into the wet clay. I can almost feel her hoarse, harsh laugh shoot through me.

Trying to find a reason not to go inside the haunted shed, I swallow hard and say, "Naw, the shed won't work. Mad Witch, I mean Mrs. Witt, told me to stay out of there. She locks it up tight."

"Then what about the abandoned skunk hole behind the shed?" Brian asks.

"That's perfect," Zach says.

The Troop marches to the empty skunk hole before I'm quick enough to think of another idea. I follow behind not wanting to show my fear.

We cram the pea shooters and raisins inside the hole. Whipping off our hats, we start to shove them in the hole. Except Joey. He cradles the night goggles in his hands. "I guess I'll take these home. They don't work so well in the daylight."

"Then you'll be ready for the next nighttime adventure," I say, giving him a gentle knuckle punch in the arm.

Joey smiles wide.

Lastly, we put Brian's hat in the hole because its green leafy vines look like nature and will hide the treasures.

So far there are no flashing lights coming from inside the shed. I relax a little and blurt out the next step for The Troop. "We need to swear to secrecy," I say.

"And seal the promise by becoming blood brothers," Zach says.

I feel my heart beat like a drum. This is not what I had in mind. After the cuts from gooseberry picking, I'm not excited about another stab wound. Usually, I'm a tough kid, but I was pricked and poked lately more times than a birthday piñata gets punched.

"Being blood brothers is a North Dakota warrior's code," Zach says.

"My warrior name is Brave One," Joey says as he sticks out his finger. "I'm ready to be sliced so blood will gush out."

My heart thumps louder now, like a tom-tom. At this rate, my warrior name will be Adam Weak-in-the-Knees.

"I know a simpler Michigan practice," Brian says. "We seal the secret with a spit oath." Like a magic medicine man, my brother saves me from Zach's war path. Brian doesn't know it but his take-charge actions make me feel better. Of course, maybe he's noticing the sting of his gooseberry wounds, too.

"Spit sounds great," Joey says. "My mom doesn't like us to play with knives anyway."

"Roger that," Zach says.

The Troop huddles up. We vow, we spit our oaths, and then leave the camouflage gear hidden in the skunk hole.

My stomach growls; it must be lunch time. We say good-bye to Zach and Joey.

*   *   *

"Hey, Mom!" we say, entering the studio.

Mom is back from her meeting and busy painting at her desk. She looks up to greet us. Her paint brush stops in mid-motion because her eyes are fixed on us and spellbound.

I glance at Brian and remember the face make-up. "We were hiding and playing camouflage," I offer.

Mom doesn't say a word. She simply taps her cheek with her fingertip.

"We used a little of your face paint," I say softly.

When Mom's not buying something, she has a quick head shake, a simple one-two. I see it now.

I feel my cheeks heat up. "It's for kids," I stammer, but keep going. "And you've painted Brian and me hundreds of times. And it cleans up with just a little soap." My words are gushing as I jabber non-stop with nervousness.

A small smile flickers across her face.

Mom understands boys.

"We'll just go wash up," I say, quietly slipping into the bathroom with Brian at my side.

After cleaning up we mosey to the kitchen to make lunch. That's our job. Mom cooks the dinner; we do lunch.

From the refrigerator, I whip out the bottle of chocolate syrup, open my mouth wide and squeeze in a big blob. Quickly, I slip the bottle back in the fridge before Mom checks up on us, and then I grab the fixings for a sandwich.

I'm smearing peanut butter on bread when Mom comes into the kitchen.

"Tell me a little more about your painted faces," she says.

I should have known the trouble wasn't over yet. Using Mom's supplies without asking is risky business, even if they are meant for kids. Without giving it much thought I swing the story in a new direction. "Oh, we were just hiding from the girls on the corner," I say.

"Girls?" she asks, saying the word slowly like there's a secret within. Her arms are folded across her chest and her eyebrows arch like a steeple. I can tell she thinks there is more to the story.

Unfortunately, she has me trapped in the kitchen. I can't escape. Her eyes stay steady, glued on mine. I feel like I'm sitting in a dark room with a huge spotlight shining on my head. I squirm with discomfort.

"Girls?" Mom repeats, not budging.

I want to turn and run. Hide in my room. Hide in the backyard. Lie low for a few days.

"Spill it," she says, waiting for an answer.

With peanut butter still sticking to the roof of my mouth, I mutter, "On ... mumph ... the corner." If I mumble enough, maybe she will just let it go.

No such luck.

"Go on," Mom says, still staring me down. Those bright blue eyes have a way of bringing the truth out of me.

I tell my story. "Well, Brian thought we should use face paint to hide from the girls so we could spy on them."

"Brian?" she asks, her eyebrows arch higher. "But, you're both wearing face paint."

"Well ... Brian, me, Zach, and Joey."

"That sounds better," Mom says.

I finish the story, telling the truth about spying and the girls not being home.

"So you really haven't met them, yet?" she asks.

"No, I guess not."

"Maybe you should invite them over and give them a chance," she says. She hasn't budged from the arms-folded stance. Now, her blue eyes look like a Popsicle that's been left in the freezer too long – icy around the edges.

Brian shoots me a panicked look. I shoot him a matching one back.

"Remember to say nice things," she says, giving Brian and me "The Warning."

Earlier, during this summer vacation, our razzing got the better of Mom. She gave us The Warning: every night, before bed we have to list three nice things to say to each other. The funny thing is, using Mom's warning, I end up feeling better about Brian and we quarrel less. Maybe Mom's right. The Warning might work for girls, too.

Luckily, for today, the girls aren't home so I won't have to say nice things to them. I'll worry about The Warning tomorrow.

Chapter 8

Spitting Like a Pro

Thump. A strange sound echoes from outside, interrupting lunchtime. I look to the little basement window squeezed in at ceiling height of the Bat Cave. No feet strolling by. *Thump.* There it is again. Still no one walks by. Usually I can tell who is outside by catching a glimpse of their shoes as they pass.

"Finish your lunch, Brian. Then we'll go find that *thump*," I say.

Soon, as we're darting to the back door to explore the sound, something strikes me. What if it's Mad Witch doing it? I freeze, not really wanting to run into the creepy lady with the crazy cat.

Then I feel it – the urge to explore. I fling open the back door and spy that the padlock is hooked tightly on the shed door. Good. Coast is clear; no Mad Witch.

Still, I take a second look at the shed to focus on the grimy windows. No flashing lights, like I've seen at night, so I breathe a little easier. But then I hear it. An eerie ping-ping is coming from the shabby old shed. Yet I know no one is inside, unless it's Custer's ghost. Naw. Only Joey believes in that old wives' tale, I remind myself. Maybe it's the wind. But I know better because wind howls, whistles or whooshes. It never pings. Besides, there isn't even a light puff of breeze right now. Even though the windless hot sun beats down on me, a shiver runs along my spine. And then I feel a bump from behind!

"Come on, Adam!" It's only Brian. He's rushing out of the apartment and dashing toward the driveway. He's moving so fast I'm sure he hasn't heard the scary ping-ping.

Brian's around the corner and out of sight when I hear it again: *Thump*. The thud is coming from the direction Brian went, which is more comforting than the possibility of meeting Custer's ghost seeping out from inside the eerie shed. I scurry after Brian, leaving the spooky *ping-ping* behind. I figure if Brian is willing to explore, I'll follow him.

I jog next door, and pull up at Brian's side. *Thump*. The thud is right behind Zach's backyard wooden fence.

Brian reaches up on the fence and unhooks the latch on the gate. "Remember to lock the gate again, Adam," he tells me.

"I know. We can't have Zach's little brothers running out," I reply dutifully, thinking about three-year-old Cole and crawling baby Ethan. I have a tough time figuring baby ages.

Little tots should have circles to count like tree rings. All I know for sure is baby Ethan scoots faster than a rabbit, so I lock the gate.

Zach is alone in the backyard. It must be naptime for the young ones. He drops a square piece of wood, turns, and begins taking long steps.

"One, two, three," Zach counts as he marches across the yard.

"What are you doing?" I ask, then notice he has another piece of wood in his hand.

"I'm counting out exactly twenty paces," Zach says.

"Why?"

Thump. Zach plops the other piece of wood on the ground. "I'm setting up Hot Box," he says. "It's my favorite baseball game."

Wow. Baseball is really, really my sport. At five years old, I was hooked at T-ball. At seven, our Coach-Pitch league was captivating. And now, Little League is first-class!

"You only have two bases," Brian says.

I'm a little confused now, and I'm glad my brother doesn't understand either why Zach is playing baseball with only two bases. Brian usually has all the answers, but for once my brother is just as confused as me.

"Two bases are all we need," Zach says.

"Not if you're playing baseball," I say.

"Haven't you ever played Hot Box?" Zach says, turning to look at us like we're from Mars rather than Michigan.

"No," I answer, standing my ground now, with my feet planted firmly. I've played baseball since I was little, and Brian's even been on the All-Star Little League team. Zach is my best North Dakota friend, but only two bases? Is he crazy?

"Grab your mitts. I'll teach you," Zach says. "I'll explain it more, but here it is: You have to reach a base before the catcher tags you out. The trick is to know when to run."

Brian and I nod in unison, following every word Zach says.

"I'll go get the mitts," I say, dashing to the apartment.

Passing through Zach's backyard fence, I whip around the corner of the shed, toward the back studio entrance. I never make it. Instead, I slam into Mad Witch.

There is no mistaking Mad Witch. She has scary written all over her, from her piercing dark eyes to her bulb-shaped nose and pointy chin – which is now only inches from my face. I take a step back.

"Slow down, half-pint," she snarls.

It takes a moment to manage an answer, and when I do speak, my voice cracks: "Ah ... sorry."

"Hogwash," she grunts, cocking one eyebrow up. Today she is carrying a cane. She stabs the end of the cane repeatedly on the cement.

Then, before I can blink, she lassos the hook-end of the cane across my arm. The cane locks on tightly, and she yanks me toward her. Within two seconds I'm nose to nose with the Wicked Witch of the West. Her hot breath spews into my face.

"Kids today! They're always in a hurry. That's why I carry this here cane. I need all the help I can to steady myself," she snarls.

Luckily, Butterscotch picks this moment to weave through Mad Witch's leg. "Oh, Precious, that tickles. Heh, heh, heh," her rough voice croaks in a harsh giggle.

I look down. The fat cat barely fits between Mad Witch's feet. The rickety old lady starts to teeter. I grab her elbow. She steadies herself by planting a firm jab with the cane.

"Humph," she growls. "I guess I better get Precious into the house. Just slow down next time, half-pint."

She shuffles away, the cane clicking with each step on the sidewalk. I'm all too happy to be going the opposite direction. I dash to the studio, snatch the baseball gloves, and then, with caution, peek out the door for Mad Witch. The coast is clear, so I rush back to Zach's yard.

I'm all ears as he explains Hot Box some more. We Michigan boys will each stand on a base. Zach will race between the two bases, and we will toss the ball to each other to try to tag him out.

"It's like Keep-away," Brian says, naming a similar game.

Zach gets ready to dart. He leads off my base with one leg forward. Brian and I fire our throws back and forth. Zach's eyes follow our every move. He's waiting for the right moment to steal Brian's base.

I arch my arm back and release a speed ball. Just then, Zach bullets off his base. The throw smacks into Brian's glove, but Zach is fast. He slides into Brian's base.

"Safe!" Brian yells.

"We need more players," Zach says. "The game is more exciting when we have more than one runner. Two or three runners are best."

"Where's Joey?" I ask.

"He's at the store with my mom," Zach says.

"Do you have any other friends who could play?" I ask Zach, winding up to pitch another speedball to Brian.

"Negative," Zach says.

Then from behind us we hear it. "Tee-hee-hee." My arm stiffens mid-throw. Zach stops mid-run, too, and our heads pivot to the sound we hear. It's the gigglesome girls from the corner house. Maybe I forgot to lock the gate after getting the baseball gloves because now they're standing on the inside of the fence, right near us.

Unfortunately, all the camouflage gear is outside the fence! With the gear still hidden in the skunk hole, I suddenly feel naked without my green and black army hat and pea shooter.

"My name's Savannah. I'm a fast runner," the taller one says, wagging one of her glittery shoes back and forth, back and forth. Her brown hair is pulled into a pony tail, and it swings behind her with each swish of her sparkly shoe. "This is my sister, Hannah," she adds.

Hannah stands just a bit shorter and without a bit of the glitz. If Savannah is a chocolate cream-filled donut, Hannah is the toast from stale bread, without jam.

Their names, Hannah and Savannah, make me wonder … if there's a third sister, is her name Banana?!

"My dad gets our names mixed up," Savannah says, "so my nickname is Georgia. Dad figures since Savannah is in the state of Georgia, it's easy for him to remember."

My snicker stops short. I can understand her dad's difficulty with the rhyming problem of Savannah and Hannah … especially if there's an Anna, Joanna, and Briana nearby!

"So, do you want to see how fast I can run?" Georgia asks. The princess' shoe wags back and forth, back and forth.

I moan. Brian sighs. Zach knits his eyebrows.

"I won a ribbon at my school's track meet," Georgia keeps boasting, glittery shoe wagging faster, now bobbing, too.

It seems to me she's a chatterbox, even if I don't know much about the inner workings of girls. "Glitzy Georgia is a motor mouth," I grumble to Zach.

"I bet I can outrun all of you," Georgia brags.

That does it. We can't let a girl boast she can beat us.

Brian and Zach take the bases. Glitzy Georgia, Hannah, and I are runners.

"Throw the ball, Brian," Zach says, pushing his glasses up his nose and pounding his fist deep into his mitt. This is serious business.

Brian scrapes his feet, kicking up dust like a bull getting ready to fight. He zings the ball and Zach catches it. Instantly, Zach tosses it back. Their pitches sail through the air as Georgia, Hannah, and I hustle, sprinting wildly between bases.

Hannah gets tagged out of the game. Glitzy Georgia is safe on Zach's base. Without warning, I'm trapped in the middle. "This is like a game we play in Michigan," I tell Zach. "We call it Pickle."

"Roger that. I can see why," Zach says. "You're in a pickle."

It's a fast moving game. I need to act quickly. My eyes dart between Zach and Brian, landing on Brian.

"Don't even think about it! I'll tag you out," he yells to me while striking a Kung-Fu pose. Zach releases another fastball to Brian. Glitzy Georgia darts off Zach's base toward Brian's. I, too, race toward Brian's base, lungs burning and my leg muscles stinging. I dive. But Georgia slides into the base inches ahead of me. How did she get from Zach's base so quickly?

Landing flat, face in the dirt, I'm tagged out. I get smoked by Glitzy Georgia. My spirit falls. I stay on my belly for a moment, sucking in the dust cloud, trying to hide the shame of losing. I wonder if General Custer felt this defeated in 1876 when the Battle of Little Big Horn broke out. If I'm lucky his ghost might kidnap me. Or better yet, maybe there is room in that skunk hole for me.

Dirt sticks to my sweaty-wet face. Struggling to my feet, I grumble under my breath about, "girls..." They appear so sweet, but watch out. Instantly, they can turn to the Dark Side of the Force. Putting it in *Star Wars* terms comforts me.

The wooden gate opens and Captain Mike enters, waving his arms through the dusty clouds of our base running. "Are you sending smoke signals?" A straight line sets across his mouth, with no sign of a smile turning up at the corners.

"It's Hot Box," Zach says.

"I can see who's in the hot seat of this box," Captain Mike says, his mouth crease deepens as he watches Hannah join Glitzy Georgia in a victory bow.

Next, the girls put their heads together and break out in a sassy chant. Their loud peppy cheer has me trapped. It's like being stuck between stereo speakers, with their voices booming into my ears. I feel my face burn, hot and red. And it's not from running. It's from getting caught with not one girl, but two.

"We'd better head home, Hannah," Georgia says before turning to Brian and Zach. "Bye-ee," she squeaks while wiggling her fingers.

"Toodles." Hannah gives a tah-tah wave as she follows Glitzy Georgia out the gate.

"Glad you boys realize Hot Box needs a lot of players to be daring," Captain Mike says. And then he adds, "So, the girls won the game?" But it doesn't sound like a question. He thinks the girls smoked us.

Today Captain Mike is not wearing his polarized fishing sunglasses. His eyes drill on each of us, one after the other. Then he shoves his hands in his front pockets and rocks back on his heels. He clears his throat and I hear his deep voice edging up. "It takes a man to play for the challenge," he says.

Wow! Captain Mike just said he was proud of us. I stand with my shoulders straight. I would salute, but the military gear is still in the skunk hole, the one I no longer want to hide in.

Changing the conversation now, the Captain has something else he wants to tell us. "Guess what?" he says. "I've got tickets to the Dacotah Speedway Auto Races." Captain Mike holds up a handful of tickets to the races.

Since I'm a whiz at math, I can see that his handful is more than enough tickets for Brian and me to come along, too. My heart speeds into full throttle 'cause I love the races. They're loud and they smell like grease and grime. The best part is the blast of oil-filled wind in your face as the cars rush by. I start to throw my baseball glove in the air, like celebrating winning a game, when Brian nudges me. Under his breath, he tells me, "Wait to be invited." My brother always remembers his manners.

"We're all going to the races," Captain Mike says. "And since kids under twelve are free, I think your two new friends who just left should come."

"You mean the two girls who just left?" I ask, hoping it's not who I think he means.

"Yeah, I'll call their mom; I'm sure it'll be okay," Captain Mike says.

And then we hear: "Yoo-hoo! We'd love to go to the speedway!"

Oh no! The girls never left. They've just been on the other side of the fence. My heart beats wildly as I realize that the girls are coming to the races, too. How can I sit with them at the races after losing to Glitzy Georgia? There must be other things I have to do tonight. I bet it's my turn to wash the dishes, or take out the trash, or pick the lint out of my belly button.

"But what do we wear?" the girls ask. Before Captain Mike can say a thing, though, they fire off some more questions. "Jeans or shorts? French braids or twists? Pink or green nail polish?"

Their yammering, to me, is a bunch of gobbledygook. The list of reasons to skip this girl-filled outing is getting longer by the minute. Maybe I'm catching a cold or have a fever. Wait, I've got dirt in my eye and won't be able to see the cars!

"The green flag goes up at seven so be at the van at six-thirty," Captain Mike tells everyone when he's finally able to sneak in a few words between the yakking girls.

"Any-whoo," the girls announce, "we'll be back!" Then they run off, tee-heeing all the way.

By this time, Brian is back from asking Mom if it's okay for us to go to the races. Out of breath he huffs, "Mom says yes! We can go!"

"Whatever," I mutter.

While eating dinner a short while later, my mind races. I have to admit, the roar of engines, the crunch of twisting metal, and the sparks from crashing cars get my motor running full speed.

I decide that a couple of girls aren't going to get me down. Half an hour early, I'm at the Grunners' van, ready to leave.

* * *

Soon enough, the girls are there too, with that hair-matches-bag-matches-fingernails look of theirs. Not us boys. Same day? Same clothes. T-shirts and khaki shorts are just fine, y'know.

We pile into the van, with Zach, Brian, and me sitting in the middle seat; just a bunch of boys with an ache to be real men at the auto races.

The girls, meanwhile, wiggle and giggle as they squeeze into the back row with Joey. Behind us, they squirm like kindergartners being forced to pose for school pictures.

Leaving Bismarck, we roll across the Liberty Memorial Bridge with the mighty Missouri far below. Next, we cruise through the city of Mandan. Outside the city limits, the prairie takes over – land so wide, sky so big.

Shortly, smack dab in the middle of nowhere-ville, I hear the rumble of supercharged engines. They sound loud and angry. Like the engines, my heart thunders in my ears. Captain Mike pulls the van into the Dacotah Speedway.

The girls and Joey scamper out of the van and head to a nearby playground. We men hike into the bleachers. The cars line up, engines racing. Craning our necks to get the best view, we restlessly wait for the start. Then it's on! The green flag goes up, cars speed off, hit the curve, and flash by.

Around the next curve tires squeal! A driver breaks hard before a turn, and smoke fills the air. We all suck in the smell of burning rubber. The car screeches through the curve, twisting and turning. A yellow caution flag waves, which means the cars have to slow down and stay in position for a while.

A cooling breeze shifts the wind, and my nose sniffs burnt burgers and oh-so-sweet cotton candy. This is what heaven must smell like – at least on the men's side of heaven, I figure.

A problem on the track is handled, the yellow flag is raised, and the rumble of engines returns. Vroom, vroom, vroom. The bleachers shake and shudder. The rumble makes my butt jiggle, and the noise is so loud I can feel the quakes up through my shoes.

Splat.

What is that? I turn my head, taking my eyes off the race.

Splat, splat. Next to me, a thin man with a bald head as smooth and shiny as a cue ball is spitting. The wad of slime lands inches from my foot. How gross. Splat. He spits again. It sails past his knobby knees. No wonder it didn't hit his legs, they're skinny as matchsticks, poking out of his shorts.

Splat. But Mr. Skinny didn't spit this time. It came from behind me. I turn around. There sits a big guy, round and pudgy like the Pillsbury Doughboy, also spitting.

Splat. My head whips forward following the sound. It's Mr. Skinny, spitting again!

I look at Zach. His cheek is puffed out on one side. I hear a crunch. He swallows, the line of his mouth tightens, and then he spits.

"What are you doing?" I ask.

"They're sunflower seeds," Zach says, reaching into his pocket and pulling out a bag of white seeds.

"The size reminds me of Halloween pumpkin seeds," I say.

"These are better." Zach pops a wad of sunflower seeds into his mouth. Crunch. Spit.

This is great, I think. A food that's proper to spit!

I take a handful of seeds and pop them into my mouth. I chomp and spit. Tiny bits of shells and seeds spray everywhere. I'm left with an empty mouth. No tasty treat.

"There's a secret. Start slower," Zach says. "Put only one shell in your mouth, crack it, separate the seed with your tongue. Once you have the seed pulled apart, you spit out the shell, and eat the seed."

I pop a shell, bite, and try to wiggle my tongue inside the small crack in the shell. But the shell stays tightly wedged. I bite again, twisting and turning my tongue to get to the seed. My cheek puffs out like I have a toothache. This will take some practice!

Defeated, I take the shell out of my mouth and use my fingers to pry the tasty seed from the tough shell.

Suddenly, Zach whacks my hand. "Hey! No hands! It's a North Dakota tradition to separate and spit," he says with a snicker.

Oh boy. Another North Dakota tradition – like blood brothers.

I sit and practice without much luck. One shell lasts until the end of the races. We collect Joey and the girls from the playground and head to the van.

"Why are your pockets inside out?" I ask Joey, who is skipping ahead of me. The lining of both of the front pockets on his shorts pokes out like floppy rabbits ears. The girls tee-hee at the sight, all tinkly like a bell.

Joey stops and spins around. "Aw, shucks. I gave Hannah and Georgia the arrowheads. I must've forgot to poke the pockets back in."

"Why'd you give them the arrowheads?" I ask, remembering that Joey believes they're a special gift from Custer's ghost.

Joey's cheeks flame red and he lowers his head.

"Joey's in love!" Zach teases in a sing-song voice.

"Am not," Joey snaps back.

The girls wiggle with glee, twirling the arrowheads in their hands.

"Be careful with those," Brian says. "They could be valuable."

I shoot a glance at Brian. He knows perfectly well that it's rare to find real-deal arrowheads. I wonder if he is trying to pull a fast one on the girls – which would be so unlike my brother, especially since Mom gave us "The Warning" that we're to say nice things about the girls.

Then, I take a deep breath and get back on track, "Yeah, the arrowheads could possibly be valuable." I figure there's nothing mean about saying the arrowheads might be worth something.

"We know it's hard to prove genuine arrowheads," Hannah says. "But our Dad has a thick blue book that tells their value."

"It's Robert Overstreet's book," Glitzy Georgia says, jutting her chin forward. This girl sounds as smart as my brother, making me wonder if the joke will be on us.

"The 12th edition Official Overstreet's Identification and Price Guide to Indian Arrowheads?" Brian asks.

Official guide? This seems serious to me. Time seems to stand still for several heartbeats.

"That's the book," Georgia says, squinty-eyed, sounding all sorts of snotty. "All Dad has to do is match the picture to these arrowheads. We might be rich!"

Now I'm worried Joey shouldn't have given away the arrowheads. But Joey doesn't seem too concerned. He's fluttering his eyelashes at the girls. Maybe he is in a love trance. Don't panic, I tell myself. There must be something I can do to help Joey get the arrowheads back.

"Hey, Joey," I say. "Didn't you tell me Custer's Ghost is hunting for lost arrowheads?"

Joey stays wide-eyed at the girls, his eyelashes blinking double-time. Always before, the word "Custer" put Joey in overdrive. I've never seen Joey not respond when I mention his make-believe superhero. And who am I kidding about make-believe? The shed lights flicker on and off and then hearing a strange *ping-ping* makes me think Custer's ghost might exist and really is talking to this little guy.

"Joey," I say with more force, not knowing if I'm more nervous about Custer's ghost or the girls getting rich from our arrowheads. The sharp calling of Joey's name doesn't shake him. His focus remains on Hannah and Georgia. I've got to act quickly or the arrowheads could be out of our reach forever. In a panic, I blurt out, "Joey, remember you told me Custer's ghost put a curse on those arrowheads."

"Curse? What curse?" It's not Joey's attention I get, it's Hannah. Her face pales. "What curse?" she repeats, biting hard on her bottom lip from nervousness.

"Calm down, Hannah," Georgia hisses, stepping up to gather her sister's arrowhead. "These older boys are just trying to scare us. We'll get Dad to tell us the truth. I'll just keep these arrowheads safe until we get home."

Cripes, I say to myself. Glitzy Georgia is smart and tricky. Even a fib about curses doesn't trip her up. It'll take a masterful plan to get those arrowheads away from these girls.

We pile into the van and Captain Mike drives us home. On the trip, Zach points out the window and says, "There's my tasty treat."

I'm puzzled. All I see is row after row of bright green stalks. The large leaves are snack-size for the Jolly Green Giant. Then, I see it – Zach's treat. At the top of each plant are brilliant yellow flowers with big brown centers.

"Sunflowers," I mutter. It is all too familiar how I failed the fine art of spitting and eating at the same time. Between that and getting beaten at Hot Box by a girl, I slink in my seat.

One of these days, I promise myself, I am going to have a regular, non-embarrassing, don't-do-anything-stupid kind of day.

When the van pulls into the Grunners' driveway, I say, "Hey, Zach, follow me." I guide my friend down the driveway to our apartment. In the kitchen I whip open the refrigerator and pull out a sliced watermelon. Mom buys the organic kind – the natural kind of watermelon with big black seeds.

I grab a slice for Zach and one for me. We go back outside with our treat. I bite into the melon. Without twisting or turning or flicking or flopping my tongue, I spit out a seed. It flies like a bullet. Success! Then I savor the tasty fruit. "This is my comfort zone," I say with Adam Moynihan Michigan pride.

Chapter 9

Not-so-smooth Sailing

I stand eye-level with his belt buckle. For a moment the two of us are silent, arms crossed, faces stern. The mountain-size man lowers his gaze down to mine and clasps a hand onto my shoulder.

"Son," he says. A slight pause. "Son." Another pause, longer this time.

Suddenly my knees start wobbling. Why doesn't he call me Adam? Or Moynihan kid? That's my name. "Son," Larry, the big guy, offers one more time.

Only my dad calls me, "Son." My Jell-O legs jiggle overtime.

"Hop inside," he finally says while turning to open the door to a monster of a motor home he's parked in Mom's driveway. And what a metal monster it is – a big tin box with huge black tires.

Mom is impressed, too, which I learn when I hear her beside me, where she has appeared. "It's a house on wheels ready to roll down the road," she says as her eyes ping-pong between Larry and me. That's the name of the big man with the big motor home: Larry. Yesterday, when I met Larry, something seemed unusual. He and Mom were shaking hands … for at least three minutes! It was like they forgot to let go. After that, Larry, Mom, Brian, and I played Monopoly for a while. But it was kind of strange: Every time Mom passed *GO*, she forgot to collect her usual $200. Instead, she would collect one look from Larry and her face would beam with a smile brighter than a shining star.

Now today, standing outside the motor home, Larry is calling me "Son." Something tells me I'm not the only one who has made friends in North Dakota. But this thing with Mom and Larry feels different than the friendship with my two buddies, Zach and Joey.

While we are in the driveway, looking at the metal monster, Mom gives me a little push in its direction, but my feet don't move. They're kind of frozen in place even though it's well over ninety degrees outside. Then, from nowhere, Brian is at my heels to check out the vehicle. In a second he wheels around me and launches up its steps. "Hey, Adam, check this out!" he calls, obviously excited about something.

Curiosity pulls me out of the frozen trance. I step up to find my brother – and bounce right off him into a teeny-weeny bathroom. Even for me, being string-bean skinny, it's a tight squeeze.

Brian moves two paces forward, allowing me to escape from the bathroom and move into the bite-size kitchen. An itty-bitty refrigerator is tucked in the corner – so small, I wonder if it can hold anything important. I tug the handle. To my surprise, it's jam-packed with my favorites – including cans of root beer and mini-cartons of chocolate milk. What a great way to travel. A kid can drink all he wants and not have to stop to go to the bathroom! This is better than the camper Papa pulls behind his truck. We can't eat, drink, or sleep until it is set up on a campsite.

Brian pulls back a curtain to reveal a snug-as-a-bug bed. I take two steps in the opposite direction, up to the front, and check out the comfy driver's seat with a mega steering wheel like on a school bus. The co-pilot chair is next to it and looks just as comfy.

"Where are we going again?" Brian asks Mom.

My mind goes fuzzy. I barely remember that Mom said something about a trip with Larry.

"Garrison Dam," she answers while skipping up the two-step entrance into the motor home. Mom twirls in the narrow aisle doing lively leg kicks like she's part of a Western hoedown. Any minute, I'm afraid she might shout "Yee-haw!"

"What's Garrison Dam?" I ask Mom, not sure if her two-step dance excitement is from the dam or from being with Larry.

Brian answers the question: "Garrison is a dam on the Missouri River. It houses huge hydro-powered turbines that generate electricity."

Well, now I'm certain Mom's excitement isn't from a dam that makes energy using engines and gushing water – which means Mom's excitement is about Larry! Larry who calls me *"Son."* My legs almost buckle as I try to take in all this new stuff.

"Hey, Adam, look what I found," Brian calls.

His voice sounds distant, but he can't be too far away because everything in here is pressed down to pint-size, like many oranges squeezed into one jug of juice. I turn a full circle while looking for Brian and, nothing. Then, I look up ... way up. Brian has climbed a ladder I now spy, so I go up the steps to find him.

"It's a sleeping loft," he says, lying back in a relaxed pose, hands behind his head. This whole loft is nestled in the front end of the motor home, a platform hovering above the captain and co-pilot seats.

Through the loft window from this high up, I can see beyond my next door neighbor, Zach's, six-foot wooden fence and into the backyard of two houses over. I wish we had these treetop seats when we were spying on squealing sisters Hannah and Glitzy Georgia, who live at the end of the block.

Scooting down the ladder now, Brian crashes right into Larry! It's no wonder Brian didn't see the giant, though, because he is so tall that his body fills the entire door frame and blocks out daylight. Brian bounces off Larry's hefty chest and lands on his butt.

"Hut, hut, hut," Larry laughs, sounding like a football lineman. "Let me help you up, Son."

Did Larry just call Brian, "Son," too?

"I'm Brian. That's Adam on the top bunk," my brother says, still sitting on the floor. "But don't worry; you'll be able to tell us apart in no time."

Instantly my knees lock tight and I'm steady as a statue instead of uncertain and wobbly. I get it now: Larry calls both of us "Son" because he doesn't know who is who.

Larry reaches out his hand, big as a gorilla's, to help my brother up. Brian clutches it, and in one quick swish, Larry springs Brian off the floor.

"The motor home is all gassed up and the fluids are checked and topped off," Larry reports. "Now we just need to test the vehicle lights and turn signals and then we'll be ready to roll. Could you boys help me with that?"

To do our part, Brian scoots outside to the front end of the motor home; I head to the back. And then we wait. I stare at the tail lights. No blinking yet. Even though it's past dinnertime, the summer sun beats down on me, making my sweaty head itchy under the baseball cap. Finally I see the left tail light flicker. "Left turn signal working," I shout out.

My eyes dart to the right side of the motor home, and I'm thinking the tail light there will blink any second.

Instead, I wait in the blazing sun. It's hot enough to toast my brain through my cap. At last, it flashes, too. "Check," I report.

"That's good news," Larry calls out. "I've adjusted the mirrors, too, so we just need to do brake lights."

Mirrors? Now I understand what Larry was doing that took so long.

Twin red tail lights glow brightly now. "Brakes, check," I call and start to head to the apartment. Maybe I can sneak in one quick video game before Every-Detail-Larry is ready to roll.

"Adam, wait," Larry calls out. "Let's go through the checks one more time." Oh boy, he's just like Mom, Mrs. Safety. Brian doesn't know how lucky he is because his job up front is done. He's already headed for the apartment.

I retreat to the rear of the motor home and again call out, "Brakes ... check. Left signal ... check. Right signal ... check."

"Thanks for the help," Larry says as he climbs out of the captain's seat. "Just have to check tire pressure now."

He thrusts his big hand into his pocket and pulls out a tape measure, three pens, a pocket knife, and a chain loaded with dangling keys of every size.

"Let's see, somewhere in here I've got a tire pressure gauge," he says, checking another pocket. Quarters, nickels, and pennies plink on the driveway. Lastly, a screwdriver and an unidentifiable, skinny metal tool appear.

Jeepers. The big guy is a walking hardware store.

While Larry locates and then fiddles with the tire pressure gauge, I manage to sneak away before he can assign another task.

Creeping past the shed, I feel the eerie silence. Instead of the usual strange *ping-ping* coming from inside, I hear nothing at all, and my skin prickles from uncertainty. The lack of flickering lights is little comfort, either. Concerns about ghosts tend to do that to me.

*   *   *

With the luggage fully loaded into the motor home, Mom takes her place up front, riding co-pilot for Larry, while Brian and I are buckled in behind them. We travel north on US 83, passing mile after mile of flat, wide-open prairie. The landscape is drastically different from my hometown of Spring Lake, which sits along the coast of Lake Michigan and features sand dune cliffs, crashing waves, and acres and acres of trees. The only similarity between Michigan and the prairie is the bright blue sky. The afternoon pure white clouds pile up here and there like puffy popcorn balls.

Traveling on, the motor home slows down and rolls into the city of Washburn. In the small downtown, a single row of two- and three-story buildings stands tall along the curb. About a dozen people roam the sidewalk, going in and out of buildings that look like they've been around for years. The movie theatre is showing a smash-hit pirate movie – but it was released *last* summer.

Mom lowers her window, and a hot, dry wind instantly rushes inside catching the scarf on her hat, whipping it out the window, blowing it wildly like a flag. People swing their Western hats high in the air, shouting, "Howdy! Ye-haw!" Maybe they think she's a movie star because we're stopping traffic now.

A tall man decked out in shiny cowboy boots and a Western belt buckle bigger than my Boy Scout Handbook yells, "Yer purr-tier than a new calf in spring!"

Mom's face glows a blushing red. But it's not from the fancy-dressed cowboy on the street. Instead, Mom is looking at Larry's ear-to-ear smile.

A minute later the town of Washburn is long gone in the rearview mirror. There is nothing but the prairie again, with its endless strand of stone soil and spiky plants as we journey north. Mom said earlier that Garrison Dam was just more than an hour's drive. What I didn't realize is one mile along that drive would look like another... and another ... and another. Highway 83 is straight as a yardstick. I have the feeling if Larry locked the wheel into position, the motor home could get to Garrison Dam by itself.

Bored silly, I decide it's time for a snack. Before leaving Bismarck, Larry gave us the kitchen tour. "Lightweight snacks are on the top," he said as he punched an upper cupboard safety latch that prevents a door from swinging open while traveling. "Breakfast cereal to the right; pretzels and chips to the left."

Brian and I nodded our approval.

Then the big guy squatted like a sprinter on the starting block and punched the bottom cupboard. "Canned fruits and vegetables are stored down low; you don't want a heavy can of green beans to wallop you in the head while you're fixing dinner on the highway," he explained.

I stared at cans of corn, peaches, and pears all tightly packed on the shelves, labels facing forward, all in alphabetical order. The cupboards were so full we could survive a nuclear war without going hungry.

Now on the road, I've got a hankering for the pizza-flavored pretzels I remember in the upper cupboard. After punching the safety latch, I reach for the snack bag just as a *thump!* takes place. The motor home jumps from a bump in the road. Instantly, I'm tossed forward. My hand crushes the bag of pretzels, and I tip a box of cereal on the shelf, sending toasted oats exploding into a motor-home meteor shower.

Luckily, Mom and Larry are yapping together like terrier pups, and they don't even notice the eruption of cereal volcano. I quickly sweep the mess together with a few wide swings of my arms and dump the cereal in the trash. Sadly, only a handful of uncrushed pretzels are left in the bag.

Maybe I'll have better snacking luck with the refrigerator, I figure. One flip of the safety lever on the handle and I grab a cold can of root beer. Snapping the ring pull, itty-bitty bubbles of fizz escape. No bumps. No spills. Life is good.

Settling into the private back seat space, I'm ready to take the first slurp of soda when a sudden roar develops. The fierce rumble vibrates around me, growling like a lion trapped in a tunnel and echoing 'round the motor home until it is louder and louder. Curious about the sound, I slip out of the seat, creep up to the front, and stick my head between the pilot seats. Straight ahead, huge cement towers stand like drawbridges. Water blasts through cement portholes, shooting into white spray and foam as it crashes below our elevated roadway. This must be Garrison Dam!

We motor just beyond the dam, where a huge lake formed from this manmade bottleneck on the Missouri River.

"That's Lake Sakakawea," Mom says, pointing toward the mass of water.

"Sock – a – who?" I stumble over the name.

"It's the name of the Native American guide who helped Lewis and Clark explore this American territory long ago," Brian says, adding to the history lesson.

"Look!" I say. "Seagulls."

"And pelicans," Brian adds.

"Those can't be pelicans," I say, thinking I've only seen them when I visit Grandma Barb in Florida, way south, along the Gulf of Mexico. "How can a southern bird live in North Dakota?" I ask.

"I bet they live here because the water never freezes. The powerful waterfall at the dam keeps the lake open year-round," Brian says.

Just then, in one swoosh, a floating pelican nearby on the lake dips its head underwater, jerks it back up and flips an enormous fish into the air to snatch into its long beak. Whole.

Having found a good spot to pull over, Larry parks the motor home so we can explore. "Be careful –" Larry starts to say, but before he can finish, I bolt from the motor home, ready to stretch my legs but forgetting I am still holding the bag of pizza-flavored pretzels. One whiff of those treats and a pelican speeds toward me. Its wings slap at me and its huge pocket beak snaps at me. If I don't act quickly, I'll be this bird's dessert ... whole, in one gulp! With the snack bag raining pretzels, I dart back into the motor home, leaving the animal with the world's biggest beak behind.

"Pelicans will scoop up anything they think is edible," Larry says, finally finishing the sentence he had started with "Be careful..." He snorts a gruff, "hut-hut" of a laugh.

"Maybe we should drive straight to the campsite," Mom says.

Larry starts up the motor home and drives onward.

"Over there is the fish hatchery," Mom says.

"Yeah, the hatchery is like an incubator for trout and salmon," Brian says. "More than 10 million fish are shipped to rivers and lakes all over the United States." Unlike me, Brian studies facts about a place before we travel. I roll my eyes, reminded that I never play Trivial Pursuit with my brother – unless, of course, we are on the same team.

We pull into Fort Stevenson State Park and roll up to the ranger station.

Mom leans over toward the ranger on duty and delivers her request: "Modern section, please; not primitive." Mom likes the royal treatment when camping – which means running hot water and an electrical hookup. If she could order room service, she would!

"We'll take the highest peak on the western shoreline," Larry adds to the request.

"Okay, folks. That's Lot Number 130, on the Elbowoods Loop," the ranger explains while handing us an overnight sticker for the vehicle and pointing toward the highest incline in the park.

Why does Larry want high ground? I have never slept in a motor home, but as far as I know, the only time it matters if you sleep on low land is when you're camping in a tent and rain starts flooding out your fun evening.

That happened to me at Cub Scout camp once. The gear got soaked in a flash and I was swimming downstream in a soggy sleeping bag. The motor home sits high off the ground, though, and the sky is crystal clear for miles too. So without a chance of rain why does Larry want the highest spot in the campground?

Hmm...

At Lot No. 130 we park, and Larry unpacks the rear cargo area. "Look what I brought," he says. "Blue Goose and yellow Sunburst."

Two model airplanes glisten in the sun. Instantly, I want the bright yellow plane with red trim. Brian can have old blue. I may be a year younger than my brother, but I'm quick on my feet and snatch the Sunburst first, with its canary-yellow wings.

"They're hand-built out of balsa wood," Larry says.

I hold the plane in my hand. It's light as a feather. The wood has been sanded smooth as silk and then painted with shiny coats of yellow, brighter than a school bus. "Where's the engine?" I ask.

"There's no engine; they're gliders," Larry explains, his crusty laugh echoing across the open field.

I wrinkle my nose. Doesn't Larry know engines are a boy's best friend? A plane without a motor is as much fun as receiving a savings bond for a present. Remote control is the thing that counts.

"The airplane is all about arm power," Larry explains.

"Arm power?" I ask.

"We'll determine the wind direction and throw the plane into the air currents," he says. "From this higher campsite, these gliders will fly forever over the flat land along the lake."

I don't understand what Larry means about wind direction and air currents, but he is right about this flat land. The only lump in the dirt is the Garrison Dam, and it's a concrete mountain. Otherwise it's a smooth slope toward the lake.

"There's a squishy blob on the tip of the plane," I say, poking my finger into a gray glob of goop on the nose of the glider.

"That's modeling clay. It helps balance the plane," Larry says.

No engine, a clump of clay, air currents, and wind direction. What a mind scrambler.

"I know how to tell wind direction," Brian says. "You can watch the ripple of waves across the lake. I learned from sailing at camp."

"Now you'll learn about air thermals," Larry says. "They happen when the hot air over the flat prairie rises above the cool air coming across the lake."

I'm great at math in school, but science is only fun when we do volcanic explosions. I lower my head a little, fighting off serious disappointment about this whole glider thing.

Larry notices my silent mood and puts his hand on my shoulder. "I'll show you," he says, guiding me so I'm parallel to the open water of the lake. He points into the air, "That's where you want to throw the plane."

I arch my arm and release the foot-long glider. The plane sails for a couple of seconds and then quickly nosedives to the ground a few feet away.

"Humph," I grumble, unimpressed with this airplane that doesn't have an engine. Annie, Zach's pocket-size dog, can run farther than that even on a leash.

"I'll try," Brian says, almost bouncing in his shoes, but I sure don't get why he's so excited.

Brian arches his arm and tosses his glider into the air. His Blue Goose sails a good ten seconds longer than my yellow Sunburst. Big deal.

"The hot air seems to be a little higher up," Larry says. "Adam, your turn. Try again, aim higher."

I take a deep breath. Larry is Mom's friend – and he does have a cool motor home – so I guess I can try a little harder.

With all my might, I hurl the yellow gilder, aiming straight up, into the sky. Three years of Little League baseball pitching should make tossing a light weight glider easy, but yellow Sunburst sails no farther than the first throw. Cripes. I don't hate many things in life, but yellow Sunburst and I are not on good terms.

"Did you see that bump?" Larry asks, his voice ringing with excitement. "It was an air current. Aim higher." Easy for Larry to say. He stands taller than a basketball superstar.

There must be some way of getting higher. Suddenly, I have an idea.

Airplane in hand, I jog to the back side of the motor home and look up. A ladder with ten steps leads to the roof. It is made for rooftop storage, but I have another plan.

I hike up the ladder. The roof is smooth and flat and empty. Since this is a one-night trip, we don't have extra gear to tie down up here, making it a perfect launch pad for the Sunburst Special.

At the top of the ladder, I crawl over the storage railing bar and stand up on the roof. The ground seems miles below me. Perfect. Larry said the higher I throw, the farther the plane will fly, so I figure being up high on the roof should do the trick.

I wind up and release yellow Sunburst – and the extra height works like magic. Sunburst sails smoothly. It takes a little bounce. I gulp. The plane doesn't crash; it climbs higher. Wow. Sunburst is so high it looks like an ant. This is the difference between hitting a base hit and a grand slam.

"It's caught an air thermal!" Larry yells. "It's been cruising over seven minutes. I've only had a glider stay up five and a half minutes!"

Suddenly, Sunburst starts to curve, heading for the lake. I hustle down the motor home ladder and sprint after the plane. Long grass whips against my legs, but I don't let it slow me down. I run like I'm jumping hurdles.

"It's near the rocks by the lake!" Mom yells.

"The plane!" I wail, my arms pumping at my sides to gain more speed.

The glider reaches the lake. The hot air from the prairie vanishes as cool air blowing across the water causes Sunburst to drop quickly.

The plane sails past the rocks, peacefully landing in the water, but now it's sinking fast, like my heart.

Racing from the long grass onto the clay shoreline, I dive in. The icy water sends a head-to-toe chill through me. I kick hard, swimming like a shark after its dinner. My arms turn numb, beating against the arctic-like water. My soaked clothes are heavy, slowing me down. Eye on the prize, I tell myself. In a few more strokes, I snag Sunburst.

I swim back, one-arm raised high in the air, balancing Sunburst to safety.

Shivering, I come out of the water. I'm sure my lips are as blue as Brian's Blue Goose glider, but the hot prairie sun beats down on me. By the time I'm halfway to the motor home, my clothes are practically dry.

*   *   *

With pep in my step, I cradle Sunburst, anxious to launch another record-breaking flight off the roof of the motor home. But as I am hiking through the tall grass away from the lake, something suddenly slithers. I catch a glimpse of gray scales, an evil eye, and maybe fangs. A puffed-up snake raises its head, opens its mouth, and hisses right at me. My heart stops. Time stops, too.

Maybe I should back away. Or stand perfectly still? No, that's what you do with bears. At least I think so. Where's Brian when I need him?

The snake's black, beady eyes cut right through me, and then its head puffs bigger. I've never seen a snake so huge. It's more than two feet long ... bigger than a Michigan blue racer. In fact, its head blows up bigger with every hair-raising hiss. This snake makes the blue racer's wicked purple tongue seem like child's play.

Brian is heading my direction. I try to shout, but nothing comes out. My brother is a few feet away, rustling through the long grass. I can't even raise my arms in warning to halt his footsteps because I'm frozen in fear.

Brian is a few feet from the snake when it flops over, mouth open, and tongue hanging out. Maybe it died. Could we be so lucky?

My brother spots the dead snake. Before I can stammer out a first word, Brian is crouching down. I can't believe it. He's getting closer to the snake. Maybe he thinks it's a dead stick. Maybe he doesn't know only moments ago it was hissing. Maybe he doesn't know I was sure the snake was shooting poisonous spit. Maybe we're both going to get bitten and die.

Brian pinches the snake's head between his thumb and fingers. He holds up the limp and motionless beast. "Puff Adder," he says, naming the snake. "They're harmless."

"Harmless?" I squeak.

With that he gently tosses the snake aside. Brian turns and walks away, saying over his shoulder, "They like to play dead if they fear their attack is failing."

I wait a few minutes for my heart to come down to Earth before walking toward the others. Then, with my first step, something shoots out of the grass right in front of me. The leopard-spotted animal lets out a shrill cry. Huge feathered wings flap wildly. Koy! Koy! It screeches again. Its fiery-red head cocks upward. Its hooked beak snaps at me as it lets out another piercing squawk. I jump. My heart rate soars. Lights dance in front of my eyes and the world spins faster. Feeling the ground tilt, I tumble into the grass.

When I wake up, Brian is hitting me on the back to start me breathing again. "You fainted at a pheasant, Adam," he says.

I can only stare at him open-mouthed.

"That pheasant spooked you and you fainted," Brian says.

"Pheasant?" I say, puzzled.

"That pheasant spooked you and you fainted." My brother won't let it drop.

I fire eye daggers at him. He fires them right back.

"That wasn't a pheasant. It was an escaped crazed rooster with rabies. A barnyard run-away, sick with mad-dog," I say, trying to make it sound like an axe murderer on the loose.

"Pheasants naturally dart when surprised," Brian says. "Face it, Adam; you were spooked by a harmless pheasant. You fainted."

"Boys don't faint!" I wail.

"Yeah, right," Brian says, shaking his head.

"I passed out," I snap.

"You fainted like a girl," Brian smirks.

"Passed out," I insist.

I see Mom charging over, feet flying, arms pumping. Larry is a few beats behind.

"Are you all right?" she asks, squatting down next to me. Instantly her hands are patting me for broken bones or some other kind of strange injury. I can't help but grin; Mom is always there to comfort me.

"Everything okay over here?" Larry asks.

"Uh, yeah, I just passed out ... from the ... heat," I stammer, trying to come up with something, anything, besides the fact I was spooked by a harmless pheasant. I hope my eye daggers make Brian wilt a little and he'll keep his mouth shut.

Larry looks down at me, casting a giant-size shadow across me. I sit up quickly, recovering from everything but embarrassment.

"Hey, Son, this heat is strong stuff out here on the prairie," Larry says. "If it makes you feel any better, I've blacked out just standing still from the hot sun."

I look up, way up, into Larry's deep, dark eyes. It was that very moment I knew I found a new friend.

Brian doesn't say a word. Instead he squeezes my hand, just like he did after the pontoon accident. I like it when he doesn't say anything at all. I squeeze his hand back. It's nice to know I have more than one friend.

By now the sun is setting and it is growing darker. The endless prairie seems to roll away, getting soft and fuzzy in the hazy distance. Mom says it's time to call it a day. Larry stores the planes for safe keeping until tomorrow. We unfold beds, fluff up pillows, and take turns in the one tiny bathroom.

Ready for bed, I'm tucked in the upper bunk. The hum of the air conditioner plugged into the electricity of Mom's modern campsite drowns out the sounds of any wild-animal that might be prowling the prairie. I sleep soundly, without dreams of pelicans, puff adders, or pheasants. And that's just fine with me.

Chapter 10

Magic Tricks

A low-pitched rumble echoes through the Bat Cave. At first I think Mad Witch's big orange cat, Butterscotch, might come crashing down on me again through the ceiling tiles. But nothing shifts or stirs above me. The deep throaty rumble continues – grows louder – and now I realize it's coming from outside. It's from the front of the house, thank goodness, and not from out back, where Custer's ghost could be lurking in the shed. Suddenly, the sound stops.

Someone in deck shoes strolls past the Bat Cave basement window. It's Mom's friend, Larry. But that rumble wasn't the sound of his motor home. At once my brain buzzes as I realize that, yes, I can name what that *fvoom-voom!* roar was all about.

I race to the studio door, whip it open – and smack right into Larry.

"Was that an H-D I heard?" I blurt out.

"So you know about motorcycles, Son?" Larry asks.

I don't wait to answer Larry. I dart past him, out the door, around the corner, and down the driveway. And there it sits! A great big Harley-Davidson motorcycle with its shiny chrome handlebars radiant in the sun, a rugged leather seat scooped low to hold two, and a fierce engine the size of an Army tank. I can feel the powerful vibes coming off the machine still oozing heat from its recent ride.

Brian and Mom come outside and stand alongside Larry and me.

"Can you do that *fvoom-voom* thing with the throttle?" I ask Larry, feeling like the bike is almost whispering to me, *"Goose the throttle and hear me roar!"*

"Sure thing," Larry says, flashing a smile so big it shows top and bottom teeth at the same time. He starts up the bike, and the engine bursts with noise, rumbling sweetly. Not the high-pitched growl of a Porsche. Not the throaty hum of a Ferrari. And not the tinny whine of a scooter. No, this is the royal rumble of the king of the road. An H-D; a Harley.

"Give the throttle a twist, Son," Larry says.

He lets me give the mighty engine some gas. With each twist the rumble explodes. I can feel the vibrations through the soles of my shoes. I suck in the smell of high octane gas and oil in the air.

"Want to go for a ride?" Larry shouts out, over the husky Harley roar.

"Yes!" Brian and I yell back immediately. Mom, meanwhile, is stammering over the monster of a bike in the driveway. "It's very ... shiny," she finally comments loudly. Her face is whiter than the time we were stuck more than forty minutes on the top of a Ferris wheel and the metal bucket seat rocked back and forth in the wind.

We can all tell Mom won't be riding this big beauty. That means rock-paper-scissors will have to settle it for Brian and me for the first ride. Brian wins.

"It's not fair," I moan to Mom as Brian is whisked off. She walks back to the apartment, and I drag along behind, scuffing disgustedly at the sidewalk with the tip of my shoe.

Mom doesn't turn back to me, even though I know she hears my grumbling.

I shuffle along and kick at anything in the way – a leaf, a pebble, a stick. Certainly no four-leaf-clovers, though, considering my lousy luck just now. Back at the apartment, the minutes of waiting drag on.

"Where can they be?" I whine to Mom.

She doesn't pay me any attention.

"This is so-o-o boring," I say. "There's not even anything on TV."

Mom stays focused on her task at hand, ignoring me. I guess this silent treatment is better than telling me Brian won fair and square. I should have said to Brian, "Best two out of three," when we played the rock-paper-scissors game.

Feeling restless, I say to Mom, "I'm going back outside to wait for Larry."

I mope my way out the door, and as I trudge past the shed, I see Mad Witch has the padlock clamped tightly across the closed door. Suddenly, there's rapid-fire of popping sounds from inside the shed. Pow! Pow! Pow! I jump, and I can't catch my breath. Is it Custer's ghost? Then, just as quickly, it's dead silent.

Still in fear, I feel my feet anchored to the cement. I try to breathe normally but find it difficult with my heart banging in my ribcage. Then, from out of nowhere, Butterscotch rockets past me, darting away from the shed and toward the front yard. His fur is standing on end, so I guess I'm not the only one startled and unsettled. Following Butterscotch's good sense, I hustle off, too, leaving the eerie shed behind.

As I come around the corner toward the front of the house, I feel her before I see her. Mad Witch, of course. Her boney fingers are wrapped around giant-fur-ball Butterscotch. The cat and Mad Witch have matching smiles – they hiss when they show their teeth. Luckily, there is no cane in sight to swing at me. She just glares at me long and hard, sizing me up with squinty eyes. For a moment I stand paralyzed under her heated gaze. I don't wait for her to talk, though. Instead, I give my ball cap a tug and nod my head in a silent hello. Then I dart to the front yard to get away from the jungle cat and Mad Witch.

Once in the front yard, I'm reminded of Brian's absence. I bet Larry and my lucky brother are carving curves and doing wheelies on the Harley the whole time I'm left here to wait. It feels like they've been cruising on that motorcycle forever, but really I know it's only been about five minutes. I should have remembered that I never win at rock-paper-scissors and should have bribed my way into a ride. That is, if I had money to buy off my brother. So far, this vacation hasn't given us a lot of opportunities for making money. And now the girls down on the corner have the arrowheads.

For a moment I flash back to holding that rugged, interesting arrowhead in my hand at the birthday party. I wonder again ... where did it come from? Is it possible that the arrowhead washed down the mighty Missouri River all the way from Garrison? Maybe it belonged to Louis and Clark's guide, Sakakawea. If it did, that arrowhead would be worth not just two dollars but two thousand! Somehow I've got to get those arrowheads back.

Before I can even begin to scheme a plan, I hear a familiar giggle. Yep; it's Hannah and Georgia. Glitzy Georgia is wearing enough jewelry to decorate a Christmas tree, but Hannah is dressed more like me, in a plain T-shirt and shorts. Both girls are twirling jump ropes, skipping at full speed while they make their way up the sidewalk. The rope smacks the sidewalk faster than a second hand ticks on a clock. The girls easily leap through the whirling rope, not missing a beat in their forward progress.

Watching their skill in motion, I make a mental note not to challenge them to a jump-rope contest to get my arrowhead back. Wouldn't win that one! When we went camping before with Mom, I learned jumping rope is harder than it looks. We played a jump-rope game one day with Grandma, who knew a silly song about school. I was winning until Grandma, with her chunky shoes and gray hair, took the lead by jumping the right amount at the right time. And right now, watching Hannah and Georgia, I can see they are into jumping with speed, too, not just to silly songs.

I start bobbing my head to the beat of the fast "*click-click*" of rope against pavement. It almost makes me dizzy. Then I start wondering again ... how can I get those arrowheads back? I shove my hands in my pockets to steady my balance. My right hand jingles a pocket full of coins. Silently, I count the coins as they roll between my fingers. Three coins – a quarter and two dimes. Suddenly, I have the answer to get the arrowheads back: A captivating magic tricks could do it! Papa's been teaching me since I was six years old.

First, I'll need to gather some information. "Hey, girls," I say, fluttering my eyelashes like Joey did the other day. I figure I better use every tool I've got.

The girls stop their jumping and turn my way. "Hey, Adam," they chirp and bat their eyelashes right back.

Oh no. What have I done? My face feels hot and my ears are burning. But I remember the arrowhead mission and keep going. "Anything new?" I ask. I need to remain calm. If I seem too anxious, they may get suspicious.

"No-oh," Hannah says, practically singing the simple word.

I swallow hard and wonder if Joey's syrupy technique is really worth it. But my heart tells me for a motorcycle ride it is well worth it. I force myself to look directly into their eyes and fluttering lashes. "So ... nothing new to report?" I ask, again, kicking a nearby rock, hoping the stone might send a message.

It works! Glitzy Georgia watches the stone spin and suddenly her eyes grow wide. "Well, our dad hasn't had time to check the value of the arrowheads. Overstreet's book has 1,264 pages to search."

"Wow! That's a big job," I say, trying to sound understanding. "Isn't there an easier way?"

"Well, I know a quick test," Georgia boasts.

"What's that?" I ask trying to keep her talking about the arrowheads.

"My dad says real arrowheads are twice as heavy as fake ones. Sometimes you can tell the difference by how heavy the rocks feel," Georgia says. She reaches in her pocket and pulls out two arrowheads.

There they are! I can't believe my luck. The flat and pointy arrowheads are right there, within reach, in the palm of her hand. Georgia hefts them a little, makes them flip and jiggle in her hand.

"So, what do those arrowheads feel like?" I ask, thinking this is my chance to sneak in my magic trick with the three coins. Inside my pocket I've sandwiched the large coin between the two small ones. This "sandwiching" technique is an important step to pulling off the magic trick. Carefully, I pull out the bundle of coins and open my palm. One dime sits on top of the quarter and the other dime I have wisely hidden underneath the quarter.

"Should the arrowheads be heavier than a couple of coins?" I ask.

"Ooooh!" Hannah's eyes shift from fluttering at me to the coins. "You're rich, Adam," she says.

Knowing Hannah's excitement is a good sign, I quickly say, "I could buy the arrowheads."

Glitzy Georgia doesn't miss a beat. "Dad should check the arrowheads first, Hannah, before we sell them," she says.

I go for my best tool now: praise. "Georgia, you said you could tell by the weight. And look at those rocks; they flip like feathers in your hand. They must be fakes," I say.

"So if these arrowheads are fakes, why would you want to spend money on them?" Georgia asks me.

Boy-oh-boy; I knew Glitzy Georgia was smart. Luckily, I've had a lot of practice with trying to out-trick my brother, who is clever, too. "I don't really want to buy them," I say. "I was going to see if the arrowheads weigh more than the two coins.

But you're an expert, Georgia, so you don't need to compare the weight to the coins."

"That's true," she agrees at my flattery.

I can tell I'm making progress so I keep going. "So are you just as good at solving magic tricks, too?" I ask.

"Of course," Georgia says with pride.

"So am I," Hannah adds.

Hip-hip-hooray! Like Brian, the girls want to prove they're smart. "I bet I can make this dime disappear and re-appear," I say.

"No way," they snap.

"I'll bet you the arrowheads that I can make the dime re-appear." I drag out the word "re-appear" trying to make it sound more bewitching. "And if I can't make the dime re-appear, you can keep the arrowheads *and* the thirty-five cents."

"It's a deal!" they say, certain I can't do the disappearing act.

"Okay," I say with my palm open, cautiously flashing the coins. "I'll take this dime away and then close my hand so I only have the quarter in my hand." Carefully, I close my fist, wrapping my hand snuggly around the quarter and the hidden dime underneath. "Next, I'll close this hand with the dime," I say, closing my hand that has only the dime in it. I give this hand a little shake. "Now you'll say the magic words."

"Which are?" they ask.

"Hocus pocus."

"Hocus pocus," they singsong together.

"Say it again," I say, waving my closed fist with the one dime over my other hand with the quarter and dime in it.

"Hocus pocus." The girls repeat.

Slowly, very slowly, I start to uncurl my fist with the quarter-dime. As I had hoped; the girls gawk at this hand. Without them noticing it, I brush my other hand with just the one dime across my side pocket, letting it slip inside. Before I uncurl my fist with the quarter-dime, I turn my fingers toward the sky so that, as my fist opens, the quarter rolls with my fingers, uncovering the hidden dime. As I open my hand, the dime is now on top of the quarter. And I flash open my other hand to show it's empty now.

"How did you do that?" Hannah asks in awe. Georgia just stands with her arms folded across her chest, knowing she has lost the bet.

"It's magic," I say, knowing Papa taught me that magic is all about misdirection. "So can I have the arrowheads back?"

"Fair is fair," Hannah says, still pondering my magic with the coins. Georgia slaps the two rocks into my hand. Again, she reminds me of my brother. Brian gets mad at me, too, but he is always honest.

"These arrowheads do feel lightweight," I say, moving them gently in my hand. I hope by saying this I chase away some of Glitzy Georgia's soreness.

Her gaze does soften a bit. Then her expression warms and there's a trace of a smile on her lips. Mom's warning to say nice things runs through my mind.

"Thanks for playing fair and square," I say, giving her my best smile.

That seems to work because Georgia breaks into a full-size grin.

Jeepers. Saying nice things really does help. The arrowheads slip in my sweaty hand, but then I remember the motorcycle. "I think I hear my mom calling," I say. "Gotta run!"

I dash to the apartment to launch the next step. How do I prove to my brother these are real arrowheads? I need him to think they're not fake so I can bribe him out of one of his turns on the motorcycle. Visions of whizzing at top speed on that big bike rush through my mind. This is the most important trick I'll ever attempt. It's even more important than when I superglued nickels to the sidewalk in front of my friend Lucas' house. When he came outside, the first thing he did was try to pick up the coins. I got a good laugh out of that one. Lucas and I are always pulling pranks on each other.

My brother, however, is smart. It will take something special to make Brian think these arrowheads are real. I need something that proves they match a photograph from Glitzy Georgia's huge book about real-deal Indian arrowheads.

I look around Mom's art studio. It's after dinner so the helpers are gone for the day. Mom is busy in the kitchen. I poke my nose into the shelves of art supplies; paint, glue, and paper are everywhere. Then I spy some gold foil circles, each one about fist-size. They look like the awards we win at the science fair. That's it! If I slap a shiny sticker on some kind of a certificate, it will look official. I've watched Mrs. Smith, my teacher at school, print certificates from her computer. Even awards like "Most Improved," or "Good Job."

"Hey, Mom," I call out, dashing to the kitchen to ask for a favor. "Can I use your business computer for a sec to go on-line and print a word game for Brian and me to play?" Mom often lets us print word scrambles and hidden-picture games off the Internet. She has bookmarked the sites we can use.

"Yes, if you stay on 'My Favorites,'" Mom says. Her hands are covered in cookie dough, rolling doughnut-hole-size drops of batter and plopping them on a tray.

"Mmm," I say, completely distracted for a moment. "You're making my favorite! Chocolate chip cookies."

For years baking with Mom has been a tradition I really love. She must have thought I was out on the motorcycle to start without me. Not thinking, I reach my finger towards the batter to swipe a big chunk of raw cookie dough.

Mom's eyes narrow. "Adam, you know uncooked eggs aren't good for you."

I quickly pull my hand back and obey. I need to stay on Mom's good side if I want to leave the bookmark websites and enter no-no land. Now is not the time for me to try to trick Mom and sneak a bite of delicious dough. Instead, I give Mom a big squeeze around the waist. Mom likes the mushy stuff. "I just need to print one game and I'll come back and help," I say.

"Does that mean help with washing dishes or help with eating the cookies?" Mom asks, letting out a chuckle. It's catchy, and instantly we're both laughing.

I slide out of the kitchen without committing to help with dishes. Believe it or not, sometimes I know when to keep my mouth shut.

Signing onto the computer, I search for *"free printable certificates."* Instantly, I get a hit, and it's better than raw cookie dough. Tappity-tap-tap, I fill in the blanks and press the print button. It looks pretty good, but it's pretty flimsy ... not the quality I need to fool my brother. This has to look top-notch.

I zip over to Mom's art paper to select a heavier quality of paper. I hit the jackpot because the new paper is not only heavy, it is the color of creamy butter – soft and fancy-looking.

The certificate shoots out of the printer. It's stiff and firm in my hand. Perfect. Next I slap on a gold, shiny sticker in the lower left corner. The certificate looks like the real-deal!

But there's one problem.

A blank line stares at me along the bottom of the certificate. To look official, this award needs a signature. I let out a low groan. My handwriting will never fool my brother. Who can I ask? Not Mom. No way am I asking Glitzy Georgia. And if I ask Zach, Joey will find out, meaning everyone in the city of Bismarck will know what I'm up to.

Cripes. I should have swiped that finger-full of cookie dough because this is shaping up to be a whole-bowlful-of-cookie-dough kind of day. In my head I can practically hear the mighty roar of the "Hog" – what H-D owners call their bikes. I can't give up now.

"Think, Adam, think," I say to myself, actually mumbling it a little under my breath. I flip the arrowheads in my hand. They're carved smooth to precise points. A real treasure. No wonder Custer's Ghost is searching for lost arrowheads. Too bad a ghost can't write. Thinking of Joey's ghost story reminds me of the shed and Mad Witch, Mom's landlord who lives upstairs.

Hmm. Mad Witch, I think. When I saw her earlier, she didn't even bark at me. I just got a matching hiss from her and her Goliath-size cat. That was pretty tame. And the other day she let us use the side entrance to dog-sit, King. But then I remember that King chased Butterscotch halfway to Minnesota so I don't know if Mad Witch will trust me if I beg for a favor. Besides, grown-ups ask a lot of questions and her wicked cane still scares me a bit.

I juggle the arrowheads in the air, tossing them high and sending them from my right hand to my left. Wait, that's it … I'll write with my left hand! Brian will never recognize my hand writing if I use my left hand.

Practicing on scrap paper, I make a big "O" for Overstreet. Slowly, I guide the fine-point marker in loopy circles for the *e's* and the *s*. I cross the two *t's* and the name looks great! Next, I do it on the butter-cream paper and finish the project just in time.

A deep rumble echoes outside. It's The Bike! I turn off the computer, gently roll the certificate and stash it with the arrowheads in my pocket. I race outside. Luckily, the girls are gone and the roar grows louder. Larry and Brian pull up, and my ears are filled with the rumbling thunder. Then Larry cuts the engine.

Brian slumps in the seat. Slowly, he slips off the big black helmet. His face is white and his breathing comes in shallow gasps.

"You'll be alright," Larry says to Brian. "You're just hyperventilating. Take a deep breath." He rubs his back. "Try to relax," Larry says, coaching and calming my brother.

Brian nods, unable to speak. Larry puts his other hand over Brian's nose and mouth in an effort to slow his breathing. Brian looks like he did when he rode the roller coaster and got sick when it was over. I guess he and Mom have the same anti-amusement-park gene.

My brother's color soon returns. "That was fun," he mumbles as he rolls off the bike to stand on wobbly legs.

"Sure, Son," Larry says, giving Brian a pat on the back. Brian shuffles down the driveway to the apartment.

Instantly I know I won't have to share any further motorcycle time. I will have Larry and the Harley all to myself. Anytime. Every time.

Even better, I have two arrowheads in my pocket that I might be able to sell. The idea of money in my pocket gets my head spinning with possibilities of how I could spend it. Maybe on a stomp rocket that blasts more than two-hundred feet high or laser-tag shooters with foam darts or …

"Ready for your turn, Adam?" Larry's voice pulls me from my daydream.

He doesn't have to ask me again. I dash to the bike and instantly straddle the soft black leather seat of the hefty Harley. This is ten times better than raw cookie dough.

Chapter 11

The Strange and the Unusual

Something is wrong – very wrong. Brian and I have to go on a field trip. A field trip to learn about history, on summer vacation no less!

After hearing the news about the trip, Mom sees me get all moody-faced as I press my lips together and clutch the cereal bowl with white knuckles.

"Now, Adam, there's a lot of history to learn about North Dakota," she says, getting a little testy. Besides, it won't hurt you to learn about government and geography."

Yuck! Social studies is my least favorite subject. It's just a bunch of facts, nothing fizzing or exploding like in science class. And right now I feel like I'm the science experiment: water left to boil on the stove. I'm steaming up a storm and overflowing my pot.

Grumbling, I take the cereal bowl to the sink. That's when Mom surprises me.

"You can bring two friends on the trip," she says.

That's all it takes for my lips to twist up into a smile. I race to the bathroom and brush my teeth in eight seconds flat. Whizzing out the door, I come up with a plan for how to sell my two best friends on joining me on a history field trip.

I rap a knockity-knock on the next-door neighbor's house. A triple rapid tap is the secret knock to let Zach and Joey know it's me at the door. When my best friends answer the knock, I burst out my genius invitation. "Do you want to come on a sleep-over in a motor home?"

"We love sleep-overs!" they shout as one and then rush off to ask permission.

Left standing on their doorstep, I'm feeling really bad. Not for myself. Well, okay, for myself, because I didn't clue in Zach and Joey about the field-trip part of the sleepover. Feeling a little worried now, I stare down at my feet and shove my hands in my pockets. My eyes sting and my throat tightens a little bit but, hey, it was just a little fib.

"Hello, Adam," a deep voice calls out and forces me to look up quickly. Towering over me now is Captain Mike. "Where are you headed for this trip of yours?" he asks, almost in a growl. It's unusual for Captain Mike to sound so gruff, but maybe he just sounds rough because it's the morning and he hasn't had his coffee yet. Mom is a bit grumpy before coffee, too. I think they both could use an extra cup this morning.

I take a step back. Then I notice that Captain Mike's gleaming dentist-smile isn't shining either. In fact, his lips are drawn tight. But he's wearing a Minnesota Twins T-shirt, his favorite team, so I relax a little. At least until I remember my fib. I probably shouldn't have gotten Zach and Joey excited only about the party-on-wheels part of the trip. My stomach feels hollow; I know I should have mentioned that we have to learn about President Theodore Roosevelt.

From behind Captain Mike, Zach and Joey appear. Wildly, they bounce like pogo sticks, anxious to hear where we're going.

I wiggle my sweaty palms in my pocket. My hand discovers the note Mom gave me with the directions for the trip, and I whip out the wad of paper, "We're going a hundred and thirty miles west," I read, thinking it seems a long way to travel to learn history. "Mom says its bad land."

"Adam, are we going to Medora?" Zach asks as he fiddles with his wire-rim glasses. It's like he's checking to see if he heard me correctly even though it's his glasses he adjusts.

I shrug a yes, silently praying that Medora isn't a bad thing. All I know about it is that Medora is some old town named after the wife of a French nobleman back in pioneer days.

"Medora is in the middle of the Badlands. It's the coolest place," Zach says excitedly. "The Badlands have huge rocks we can scale. It's almost like mountain climbing. And when you pitch a stone over a cliff, it never hits the bottom!"

I find it strange and unusual that my friends want to go on this field trip about a town built in 1883. But if there are boulders to climb, I'm getting excited about this trip, too.

Captain Mike reads Mom's note. "It sounds like a fun overnight. Tell your Mom it was nice of her and Larry to include the boys on the motor home trip." No longer so coarse and rough, his voice now sounds as smooth as caramel. "The boys will be ready for your leaving time at four o'clock," he adds, reading more details from the note.

"Roger that," Zach says. "I'll start packing right now." He whirls away and is out of sight in a snap.

*   *   *

At twenty minutes to four, I hear a dragging sound along the driveway and then our secret knockity-knock. I rush to the door and swing it open.

"We couldn't wait any longer," Zach says, his eyes dancing behind his glasses.

"Yup! We've rustled up our gear for the Wild West!" Joey says, sporting a coonskin cap. As he tugs his overstuffed backpack a little closer, Joey makes me grin to see that he packs big-time for a trip, just like I do.

Brian and I grab our overnight bags and, all together now, The Four Tenderfoots – a North Dakota word for cowboy-in-training – hustle down the driveway to where Larry's motor home is parked.

Joey has to stop twice to adjust his coonskin cap. It keeps sliding off his head as he hunches over to drag his jam-packed backpack. Finally he hoists the bag by the straps onto his shoulders and waddles the rest of the way to the motor home.

"I'll give you a tour of the RV," I boast, using the travel slang I learned on the recent trip to Garrison Dam in Larry's motor home.

"RV?" Joey gives a puzzled look.

"RV stands for recreational vehicle, which is the same thing as a motor home," Brian says.

Single file, we hike up the two-step entrance and squish together into the narrow aisle of the kitchen. Joey, who is too heavy with his bulging backpack, topples over and lands in the front area near the driver's seat.

Flat on his back, he giggles through a totally goofy grin and we all burst out laughing. I give Joey a helping hand as he struggles to his feet.

"It's certainly tight quarters in here," Zach says, trying to get some elbow room.

"You can store your gear in this closet," Brian says. "There's a latch that snaps in place so things won't fall out when we hit a bump in the road."

With the backpacks tucked away, there's a little more wiggle room, so I give the guys a quick tour. "Mini fridge with cold drinks in here," I say, flipping the lever and opening the refrigerator. Cans of cola, orange drink, and root beer all stand in a row. I notice that Larry has them in alphabetical order again.

I snap the fridge shut, turn a half circle and take two steps. "This is the mini bathroom," I say, opening the door.

"What's up there?" Joey asks, pointing skyward, above the driver's area.

"That's where we explore the wild frontier," I say, starting to scale the ladder to the loft. "Come on! Let's go to the upper bunk."

The tenderfoots are right behind me. We gaze out the huge windshield that spans the entire width of the front end of the motor home. That is, most of us are gawking out the bird's-eye-view window. Joey is bouncing on the soft bunk cushions.

"Is this where I sleep?" he asks, springing up and down and then side to side, like a pinball.

"All of you boys will sleep up top," booms a rugged voice as deep as the lowest note on a piano. It's Larry. He stands so tall his head is eye-level with the loft.

We nod in unison and are pleased to know we will all camp out together in the bunk with a window on the world.

"Daylight's a-wasting," Larry says, flashing a little smile at the Four Tenderfoots. "Let's hit the dusty trail." And with that he holds up his large hand for high-fives. We slap at it and it captures all four of our hands at once.

Soon enough Mom and Larry are ready to roll. They wedge into the front captain and co-pilot seats. Larry motors the big house on wheels out of the driveway and, after just a few turns in town, we are heading west on I-94. The road is straight as an arrow, stretching far ahead off into the horizon. The flat, brown land is pretty boring.

"It looks like Paul Bunyan flattened this ground with a rolling pin," I say being as bored with history on the highway as I am in school.

"Adam, do you know the best part about the prairie?" Joey asks.

Before I can utter a sound, Joey answers his own question. "You only have to use two colors to paint a North Dakota picture, gold for prairie and blue for sky."

Joey double ups in laughter. I wonder if he thought it was a joke. Unsure, I say, "Well, you can save a lot of money on art supplies so that's a good thing."

Still bored, I pull a brown paper sack out of my pocket, give it a shake and make its contents rattle around. "Guess what I brought?" I ask my fellow Tenderfoots.

No one answers, but the rattle has all eyes peering at me.

"Let's do a blind taste test," I say, giving the bag of thirty-three flavors of jelly beans another shake. "Close your eyes and then guess the flavor of the treat!" I pop a jelly bean into Zach's mouth.

"Mmmm ... Marshmallow," Zach says, chomping on the jellybean.

"Nope; guess again," I say.

"Banana Split."

"Yes!"

"Close your eyes, Brian," I say. "You can be next." After he shuts his eyes I pull out a tan jellybean with dark brown spots.

Mom says it tastes like the best cup of coffee in the world, calling it cappuccino. I call it cup-of-yuck-o.

"Blah!" Brian chokes, and then snorts. "It tastes like dirt!"

Zach and I crack up. And Joey, as usual, is rolling in laughter, ding-a-ling happy. Putting Joey in a cool bunk with a window and expecting him to stay calm is like plopping a baby in a church pew and telling him not to fuss.

"Settle down," I say to bouncing Joey, hanging on tightly to the paper bag of jellybeans.

Trying to control his laughter, Joey curls his knees up to his chest. Oh no! Larry hits the only curve on I-94. Joey's tightly squeezed body turns into a bowling ball. Suddenly he's rolling toward me, full speed ahead. I try to scoot out of the way. Too late. Joey knocks into me and the bag of jellybeans flies into the air, exploding like fireworks! Blueberry, butter popcorn, and chocolate pudding pellets rain down, bombarding Mom and Larry below.

Immediately, Larry's face wrinkles. His eyes bulge. The big guy looks like he bit into a sour pickle. Mom looks at me like I've given the wrong answer to two plus two and have failed the math test. Or in this field-trip case, history.

Luckily, I'm quick to act. "We'll pick up every bean at the first stop," I say, backpedaling a bit to get out of trouble over "spilling the beans."

Brian's brain quickly clicks onto something: "Breath-holding contest. Let's see who can hold their breath the longest. Ready. Set. Go!"

In less than five seconds Brian has all us boys still and quiet. Larry and Mom's pinched faces soften a bit.

Brian wins the first breath-holding contest. "Let's play best two out of three," I say.

We Tenderfoots all suck in a deep breath. Then, with my mouth clamped shut and my cheeks puffed out, I spy an odd-shaped thing far off on the horizon. Something huge and dark is standing atop a small hill. Maybe it's a creature from Mars, I think in a panic, and it makes me blow out my lungs filled with air. A breath-holding contest can't compete with a creature from outer space. Unable to find my voice for the moment, I point excitedly at the mass on the hill.

"That's New Salem Sue," Zach immediately says.

"New what? Sue who?" Brian asks.

No one is holding their breath any longer, and Joey is bouncing as he chatters about New Salem Sue.

"She's a big, big, big cow! A statue so tall I can stand between her legs. Even on tip toes, I can't reach her belly. Or even when I jump!" Joey yaps nonstop.

Feeling better because no Martian attack is coming, I ask, "But why a giant cow in the middle of nowhere?"

"The cow is a landmark for the town of New Salem," Zach says. "They celebrate milk."

"And milk is the state beverage for North Dakota," Brian adds.

"Can we stop and explore?" I ask Mom, not too interested in random facts but full of curiosity about a mountain-size cow.

Mom looks at Larry.

"Well, it's not a scheduled stop," Larry says, glancing at the GPS device on the dashboard. He has it programmed with not only the planned miles per hour we should travel but the miles per hour until we need gas, and every other detail a traveler might want.

Near an exit I see a sign that shows pictures of dancing, chocolate-dipped ice cream cones. Knowing how the big guy loves sweet treats, I have an idea. "According to the local history, Lewis and Clark stopped here in the winter of 1811."

Mom's eyes fix on me in amazement as I spew out a fact about "ancient times" that we learned on our trip to Garrison Damn.

"This was where their Indian scout, Sakakawea, made friends with Lewis and Clark for bringing soft-serve ice cream to the Native Americans," I add.

"Very funny, Adam," Mom says, "soft-serve ice cream in 1811."

I glance at Larry. He bursts out in his hut-hut chuckle. Oh, how I'm beginning to enjoy that laugh. In fact, I might even be finding ways to draw it out of him a bit more.

With a smile plastered across his face, Larry takes exit 127S toward the town of New Salem and the statue of huge Sue. The closer we get, the bigger the cow gets. This is strange and unusual.

Larry parks the motor home. We tumble out of the loft and head full speed for the door. "Wait a minute, boys!" Mom says, arms folded across her chest. "You're forgetting something, aren't you? There are jelly beans to pick up."

I'm ready to moan and groan, but then recall I was the one who brought the beans. The barn-size cow will have to wait. As it turns out, the pick-up job isn't too tough. Pint-size Joey squeezes in between the front seats easily to snag the morsels scattered around the gas and brake pedals. Brian gives each front seat a big swoosh to scoop up more beans. And for the aisle area, Zach swishes the broom while I hold the dustpan.

Minutes later we are tumbling out of the cool motor home and into prairie heat that feels like a pizza oven. The wind whips hot air around us, yet I hardly notice because my eyes are taking in the giant black and white cow. Sue is a big Holstein sculpture made out of something strong – maybe painted cement – because it stands tall and solid even in this wind.

We scurry up to huge Sue. Standing under her now, I can see that Joey is right; her belly is high above my head.

In the distance I see real cows grazing on the range. I'm learning North Dakota grows more than wheat and sunflowers.

"Tag, you're it!" Zach suddenly says to me, darting away. I chase after him, circling around the monster-size legs. The funniest part, though, isn't weaving in and out of the cow's four legs. The funniest part is under the belly of the cow. Hanging high above my head are giant milk udders, all pink and white. I laugh every time I race under the utters.

Soon, we're all sweaty and panting.

"Ready to call an end to your game of tag?" Larry asks.

We nod, hands on our knees, trying hard to catch even a tiny breath.

"Then let's grab some of those dancing chocolate-dipped ice cream cones," Larry says.

"Yee-haw!" all us Tenderfoots yell and pump our fists in the air.

*   *   *

We pile into the RV and drive to Road Warrior Gas Express. Scribbled on a weathered board here is a sign that says: *ICE CREAM, COLD POP, PORK RINDS.* What are pork rinds?

Larry steers the motor home onto the dirt drive leading to the station, and a funnel cloud of dust forms behind us that is bigger than Dorothy's tornado in Kansas. One lonely gas pump stands on a tiny cement island, and the station itself is just an old wooden building. The wind has whipped the paint right off the wood, but you can tell that the building once was painted white.

We file out of the RV. Next to the front door of the station, sitting outside in the heat of midday, is a very sun-faded red chest. The brand name *"COKE"* is barely readable on its side. I step up to the waist-high, chunky tin box and soon learn that the closed lid is locked tight.

"What's this hole for?" I ask, gazing at a side opening smaller than my fist.

"Adam, look inside the hole," Brian says, giving me a shove as he stays a step behind me. My brother likes to volunteer me for certain things.

Slowly, I bend down for a closer look. "There's a metal hook at the top and no bottom," I say.

"What good is that?" Joey asks.

Just then, an old guy with a sun-wrinkled face that is leathery brown strolls out of the station. "It's a Coca Cola bottle opener," he snickers showing off a three-tooth smile.

I catch on, then explain to everyone. "It's for glass bottles of pop, like in the olden days. The opener pries off the metal bottle cap."

"Can we get a cold drink?" Joey asks. "I've never had a real bottle cap before."

Already Joey's pockets bulge from his collection of keepsakes. At least this time a bottle cap can't jump out of his pocket like a frog or cricket or who-knows-what else that usually springs from it.

"Yeah, can we get an ice cold bottle of pop?" I ask. "We can get ice cream anytime."

Mom gathers her coins while the old guy waits, leaning against the door frame, hands shoved into his pockets. His funny face seems a little suspicious, but I'm mostly focused on a frosty bottle of pop to chill my hot, dry throat.

Clink, clink, clink. The coins drop into the machine.

Clunk. Out rolls a can of Coke.

"What? Who put cans in the bottle machine?" I ask.

The old man slides a sideways look our way. "That machine was switched to cans years ago," he says.

Jeepers. The only part of history I care about has been updated to cans.

"But you're in luck, cowpokes," he says. Then he spits. But it's dark and thick like black tar! How unusual. Next his jaw jerks and his cheek puffs out on one side. That's when I get a glimpse of what must be a wad of chewing tobacco wedged in his mouth. "Step inside for the bottles of pop," he adds as he chews again and squirts out another stream of black.

Mr. Spit pushes the door farther open, and it makes a cowbell clang to announce our entrance. I look up and see the cowbell swinging above my head, like a piñata at a party.

"Actually, you can leave the door open," Mr. Spit says. "There's no air conditioning inside."

The small station is packed with wooden shelves of motor oil and some kind of farm or tractor parts. The floor is brown with a layer of dust so thick it makes my shoes slide. We could play floor hockey on it if we had four brooms and a can of cat food. On second thought we'd probably sweat to death after one round around the center aisle of shelves. It must be more than a hundred degrees inside this gas station. With my T-shirt I swipe away beads of sweat dripping off my nose.

"The bottles are this way," Mr. Spit says, pointing to a metal tub.

I peer into the waist-high tank. Rows of bottles stand upright, bathing in ice. On the metal bottle caps, I read Nehi Grape and Nehi Orange.

Mr. Spit thrusts out an open palm wanting coins before we fish out the cold pop. I plop three quarters into his hand and then plunge my whole arm into the icy water. I dip for a long time to let my arm freeze among the ice cubes. It's the coolest I've felt all day.

"Grab grape, Adam," Joey says. "We can all have purple tongues."

I've never had a Grape Nehi before. It seems like the choice to make, being in North Dakota with all the other strange and unusual things. Besides, I'm up for anything that makes me into a purple-tongue oddball.

Finally, I grab a frosty Grape. On a rope tied to the side of the tub, swings a silver bottle opener that I use to pry off the bottle cap. Joey is quick to snatch the cap and save it in his pocket. It jingles with all the other treasures he has socked away.

Soon, The Tenderfoots, Mom, and Larry all are sipping on chilly Nehis. That's when Mom asks Mr. Spit, "Aren't you going to have a cold drink?"

"Nah, soda gives me gas," he says, patting his stomach. Looking at his scruffy clothes, worn cowboy boots and frayed hat, I think anything that costs money would give this old guy gas.

We sip a few minutes longer. "Hey, where's Joey?" I ask, noticing he's not in the group.

"He's probably wandered off," Zach says.

Unexpectedly, we hear a thump and clatter. We hustle toward the racket and find Joey buried beneath a pile of souvenir cowboy hats.

"Har, har," Mr. Spit starts to rumble up a laugh. "The little cowpoke is like a barn cat, slinking off because he's itching to hunt."

"I was just going to try on a hat," Joey says, struggling to get out from under the pile of cardboard hats.

"No harm done," Mr. Spit says. "These two-dollar hats are meant to be used for a little whooping and hollering."

We get the rack upright while we boys try on hats, too. Even though they are made of cardboard, they have a real cowboy feel just the same. Cripes. It's too bad I left the arrowheads and homemade certificate in the Bat Cave. Right now I'm thinking it would be a great idea to try to sell them to Mr. Spit. I'll bet he'd trade me one arrowhead for one hat.

Forgetting to take spending money on a road trip is a New Salem Sue-size mistake. I count three *Mississippi's* to myself to settle my frustration.

Just then I catch sight of myself in the store mirror. I'm sporting the soft brown hat that makes me look better than the Lone Ranger. I forgot the arrowheads and don't have any spending money, but there must be another way to get a hat. I run my fingers along the brim. This baby is a real bargain at two bucks!

"Hey, Mom," I say, tipping my hat to her. "These cool hats are only two dollars."

"Two dollars more than you have from forgetting to take the trash out for pickup," Mom says.

Jeepers. That was more than three days ago when I lost my allowance. Mom remembers more details than there are in a five-thousand piece jigsaw puzzle.

But I don't give up easily. "Ah Mom, I promise I won't make the same mistake twice," I say in my sweetest voice.

"Yes, well, I've heard that before," Mom says, not budging.

I drop my head and stare at the floor. The brim of the hat covers my flushed face. I can feel it turning red as I imagine

Mom reminding me I forgot to turn off lights or put the milk away.

"I have an idea," Mom says. "Since you can work the computer and get to the last level in Mario, I'll bet you can learn how to operate the dishwasher."

I raise my head and look at her like she is speaking Latin or something.

"Load and unload for one week," Mom explains firmly.

Cripes. Most times Brian and I are begging for fifty-dollar gym shoes. Two bucks is a real steal for a Western cowboy hat. But I know when not to argue with Mom. "It's a deal," I tell her, very happy to snag a new hat.

Leaving the gas station, three heads are covered in velvety brown cowboy hats. It turns out Joey is too proud of his Davey Crocket real-fur raccoon skin cap to wear a cardboard cowboy hat. This is fine by me because it is one less week of dishwasher duty I have to do, since I bought Zach's hat too. Brian agreed to do his own dishes.

On the way out the door, I give the cow bell overhead a *clang, clang, clang,* wave my hat high in the air, and let out a whooping "Yee-haw!"

Mr. Spit simply shoots me back a stream of black spit and then cracks his toothless smile.

Outside, I spot the handwritten sign reminding me of the main reason I was curious to step into the service station. I spin around to ask my big question before we leave: "What are pork rinds, Mister?"

"A crispy snack made from the fried fat of a pig," Mr. Spit says.

Like I said earlier, there are some strange and unusual things way out on the northern prairie!

* * *

We travel west along I-94 about an hour and then I see some kind of lumps far off on the horizon. I nudge Zach and point in their direction out the upper bunk window.

"Those are the Badlands," Zach says.

As we drive closer, we see that the Badlands stretch far and wide ahead of us. They are brown, flat, rugged cliffs, like mountains with the tops chopped off.

Larry drives into the small town of Medora. We roll by the post office – a building with wagon-wheel trim. Next we pass a white wood building. Zach reads out the old-fashioned lettering on its sign: "Theatre / Town Hall."

"This town is so small one building has more than one purpose," Brian observes.

"Yeah, you can have a town meeting and watch a play all in the same building," I say, thinking how strange and unusual that would be.

The only building that looks newer than a horse and buggy is the Billings County Courthouse. It's built of brick with tall sharp angles. Next to it, like a midget, sits the original 1913 wood courthouse.

Just outside of downtown, Larry parks the motor home in front of a massive wooden playground. It's a maze of forts, stage coaches, and train engines with hidden rope traps, tunnels, and slides.

I step out of the motor home, and the burning pavement sizzles the soles of my shoes. Hot steamy air crowds close, all around me, but I don't let it slow me down. To swing from a jail cell, I'm willing to bust through the blazing heat.

"Yippy-ky-oh," Joey yells. His excitement sums it all up. We rope and ride in the Western land of make-believe, kicking up a cloud of dust with every rustling move. Sweat streams down my face, leaving dirt-trail streaks on my face.

Then it happens. The cardboard hat starts to melt from my sweat, flattening on my head. I slip it off my head and punch it dead center. It pops back up but it takes only two more swings on Hangman's Noose for my sweaty head to turn the hat into a soggy brown Kleenex. I wad up the shrunken wet blob and sadly toss it in the trash. It was fun, though, and well worth my promised two weeks of dishwasher duty.

*   *   *

We pile into the motor home, driving west into the huge rocks of the Badlands in Theodore Roosevelt National Park. A billboard shows off a photograph of President Roosevelt in his old-fashioned wire-rim glasses.

"Hey, four eyes," Joey says, pointing to Zach's eyeglasses. "Storm windows, space creature, spectacle," Joey teases Zach in a sing-song voice, using all the same names Roosevelt was called.

"I bet Zach is as smart as President Roosevelt," Brian says, quick to cut Joey off from his razzing. That snaps Joey's mouth shut, at least for a while.

Then Joey is all happy-face again, busting out with giddy energy, sitting up, sitting down, shifting right, shifting left. "Do you think we'll see the elf?" he asks.

"What elf?" I ask.

"Dad said we'd see an elf in the Badlands," Joey says, wearing a big smile of anticipation.

"Did your Dad say why there'd be elves in the Badlands?" Brian asks, rolling his eyes in Zach's direction. Zach points his finger to his head and twirls it, indicating he thinks his brother is a bit crazy.

"Dad told me they like to drink the water from the Little Missouri River," Joey says. "So are we almost there, so I can see the elf?" Joey bounces in his seat and presses his nose to the window.

"Sure, Joey, we're almost there," I say, not wanting to crush his field-trip dreams of spotting an elf. I wonder if he thinks we'll find Santa Claus, too.

The rocky cliffs of the Badlands are just a mile ahead when Larry steers the motor home into Juniper, the North Campground of the national park.

At the Juniper station Larry rolls down his window to ask, "Can we have a campsite along the Little Missouri River?"

"You betcha; yah," replies a man in a green uniform covered with nifty badges. "You can have Lot Number 40. It's the best sunset and breakin' dawn campsite."

"How close is it to the hot showers?" Mom asks, leaning over to talk to the ranger.

"Sorry, ma'am," the ranger replies. "This here campground doesn't have any showers. Flush and pit toilets only."

Uh-oh. I give Zach a jab in the ribs with my elbow. "I don't think our mom has ever used an outhouse," I say to Zach with my hand covering my mouth so Mom can't hear. Usually when traveling, Mom prefers a fancy hotel room, especially one with a lot of pillows on the bed so when I run and jump and land a belly flop I don't even feel the bed springs.

"There's no electricity or water hook-up either," the park ranger adds.

Oh boy. When we camp in Papa's trailer at Muskegon State Park in Michigan, we have all the hot water and power we need. Even then Mom thinks she is without her basic needs of bubble baths and remote controls. Camping in the Badlands ought to be an interesting night for Mom.

"How about the south campground, Cottonwood? Do they have showers?" Mom asks, her voice rising higher than Minnie Mouse.

The park ranger shakes his head no. It's as backwoods as when President Roosevelt hunted buffalo.

Mom presses her lips together in thought and her chin quivers a bit. She's almost frozen in place over the situation, and I'm not sure even the hundred-degree heat can melt Mom's icy stare.

Quickly I dart to Larry's organized cupboard. Earlier I spotted the perfect thing for Mom. "Here, Mom," I say, handing her the rope-handled shopping bag from the cardboard cowboy hats.

She peeks inside and erupts with laughter.

Inside I put a roll of toilet paper wrapped in fancy tissue paper with the words: Best for *bear* bottoms ... comfort where you want it.

Mom pulls out the roll of toilet paper, winks at me and waves it in the air. "Now this is the royal treatment."

Even the park ranger is hooting and howling with the rest of us.

Larry goes ahead and pays the ten-dollar fee. Gosh, camping in Michigan is three times more expensive. I guess it doesn't cost much to sleep in the ruff-'n'-tuff prairie.

Once the motor home is parked at Lot No. 40, the Tenderfoots scamper outside.

"Mom, can we go down to the river?" I ask, knowing Joey is thinking about the elf and itching to look for it worse than if he had poison ivy.

"You can go to the river as long as the four of you stay together and back from the water," Mom says, clearly in Mrs. Safety-mode again.

By now the lowering sun is a huge fireball turning the sky cotton-candy pink and casting our shadows long and dark across the flat prairie. Up ahead as we walk, we see the wind wrinkle the surface of the river and make it sparkle like tiny gold nuggets.

"Come on," I call the boys. "Let's go down to the river."

"And look for the elf," Joey sings out.

We march along the dusty path toward the riverbank. It's narrow, so when the wind whips, the nearby waist-high grass tickles my bare legs. Grasshoppers jump about, crisscrossing our path. The brittle grassland is a-buzz with their crackling song.

I'm first to reach the river. Its muddy shoreline is like the big Missouri, back in Bismarck, but the river itself is half as wide. Unlike in Bismarck, however, I see a four-legged beast sucking up water.

And it's enormous! My breathing does a stop-start kind of thing as my heart quickens. By now the other boys are alongside of me.

"Uh ... Joey," I barely push out the words.

Up ahead, a mammoth elk stands. It's twice as big as a horse. On its monstrous head is a rack of man-eating antlers that are wider and broader than its body length.

"I think your Dad was saying elk, not elf," Brian stammers.

Quickly a herd of six gathers to drink from the river. Their heavy feet smack the water and their antlers let out a thunderous clang as they brush one another when they drop their heads to drink.

The elk are more than a football field away; but when one of them screeches a shrill, ear-splitting cry, the hairs on my neck stand up and prickle. Another elk lifts its head high, towers over the others, snorts and lets out a deep powerful grunt. We beeline it to the motor home.

"Glad you're back," Mom says. "You're just in time to gather wood for a campfire."

"We'll head over to that group of trees," I say, relieved a stampede of elk wasn't chomping on our heels.

I lead The Tenderfoots away from the river, toward the North Dakota forest – a dozen trees among a field of grass. From behind, I hear it. Something snaps. Spinning around, I see Joey is simply breaking a branch.

"Look, it's where the stars hide during the day," he says, pointing to the star-shape in the center of the cottonwood twig.

"Affirmative," Zach says. "Go ahead. Snap one, Adam. It brings good luck according to the Native American legend."

I crack a branch. A star appears. Excited energy tickles my stomach. I could use a little luck my way. Maybe I should take a bundle of cottonwood home. This is one unusual prairie myth I need.

We gather more sticks and bring them back to camp. Brian piles the sticks into a teepee shape. One match and the fire roars. My brother has a Boy Scout Merit Badge in fire building. When the roaring campfire blaze gives way to a good mound of hot coals, Larry piles on tinfoil hobo pies for supper. After we all enjoy the tasty beef, potato, and carrot stew, I decide Larry should get a merit badge in campfire cooking.

"I'll do dishes," I say. And with that, I crunch the tinfoil into a wad and toss the small ball into the recycle bin.

In minutes we're playing a game of basketball and everyone has scored two points apiece as their tinfoil sails into the bin. This is my kind of cleanup duty!

The pink-cotton-candy sky has turned from candy-apple red to a plum-pudding hue to its present state of pitch-blackness. All around us a thousand stars shine brightly. They look so close I think I could climb a cottonwood, reach up, and pluck one out of the sky.

We stoke the fire again until it blazes in the night. It reminds me of the lighthouse beam back home on Lake Michigan. And when I reach my hand out behind me, it disappears completely into the darkness. Like the lighthouse the campfire light is a tiny speck in a sea of black.

Speaking of the deep, dark night, Zach suddenly holds a flashlight under his chin, casting creepy shadows across his face. He lets out a ghostly moan and gives Joey a poke. Joey jumps and then curls up his knees, wrapping his arms around himself as he huddles tight.

"Quit teasing, Zach," I say, trying to steady my voice. A breeze kicks up and whips the crackling flames of the campfire, making them dart and dance while sending an eerie sound through the fire. Next a coyote howls, and the spooky moan echoes off the rocky Badlands. It sounds so loud I think the coyote's sharp fangs are right behind me. A shiver creeps up my spine.

"That's right, Zach, we don't need spooky stories," Brian says in a firm voice that brings me comfort. I scoot a little closer to him.

And then, he says it.

"Who needs ghost stories when real spirits are still alive out there?" His voice is deep and dark. "Native Americans believed in the spirits of the sky, the moon, the sun, and the wind."

And if that's not enough, my brother stands and casts his arm in a full circle in front of the fading campfire light. "It's said their spirits still haunt this area."

Great. Just great. My sensible older brother now has me shaking in my shoes.

"Do you believe in spirits, Adam?" Joey asks me. There's a quiver in his words.

"Nah," I say. My mouth feels as dry as the dirt that's blowing in my face. Who am I kidding? Thoughts of Custer's ghost haunting the scary old shed behind the apartment buzz through my brain. I've seen lights flicker on and off and I've heard strange pinging sounds. And then I was startled by a frightening, rapid-fire popping sound. Now Brian is telling us dead spirits live in the Badlands.

Suddenly, to the north, the black sky lights up! Spokes of strong white beams with shimmery gold and rays of green shoot up! The long, eerie streaks seem to pulse and breathe, exploding the dark with chaos.

"The spirits are attacking!" Joey cries.

"Calm down, Joey," Brian says, patting the little guy's shoulder. How can Brian tell Joey to calm down? The entire sky is lit up like it's on fire.

"Those aren't spirits; those are the amazing northern lights," Brian explains. "They're one of the miracles of charged atoms in this high latitude."

This all-too-familiar science mumbo jumbo erupting from Brian's mouth relaxes me. He is the only person I know who can use science to chase away fear.

"Besides, spirits are more in the sounds of the wind," Brian adds.

Now I wish my brother would stop talking. Luckily, the spooky wind dies down. Since there won't be any spirit hocus-pocus in the air, I'm content to gaze at the brilliant northern lights fireworks. The sky is glowing like it is raining liquid rhinestones of color, yet another strange happening on the North Dakota prairie.

Chapter 12

A Hiccup in a Bad Land

Minutes before we're ready to leave the overnight campsite in Theodore Roosevelt National Park, my shoe gets stuck. I tug hard and yank it free. Now sticky white slime strings down from the sole. "What is this goop?" I wonder aloud.

"It's your marshmallow from last night's campfire," Brian says. "Don't you remember? Your toasty treat became a ball of flames in just seconds."

"Yep, Adam. Then you flicked your stick," Joey pipes up, giving his arm a big wave to show how I whipped the fireball into the air and sent the marshmallow sailing away.

"And that trick of a flick could've started a forest fire," Brian reminds me in a serious tone.

Cripes. He's right. Last night's flick could've turned this dried-up prairie into an awful blaze. And there'd be no one to blame but me. I've been in trouble once or twice before, but those incidents would be nothing compared with starting a prairie fire with a marshmallow meteor.

I scan the ground and grab a twig to scrape the goop from my shoe. Now the slime is stuck to the stick. Trying to clean the tip, I flick the stick. The goop goes flying, and a blob of it lands on Joey's coonskin cap. He reaches up to the blob, of course, and then cries out when his hand just sticks there to the fur.

And just my luck, Larry calls out to us at that moment, "Gather 'round, boys."

"What should I do with my cap?" Joey asks, trying to shake off the yuck-stuck cap from his hand.

Jeepers. Trouble seems to stick to me like glue.

"Hide it," I say, grabbing Joey's fur-clad hand and showing him to tuck it in his armpit.

"It's time to shove off," Larry says. "We're scheduled to motor out of Juniper and make our way into the Badlands of the park. Daylight's a-wasting."

I turn to Joey and hustle him along, saying, "Come on; we'll fix it in the motor home. Let's sneak into the bathroom."

We let Larry and the others settle into the motor home; then we slip off our slimy shoes and slide into the wee-size washroom as the RV begins to roll along.

"Put your hand in the sink," I say, yanking his slime-stuck hand out from his armpit.

"Wait, Adam. We can't get my Davey Crocket cap wet," Joey says, hiccupping with nervousness.

"Don't worry. The cap is made of raccoon. When this critter was alive, it played around in the mighty Missouri lots of times," I say.

"Okay, I guess." Joey hiccups again while chewing on his lower lip and casting his worried eyes in my direction.

"Suds up the soap, say goodbye to the slime!" I say, trying to ease Joey's concerns. "This cap is gonna slide right off your hand!"

Oops. The soap bar slips onto the floor. I begin to bend over, but find it hard to wiggle in this itty-bitty bathroom. I twist like a pretzel to stretch for the soap. My fingers are only inches away. Closer ... almost there. Thump! The motor home hits a bump. The soap shoots between my feet, bounces off the corner, slides through Joey's legs, and slows to a stop just out of our reach.

"Let's trade places," I say, uncurling from my twisted squat. "I'll stand and you try to snag the soap."

Joey shifts. He whacks me in the face with his cap and hand; I spit out sticky raccoon fur. Meanwhile, Joey manages to slip down and snatch the soap.

We run the water and suds up the soap.

"Rub a little harder," I say, hoping more scrubbing will cause the soap to soften the slime and free the cap.

"Maybe this brush will help," Joey says.

"No! Wait! That's Larry's toothbrush!" I cry as my trouble magnifies.

Too late. Joey snags the toothbrush from the holder and scrubs it on the soaped-up cap. "Uh, maybe he won't notice," Joey says.

Not notice? Larry has the shape of every tool in his repair kit outlined so each tool is put back in the correct spot. He'll be sure to notice a change in his toothbrush. Suddenly I feel like I'm over my head in hot water.

"Look, the toothbrush worked! My hand is free!" Joey says as the slime slides down the sink drain.

I clean off the toothbrush and dry it the best I can, hoping it will be months before Larry needs his toothbrush. After all, this is our last day in the motor home since we head back to our apartment in Bismarck tonight. I say a silent prayer that I could only be so lucky. Joey and I squeeze out of the bathroom.

From the kitchen aisle we see Mom and Larry in the pilot seats and hear Brian talking to Zach from the upper bunk: "Hey! Are those the secret caves that bandits used as hideouts?"

Hideouts. Outlaws. Gunslingers. Wild Bill Hickok. My mind circles through a list of cowboy heroes and Wild West tales – and I quickly forget about Larry's toothbrush.

"Where are the secret caves?" I ask, hopping up the ladder to the upper bunk.

By this time the motor home is in Cottonwood, the name for the southern section of the park. Giant purple rocks almost scrape the sides of the motor home as we drive along a narrow

234

path, going higher into the mountains of the Little Missouri Badlands. The huge rocks are everywhere I look, and only a few little pine trees cling by their roots to whatever soil they can find.

"This looks like snake country," Brian says.

Snakes? Did my brother say snakes? The very thought makes me feel like a wad of Joey's coon-cap fur is stuck in my throat.

Then Zach says, "Roger that. Snakes like to lie on these rocks and soak up the sun's rays."

Small beads of sweat form on my forehead. Quickly I slap on a baseball cap to cover them because I can't let my friends see my jitters. Using the steadiest voice I can muster, I ask, "Hey, Brian. Are you going to toss another harmless puff adder snake when it plays dead?"

"These cliffs aren't like the tall grass at Garrison Dam, Adam," Brian says. "There are no puff adders here."

"Affirmative. The Badlands have poisonous prairie rattlers," Zach says.

"Rattlesnakes!" I cry, beginning to understand why they call this land "bad." Hissing, biting, poisonous snakes are one reason why. I can only hope the broiling sun will sizzle the snakes into crispy critters.

"Is this the scheduled stop to hike?" Brian asks Larry.

"Maybe it's too hot to hike," I butt in, trying desperately to think of an excuse to whiz right by these Badlands.

"Negative," Zach says. "It's never too hot for the excitement of hiking the Badlands."

Right on cue, Larry says, "This is the scheduled stop; have fun!"

As Larry parks the RV, Brian whoops his hat over his head and Joey jumps and kicks up his heels. I'm the last one to climb out. My legs are a little wobbly from my nerves, but at least I see no snakes so far.

"Tag, you're it!" Zach blurts out as he taps my arm and darts away, scrambling up a rock like a lizard.

Joey and Brian race away, too. I chase after Zach, taking huge leaps from boulder to boulder. Happily, the game takes my mind off the subject of snakes.

Just as I'm ready to tag Zach, that's when I see it. Dark and round. I stop dead in my tracks.

"Snake hole!" I yell – and then my voice booms off the ridge into the canyon. "Hole! ... ol-ol-ol!" The echo startles me. I suck in the furnace-hot air of summer. Jeepers. If I don't die from a snake bite, I might die from thirst.

Zach has run ahead, but from behind, Brian catches up to me. He peers at the dark, softball-size opening in the rock.

"Adam, this hole is for a jackrabbit, not a snake," my brother explains.

I'm quick to recover from the mistaken hole. "Just kidding ... tag! You're it," I say, giving him a shove.

Before Brian can react, I scale the rocks fast as that jackrabbit. If Brian were telling this story, of course, I'll bet he'd say I looked white as a ghost and my shaky legs barely held me steady to trot away. But this is my story and the way

I tell it is this: I easily escaped the false alarm of mistaking a rabbit hole for a snake's lair.

The game of tag continues as we race, leap, and climb higher up the rocks. The buildings in the nearby town of Medora are dollhouse-size from here. The few city trees look like heads of broccoli. Way off on the horizon, I swear I can see the curve of the Earth.

"It's time to hike back," Mom calls from her comfy shady spot near the RV. This is Mom's way of beating the heat.

Climbing down the rocks is not like the slide-like ride of running down a giant Lake Michigan sand dune. The Badlands cliffs are rock-wall scary. I check each foot placement on every big rock. After crisscrossing our way down the boulders, we find Mom and Larry at the motor home working closely together, huddling at times.

"Do you think they're going to kiss?" Joey asks.

"Nah. Not while we're around," I say.

"Then let's hide," he says.

"Where?" I ask, scanning the flat prairie with my hand on my forehead to screen the scorching sun.

"I saw a blanket in the motor home," Zach says.

"I'll go get it," Joey says, rushing off before we can work out the plan.

In no time at all, Joey is back. We tiptoe along the opposite side of the motor home and gently shake out the blanket. But something is wrong. A baseball-size hole is cut out of the middle of the blanket.

"That's the peek-hole," Joey says, with a smile scribbled across his face.

"Did the blanket always have this hole?" Brian asks.

"Well, no," Joey says.

My heart stops. I look at the hole in Larry's blanket, which is part of Larry's motor home, which Larry is kindly letting us borrow for the sleep-over with my friends. It is the same motor home in which Joey used Larry's toothbrush to clean slime off his coonskin cap. So right this minute, my heart feels like it's lassoed, roped in, and rustled up so it can't beat any more. What are we going to do?

"I had to cut it," Joey squeaks out. "How else could we spy without being seen?" His hiccups are back and he tilts his head up to the sky so the tears won't slip out.

I look into the watering eyes of my seven-year-old-friend. If it wasn't for our funny little friend Joey, this would be an ordinary field trip with ordinary history with ordinary dates and numbers.

"Don't worry, Joey. We can buy him a new blanket," I say, hoping he can't hear the sadness in my voice because I am sure I will be on dishwasher duty for the rest of the summer.

"So can we spy now?" Joey asks.

"Sure, partner," I say. The word "spying" always distracts me.

We quietly nestle in the grassland using the blanket to hide us. I am the first one to peek through the hole. Zach is at my side while Brian and Joey peek out each end.

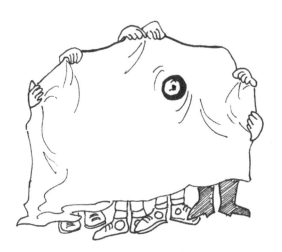

Suddenly, I feel a tickle on my neck. I hold still, thinking maybe the prairie wind is making my collar flutter and tickle my neck. But the air is dead calm. I swat at the tickle and check my hand. Nothing, no blood or guts from a mosquito or gnat.

Again I feel a light tingle brush across the back of my neck. I squirm in my stance and swat once more. Nothing. Nada. Zilch. Then it happens again. That tickle. Instantly, a bone-numbing chill grows from deep inside me as Brian's tale of the Native American spirits swirl through my mind. Worse yet, what if Custer's ghost followed me here? Maybe it knows I fudged the arrowhead certificates.

The itch is back. I whip my head around. Straightaway, I'm eye-to-eye with a fur ball. "Yikes!" I yell and jump. The blanket sails sky high.

"What's wrong?" Mom calls to us, wondering what all the howling is about.

I look around. Brian is waving Joey's coonskin cap. How could I have forgotten? My cheeks redden.

"Uh ... nothing much, Mom," I say, trying to think fast. Mom knows I don't startle easily. "I thought a gnat flew up my nose."

"Yeah, they like to dive bomb your ears and mouth and can buzz right up your nose," Brian calls out.

"It tickled me silly," I say, trying to make a joke so Larry won't notice the "hole-y" blanket.

Quickly, I bundle up the blanket and put it behind my back. I take a step, wedging myself tightly between Brian and Zach. For now, the blanket is out of sight.

Zach notices my fast actions. Realizing I'm trying to save the day, he adds to the story, saying, "Once I had a gnat fly up my nose. I sucked in so hard the critter went all the way through my nose and into my mouth!"

Zach starts choking up with laughter at that point, so Joey finishes the story: "Yep. Zach coughed and had a bug booger fly out his mouth!"

Zach tries to clear his throat like Mr. Spit from the service station in New Salem, but he can only dribble out a sputter of slime.

There is no problem of Larry discovering the blanket right now because he's in an uproar letting out his deep *hut-hut* laugh.

Mom smiles so wide it covers her whole face. She's very used to all this gross boy stuff.

Once the laughter quiets down, Larry gives us the next scheduled stop: "It's time to drive into Medora for lunch. We're eating at the Pitchfork Fondue."

"I thought pitchforks were for stabbing hay," I say, trying to keep the humor going so Larry doesn't notice the blanket.

"It's an outdoor barbecue place," Mom says.

"With steaks!" Joey adds. "The steaks are hooked onto pitchforks and cooked over a campfire. It's the cowboy way."

"Yeah, President Roosevelt made Medora famous when he started a cattle ranch and beef processing in 1906," Brian says.

"Unfortunately the beef-packing plant had to close because of poor train transportation," Zach adds. "But beef and cattle ranching is still big business today."

I smile to myself, thinking Brian and Zach must eat encyclopedias for lunch while the rest of us munch on hamburgers.

We climb aboard the RV and I quickly stash the blanket in a lower bathroom cupboard. Larry guides the big house on wheels through the switchback road as we inch our way out of the rocky Badlands.

*　*　*

We're back in Medora now, and Larry is pulling into the eatery parking lot. Right away we see that smoke is rising from the fire pits, and then we see the steaks sizzling there and smell the mouthwatering barbecue a second later. Pitchfork Fondue is a real chuck wagon of an outdoor restaurant. We practically gallop our way over to the host.

"Howdy, partners," says a young man sporting a black felted cowboy hat and black shirt studded with fringe and fancy buttons. Standing in front of us, he looks broad and strong like a stallion.

"Are you a cowboy?" Joey asks.

"You betcha. My name is Cowboy Kevin, but you can call me Bad Bart," he says, straightening his cowboy tie with pride. This is not like Dad's necktie, though. This guy's tie is a skinny black rope with a small silver bucking-bronco on it.

"Is that a bolo tie?" Brian asks.

"Darn tootin' it is. I won 'er at the rodeo, bareback ridin'," Bad Bart says, sounding as tough as beef jerky.

Our jaws drop wide open with wonder as we listen to every word he is saying.

"Now, I have an important piece of cowboy equipment for each of you greenhorns," Bad Bart says, reaching into his back pocket and pulling out red bandanas.

"Are bandanas equipment?" Joey asks.

"Absolutely," Bad Bart says. "Pull a bandana across your nose, for instance, and you'll breathe easier during a dust storm. This here, boys, is one piece of valuable cowboy gear."

This over-the-nose trick is one I know. Mom and Brian already teased me when I choked on the first dust cloud at the Bismarck Airport parking lot. Back then I thought the bandana was for bank robbers. I know better now, but Bad Bart's big booming voice captures my full attention.

"Here's another one, boys: Tie a wet bandana around your forehead on a hot day and you'll avoid sunstroke," Bad Bart continues. "And most importantly ..." he pauses.

We can only nod.

"If a rattlesnake strikes," Bad Bart continues, "a bandana makes a good tourniquet to stop the poison from headin' to your heart."

My mouth has been open so long I begin to drool. I don't think even a hot branding iron poked in my butt would get me to ditch this cowboy.

"Hey, cowhands!" Mom's voice startles me a bit. "It's time you move your herd over here," she says, waving us to benches and a picnic table.

Bad Bart leads us toward Mom. His spurs on his boots jingle-jangle when he walks. "You-all young saddle pals enjoy your dinner now, you hear?" Bad Bart says, tipping his hat to us as he ambles away.

We sit at a weathered wooden picnic table, and soon our food arrives on dented tin trays bigger than wagon wheels. They're piled high with steak, beans, and ears of corn on the cob, all fresh off the grill. A real cowboy's feast, it is.

"Hey, Bad Bart forgot to tell us that a bandana also makes a great napkin," Brian says, dabbing the red cloth on his chin dripping with butter from the corn.

I give my chin a good cowboy wipe, too. Getting a whiff of smoke from the fire pit, I feel like a real cowpoke while chomping on steak with a bandana tied around my neck. Then I remember ... a real cowboy who will be on dishwasher duty because of a certain "hole-y" blanket. But wait, I still have the get-rich-quick arrowheads and certificate. So long, kitchen-duty, I think.

Chapter 13

Dog Developments

I should have realized something was up when I heard the word "kiss." Outside, huddled together, Mom and Larry are chatting. The summer sun here in Medora is low on the horizon, sinking like a big orange fireball.

"This is magic hour," Larry says. "It's when the sun kisses the horizon."

"Are they going to kiss, again?" Joey asks. It's like the word "kiss" makes us boys kind of brain dead.

"They never kissed the last time," Zach says.

"Yeah, because they caught us spying," Brian says.

"Shh, quiet," I say. "Larry and Mom still don't know his blanket has a hole." The double-trouble mess we're in flashes through my mind. First is the blanket with a baseball-size spy-hole cut out of the middle and second is Larry's toothbrush with marshmallow-slime cooties.

"Well, if they aren't going to kiss, why are they talking about it?" Joey asks.

"They're talking about photography," Brian says.

"It's called bounce light," Larry says to Mom. "Just before the sun sets, there's a color in the sky that bounces from the fading light. It casts a magical glow."

"I like sunsets," Brian says, stepping closer to them. "Can we take some pictures?"

"Sure," Larry says, turning toward us. "I brought an old Nikon camera. It uses Kodachrome film. I thought it'd be fun to shoot out here and then develop photos in the darkroom when we get home."

"Darkroom?" I ask.

"Yes, it's where I develop film," Larry says. "When we shoot black and white film, we can process the prints ourselves."

"Black and white?" I ask, thinking this must be a really old camera.

"That's right. Black and white photo developing takes just a few simple chemicals," Larry says, rattling on and on about stop baths and fixers.

My brother eats up Larry's camera talk. Before we can blink, Brian has a camera in his hand and is snapping pictures of the setting sun.

The rest of us boys – Zach, Joey, me – grow bored and wander off to find some fun. Inside the motor home kitchen we snatch cheddar cheese popcorn and ice cold root beer and chomp happily away. Just as we finish the snack, Brian, Larry, and Mom join us inside.

"Daylight's a-wasting," Larry says, using his favorite phrase and climbing into the pilot's seat. He puts the big rig in gear, steering east toward Bismarck, away from the Badlands.

"Let me see your photographs," I say to my brother.

"You can't see them," Brian says.

"Come on. Give it up. Don't be shy," I say and give him a playful punch on the shoulder.

"No, really. You can't see them, Adam," he says.

"Hey, Mom," I call. She's up front in the co-pilot seat. "Brian won't let us see the pictures he took."

"He can't," she calls back. "Remember, Adam, the camera isn't digital. It's film. And film needs to be processed and developed before you can see the pictures."

Oh, yeah, I forgot. This really is an old camera.

Brian scoots to the edge of his seat, leans toward the pilot seats and starts talking lens settings, timers, and other photography gobbledygook with Larry.

This is as much fun as watching a turtle race. Before Larry and Brian put me to sleep, I hustle up the ladder with Zach and Joey in the upper bunk. There must be something ... anything ... to do that is more interesting. Looking out the window, I see tiny moon craters scattered across the flat ground.

"Hey! Did you see that?" I poke Zach and point out the window.

"What? I don't see anything," he says.

I squint into the setting sun. The only movement is a swirl of dust from the blowing wind. Certain I saw something brown and furry come out of one of those moon craters, I push my nose flat against the glass.

"There! Up ahead! Where did it go?" I ask, as something hairy disappears into one of the craters.

"Negative, Adam. There's nothing there," Zach says.

"No, wait. Watch ... and don't blink," I say.

Our heads are fixed, staring. Yikes! Out of the corner of my eye I see a flash.

"Over there. This way! Look! It's a squirrel!" I say, tapping on the side window. But instantly it's gone. "I know I saw something."

Then I hear it. A soft giggle. It's Zach and Joey. "What's so funny?" I ask.

"That's a prairie dog," they snicker pointing out the other side window.

A squirrel-size critter is standing upright on his short back legs. "It doesn't look like a dog to me," I say as my friends' giggles let loose into whoops of laughter about me thinking the critter is a mutt.

Then the RV rolls smack dab through an area with hundreds of moon craters. Looking out the north-side window, a prairie dog sits up on its hind legs. Its tiny tail flicks and jerks. I wonder if I can pet one. Wouldn't Zach and Joey be surprised if I was first to cuddle one of those furry little guys!

Larry parks the motor home. I launch out the door and leap into the air, flying at jet-speed. The prairie dog zips into a crater. I land belly flop style, leaving me with nothing but a face full of dirt.

Before I can blink another prairie dog pops out from another crater. Then, just as quickly, it ducks back in. I'm still lying in dirt, spitting dust, when I spy another critter pop up, dart two feet and quickly disappear into the ground.

"It's a prairie dog colony," Zach says as he jogs up to me. "Prairie dogs dig tunnels with thousands of passages that make up an underground town."

"Hear their chatter? That soft squeaking is their warning sound. It's like when a dog barks," Brian says. "That's why they're called dogs even though they're in the rodent family." My brother now towers over me.

Looking up at him, I realize I've caused enough drama to give Brian a reason to leave his old-fashioned camera talk with Larry. I get up off the ground and slap off all the prairie dust on me. Even when I try to appear normal and put together, I always seem to get myself into embarrassing situations. This time I shove my hands in my pockets and slither away.

In front of us is an endless field of critter craters revealing prairie dogs popping up and down. It looks like a carnival game, the one where it's a contest to bop the appearing, then disappearing, clown heads. Like the clowns, you never know where the next prairie dog will pop up.

Luckily all the prairie dog fun takes the attention off my face plant in the dirt. Then I get a brainstorm: If I can't catch a prairie dog, at least I can capture one on camera. I grab Mom's digital camera, which is a pretty simple, point-and-shoot model. I hold out the camera and frame a little critter into the viewfinder. Click. I flip the screen to display my picture. No prairie dog! Just dirt. Hmm. There aren't any fancy buttons to fiddle with and slow me down, and no lens twisting or fussy flash attachment like Brian with his sunset pictures. This quick digital camera should snap that prairie dog in action. I aim the camera again and click again. View – just a brown blur this time!

Brian sneaks a peek at the nothing-but-dirt picture. "Nice photo, Adam," he smirks.

Instantly I feel the punch from his zinger; my brother knows exactly what he's doing when he teases me. It's like he lives for my failing moments. Then I see a hint of a smile rising from a corner of his mouth. My face goes from blush pink to beet red as I picture him howling out loud at me. I squeeze my eyes shut to wipe the thought from my head.

"Adam," Brian speaks my name. No laughter yet. I open one eye, just a slit. My brother is sitting on the ground. I open my eyes wide. What's he doing?

"If you shoot from this angle, aiming across all these craters, you'll be sure to catch a dog in action," he says.

Sometimes I hate to admit it, but my brother is smart. He just solved my problem in two seconds flat.

"Besides, it's no wonder you're having trouble getting their picture; prairie dogs run thirty-five miles an hour," Brian adds. Sometimes his textbook wisdom comforts me.

Suddenly we hear a shriek! Turning around, I see someone, or something, holding up a blanket. Not just any blanket – the blanket we cut a baseball-size hole in to spy on Mom and Larry. And through this hole, one big ugly eye is staring at me – and it's not winking.

The one-eyed monster growls, "How did this happen?" It's Mom. I can tell from her howl she's pushing out more hot air than a steaming tea kettle. Her spout is short and hot. She drops the blanket. Mom's chin quivers. She's a heat wave spreading into a wildfire.

"How did this hole get in the blanket?" she asks again, now with a bite to her words.

"Could it be from a moth?" I ask. "There are a lot of bugs out here in North Dakota."

Mom stares, tightening her lips. No words come out.

"I know how the hole got in the blanket." It's Brian talking. Oh, no. My brother never invents fairy tales or fibs. Not Brian.

Zach and Joey watch Mom's fists turn white as she clenches the blanket. Her breathing gets deeper, blowing out more hot air.

"We were trying to spy," Brian says.

I've got to do something. I know he'll tell the truth, the whole truth. I sneak behind Mom and give Brian a big, call-it-off signal, wildly waving my arms, silently mouthing, "Stop! Stop! Stop! Don't do it."

That's when Larry sees me.

"Adam, you look like you're trying to flag down the cavalry," he says as he wanders closer to all of us.

Uh-oh, I'm caught. It's too late to tell a fairy tale ... too late to stop Brian ... too late for me to ever be able to play with my friends again.

"Kate," Larry says to Mom, "what are you doing with that old blanket?"

Old? Did Larry say old? Now, I'm not a superhero, but I know when to take charge and save the day.

"What do you use that smelly old horse blanket for anyhow, Larry?" I ask, marching out in front of Mom toward the big guy.

"Nothing really," Larry says. "I just keep it in the under-carriage of the motor home with the spare tire. You never know when you might have to crawl under this rig to make repairs."

"Then it's okay if it has a tiny hole it?" I ask. My soccer coach always says the best defense is a strong offense, so I spill the truth up front.

"Sure, no problem," Larry says. "Give it here. If no one needs this wool rag, I'll just toss it back with the spare. We should start heading to Bismarck before it gets much darker."

Mom's fists uncurl and her breathing slows to normal. She hands the old blanket to Larry.

"Come on you rustlers, let's ride the range home!" I call out, making sure to get the gang moving before Mom asks anymore blanket questions. "Daylight's a-wasting, right Larry?" I add, knowing he'd get a kick out of me using his favorite saying.

His lips twitch with amusement as he waves us single file into the motor home.

The journey home is uneventful. Brian and Larry chat more about photography, stuff like chemical dips and developer baths. I hear so much about photography that I'm actually getting interested. My curious nature kicks in, and I decide to go with Brian to develop pictures at Larry's studio the following day.

*   *   *

The next evening, before we leave for Larry's photo studio, Mom gives us specific instructions. "Follow everything exactly how he asks you to do it. No exceptions," she says firmly, giving us a warning look that tells us to use restaurant manners and indoor voices, too.

"Sure, Mom, we'll do everything exactly how he asks," we tell her.

Larry's photo studio is in downtown Bismarck, six short blocks from Mom's apartment. But before we get to the first corner, I freeze. Straight ahead is a skateboard ramp in Hannah and Glitzy Georgia's front yard. It's home-made out of left-over lumber. The structure is crude with jagged rough edges, but the ramp is awesome for speed with a sharp edge for grinding, too.

All I can do, as we walk past the ramp, is rotate my head like a zombie and point it out. "Do you think the girls are learning to skateboard?" I ask Brian.

Brian shrugs.

Visions of Hannah and Georgia pop into my head. I imagine the girls doing fancier skateboard kick-turns, board-slides, and stalls than I can do. Just then their neighbor pokes her head out the door of her house.

"Yoo-hoo! The girls are gone on a day trip," she yells across the yard. As quickly as she poked her head out, she darts back inside. I don't get a chance to ask about the skateboard ramp. I shift from foot to foot, no longer feeling so certain about things. Jealousy can unglue a guy.

"Adam, we need to keep moving or we'll be late getting to Larry's," Brian says, giving me a good nudge to get back on our walk.

We quick-time it to Larry's, crossing the alphabet street names, Avenue C, B, and A. After passing Broadway and Rosser, the next avenue is Main, where we turn left, pass First Street and easily find Larry's place of business. It's a sprawling, one-story building. The outdoor sign lists a handful of different businesses.

It's after dinnertime, and the parking lot is empty except for Larry's car. The people in the other offices must have already left for the day.

A door opens, and Larry lets us inside to a small waiting room with a handful of chairs, and then into the next room.

"This is my office," he says.

At a desk sits a computer so powerful that it could probably e-mail Mars and a phone that has a ton of buttons. A comfy-looking leather chair is pushed up to the big desk. I can't help myself. I plop down in the chair and give it a spin, twirling merry-go-round style.

"Daylight's a-wasting," Larry declares, "so let's continue the tour."

I stop my wild spinning just this side of Vomitville, and then step dizzily out of the chair. I wobble as I follow the sound of Larry's voice into the next room. I can only hope there will be a chance to spin in that chair again!

"This is the shooting studio where I take pictures," Larry tells us. The room is filled with big round spotlights on adjustable poles.

Pointing to huge white panels on wheels, Brian asks, "Are these for bounce light?"

"Good memory," Larry says to Brian. My brother eats up tech-terms like I eat M&Ms.

"This is the darkroom where we'll process the film," Larry says, leading us into a narrow space featuring a long counter with tubs of water and a clothesline strung across. That's when I get a whiff of stinky chemicals.

"Any questions before we get started?" Larry asks.

"Is there a candy machine in the building?" I ask.

"I meant questions about film developing," Larry snaps back.

I shake my head no, give the brim of my ball cap a tug so it slips down over my eyebrows, and stare at my shoes. Hiding under my cap, I figure I should just watch for a while from a safe distance, like maybe the North Pole.

"Can we get started?" Brian asks.

"Right after you get three root beers out of the pop machine down the hall," Larry says, tugging the cap off my head and beaming a big smile at me. "We don't have a candy machine in the building, but there's a pop machine out this door. It's a dollar a can."

Twelve quarters soon jingle in my pocket as Brian and I dart down the hall. I drop one quarter into the machine and plunk, plunk, plunk. Three ice cold cans of pop roll out!

"How did you do that?" Brian asks.

I'm dazed; I have no idea how that happened! We gather the soda and head back to the studio.

"Is this the door we came out of?" I ask, staring at a sign on the door that reads: *Knock before entering.*

"I don't remember this sign on the door when Larry greeted us," Brian says.

"Let's go this way. Maybe there's another door," I suggest.

We carry the pop around the corner. Oh, no, there must be ten doors to choose from. And most of them don't have any signs.

"What do we do now?" I ask, really confused.

"Check and see if they're locked," Brian says.

I juggle all three icy pop cans into one hand and start to twist the first doorknob.

"Wait! Stop, Adam!" Brian grabs my wrist so hard he knocks me off balance. The pop cans fly out of my clutch, hit the ground and roll around.

"Why did you do that?" I snarl.

"Look," Brian says, pointing to a sign that says, "*Protected by video cameras.*"

"It's bugged!" he says.

"You mean like someone can spy on us?" I ask.

"Yeah, like a wiretap," my brother whispers.

"Why would Larry's photography studio need to track criminals?"

"He wouldn't, but you just stole three cans of pop."

"I didn't steal them; they rolled out of the machine!" I cry.

"You can still be arrested because you didn't pay for them. Let's get out of here," Brian says.

We scramble after the rolling cans, pick them up and hustle around the next corner. Oh, no! Another hallway – with only one door. There's no other way to get out of the building. The sign on the door reads like the first door we saw: *Knock before entering.* A sense of doom spreads over me as I figure I'll be getting arrested any minute now.

I look at Brian. He's trying to speak, but he wheezes instead. He stabs his finger into my chest, still trying to get words out. His jabs are quick, and they send my nerve endings sizzling. My heart thumps the chant: be brave, be brave, be brave, but my hands are getting sweaty, even though I'm holding three chilly cans.

"What are we going to do?" I ask.

Brian stops jabbing me in the chest but stays silent. Usually Brian can rattle off a plan as fast as he fits pieces into a jigsaw puzzle. Judging from the look in his eyes, though, I'd say he hasn't even started solving this puzzle – not even the straight-edged border of a puzzle that Mom taught us to do first. So this time Brian's silence is not good. In fact, it's bad.

Then, out of nowhere, Brian beams with an idea. Not just a smile, his face lights up and he starts chattering. "I know what to do," he says. "We're not going to get arrested. We're going to trick Larry."

Huh? Has my brother lost his mind? We're lost and locked out. Cameras are spying on us as we steal root beer from a pop machine. And now he wants to play a trick?

Brian continues, "I just figured it out. The knock-before-entering signs are to Larry's darkroom. It's a safety feature so no one comes in while the film is being processed. Natural daylight will expose the film. That's why they process film in a darkened room."

"I get it," I say. "But how do we play a trick on Larry?"

"Mom told us to do exactly what Larry says. It says here to knock first ... so we will!"

"How is that tricky?" I ask.

"You stay here and count to twenty. I'll run to the other door with the similar sign. We'll both knock at exactly the same time. Larry won't know which door to answer first!" Brian beams.

I count to twenty and then pound three times on the door. I hear Larry's feet scuffle toward me. Knock, knock, knock. I hear the faint rap of Brian's knock from around the corner. Larry's footsteps stop and then start to move in Brian's direction.

I may be a North Dakota newcomer when it comes to prairie dogs in the Badlands but I'm a master at jokes. I wait a few more seconds and knock on my door, smiling as Larry's footsteps turn and come back my way.

Suddenly, the door flies open. Hulk-size Larry fills the entire door frame. I'd forgotten how big he is as he towers over me. I yelp, in surprise. A devilish frown darkens his face. Then, like the sun coming out after a thunderstorm, he smiles, chasing away every dark cloud as he breaks into a wonderful, head-held-back laugh.

From around the corner I hear Brian's rushing footsteps. Half a second later, out of breath, I hear him cry out, "Adam, what's wrong? I heard you yell!"

"False alarm," I say, trying to hold back laughing as loud as Larry.

Between laughs, Larry says, "Yeah, it's a false alarm. At first, you boys had me fooled with the double-door knocking. Then I remembered the knock-first signs."

By now Brian has a silly grin on his face, too.

The ice-cold root beer is freezing my hands now. That's when I remember the secret camera.

"Uh ... maybe it's not a false alarm," I say as my voice turns shaky.

Brian and Larry stare at me.

"We only paid a quarter for three cans of pop, and the sign that says, 'protected by video cameras,' well, we can be arrested!" I say with a nervous edge to my voice.

Larry lets out a snort so loud I yelp again.

"I guess we've all been fooled," he says. "There aren't any cameras. It's a sign left from the building owner before me. Now let's not worry about the price of the pop. Let's go develop some pictures," he says with a smile.

In the darkroom there is one roll of film apiece for Brian and me to process.

"I have already mixed the developer, stop bath, and fixer to the exact proportions," Larry says as his arm sweeps across the narrow counter holding the various trays of chemicals.

"And the correct temperature," Brian comments, pointing to a thermometer.

"That's right, Brian. The next step we do in complete darkness."

"That would be moving the film from the camera into the reel case," Brian pipes up with pride.

My hands are a little twitchy as I think about working in the dark, needing to juggle the film and reel case.

Larry flicks off the lights. Soon I feel the stiff and ridged film in my hands.

"In front of you, boys, every tool is in its exact place," Larry instructs. "First tool is the bottle opener."

Following Larry's directions, I feel for the opener and pry off the film cap. Like a relay race, I work left to right. Next, as instructed, I pick up the scissors and snip the film end. Following the last command, I wind the film into the reel case and secure it tightly.

"Ready for lights?" Larry asks when he hears the snap of the reel cases closing.

"You bet," Brian and I sing out.

We blink our eyes while adjusting back to the bright light. Before I can even see straight, Larry slaps a stopwatch in my hand.

"We agitate for thirty seconds," the big guy states.

Brian sees my puzzled look. "Agitate is to roll the film around and mix it up," he says.

My shoulders relax now because I'm good at mixing things up and rolling around.

We click the stopwatch on and off during the stages of developer, stop bath, and fixer. Lastly, it's plain old bath time, which is running plenty of tap water over the film.

After ten minutes of running the water, I gently pick up the strip of film with rubber-tipped tongs and clip it to the clothesline overhead. On the dripping film, I begin to see negative images of Brian's sunsets and the crazy prairie dogs.

"We have to let the film dry for two hours," Larry says. "Then I'll scan the negatives and print the pictures from my computer onto high-quality photography paper. Tell your mom I'll bring a set of prints over in a little while," Larry adds, letting us know that we are done with our darkroom adventure.

*   *   *

We say good-bye to Larry and start the short walk home from his studio. Next to their house, Glitzy Georgia and Hannah are jumping rope on the sidewalk. And Georgia, of course, is wearing her trademark color and style: frilly pink.

My heart pings against my chest as my eyes stare at the skateboard ramp.

"Hi-ee, you guyeeez," Georgia calls out to us. When she sees me size-up the ramp, she nails me with those hot hazel eyes.

"It's my –," Hannah starts to say, then Glitzy Georgia holds a finger to her lips to shush her, acting like the ramp is a big secret.

But it's too late. Hannah yakkity-yaks, "My cousin was here yesterday; he's a skateboard whiz. In one day he built a ramp and did tricks."

"Just for one day?" I ask.

"Yup. My dad said he'll recycle the wood at work," Hannah says. "He's bringing a truck home tonight to haul it away."

Not realizing I was holding my breath, I exhale slowly. I can stroll home standing straighter because it's a relief knowing there aren't any new skateboard superstars – girl or guy – on the block.

"Too bad you missed the show," Glitzy Georgia snips at me, folding her arms across her chest, which makes all of her bracelets start to jingle. We're faced off now like two gunfighters who are fifty paces apart and staring at each other.

"My cousin is the best skateboarder around these parts," Georgia brags. Her words fire at me like a dare.

Brian gives my arm a little tug. My brother is the type to blend into the background, but I can tell he's stepping forward before there's a shoot-out on Second Street. He knows I can't turn down a dare. He knows Zach's skateboard is sitting there, only a couple houses up the block. He knows in minutes I could be doing a 50-50 grind, showing off how I can slide across on the bottom of the skateboard while being half on and half off the edge of the ramp.

Just then, Georgia's dad pulls up, driving a pickup.

"I'm ready to load the ramp," he says, hopping out of the truck.

"Sure thing, Dad," the girls say. Glizty Georgia's feistiness is suddenly gone, ending our gun fight in a draw.

Brian, the peacemaker, offers to help Georgia's dad load the ramp into the truck. I bite my tongue and help too. The girls and their dad ride off in the sunset to recycle the wooden ramp. Brian and I finish walking home.

Later that night Brian and I are busy playing Nintendo when Larry steps into the Bat Cave. From an envelope, he shakes out slick paper and passes a sheet to each of us. In my hand I hold a glossy black and white image of a prairie dog. The critter sits up high on his hind legs, and I swear he's smiling at me.

I may be a newcomer to North Dakota who can't catch a prairie dog, but at least I can shoot one ... with a camera!

Chapter 14

Riding the Range

My eyelids grow heavy. Then my head nods forward. The smooth, rolling motion of the minivan lulls me to sleep as we hum along mile after mile in the dim light of dawn.

Pow! Thump! Suddenly, the front end of the van dips and scrapes the road, and instantly, I'm wide awake. Behind us sparks fly like fireworks down on the highway surface, and the stink of burning rubber quickly hits my nose.

"Mom, we blew a tire! Grip the wheel!" Brian shouts from the back seat, his voice so loud it echoes in my ear because I'm up front, riding copilot. "Don't slam on the brakes, Mom, or we'll crash!" Brian is practically in the front seat with his head wedged between the two front captain chairs.

Then he puts his hand on Mom's arm: "Sloooowly take your foot off the gas." My brother's voice is now smooth and unshaken as he continues to lean into the front seat. "Now, turn into the skid."

The van is sliding at race-car speed – yet the nightmare is happening in slow motion. Even the thundering thump of my heart is slow and steady in my ears.

Mom steers the wheel into the skid, but it doesn't help. We slide sideways.

"Hang on!" I shout.

The van sails onto the gravel shoulder, where the wheel rim rams into a rut. We're jerked, bucked like a bronco. The seatbelt tugs my chest as I'm whipped forward and then back against the seat.

Now we're sliding forward again, nose diving into a grassy ditch. One more yank on the seatbelts and we come to a full stop. I feel like a lunch box that got run over by a school bus!

"Is everyone all right?" Mom calls out. Her hands are still glued to the steering wheel even though we're at a dead stop.

"I'm good," I say, even though my heart is still hammering in my ears.

"Me, too," Brian reports from between us.

Mom's eyes stay fixed straight ahead. Trance-like, she simply mumbles, "Thank goodness." Finally she lets out a long, slow sigh. "What a relief! For a minute I didn't know what was happening. I wonder what caused a blowout! I just had the tires rotated and the treads checked."

"A tire can overheat when it loses pressure from anything sharp, like a nail in the road. The tire overheats and, ka-boom, it bursts!" Brian explains.

"Hmm," Mom says nodding, but the look in her eyes makes me think she's still a bit dazed. She lets out another long sigh. "Well, thank goodness everyone is okay," she repeats, but this time she turns to gather her two boys into a wrap-around hug. Her breath tickles my ear. I can tell she's feeling a bit better.

Then Mom turns back to my big brother and says, "Brian, how did you know not to slam the brakes? You don't know how to drive, let alone get out of a skid."

"Xbox has a speed wheel," he says, mentioning the videogame system we know so well.

"Lucas, our friend back home, has Split Second, the racing game," I add.

Any day of the week I can beat my brother in Split Second. I play for speed while he plays with caution and accuracy. I guess his method paid off this time.

"Well, it's good to have a computer whiz onboard!" Mom says.

"Yeah, but I don't think the computer game will help us with what's outside," I say, suggesting that it is time to check out the tire damage.

Inspecting the situation, we see that the van sits with its front end buried into the soft green grass along the roadside. From this angle the van appears much larger and heavier, like a tank bulldozed into a foxhole. Happily, the right front fender area, above the blown tire, is not even bent or scratched.

The tire, with just a speck of rubber left clinging to the metal wheel rim, is the wounded warrior. Having made its last stand, it is now dead in the dirt. Only the rim is left, looking shiny as it reflects the early morning sun here on the highway.

Looking away from the ditched-van scene, I see miles of rolling hills all around us ... not a building in sight; not even a road sign or maybe a billboard advertising the South Dakota horseback-riding ranch where we were headed on an adventure.

I wonder how far the barns and horses and ranch hands are from here. Not one car, pickup, tractor – or even a horse and buggy – has rolled by in the minutes since we nosedived into the ditch.

"I think we can fix this," Brian says while leafing through the van owner's manual already in his hand. This is typical Brian – already determined and working on the problem.

"Fix this? With what tools?" I ask, remembering Mom's way-too-simple toolbox. Her "toolbox" doesn't deserve to be called that because it contains mostly safety pins and twist ties. If a project is much more complicated than changing a light bulb, well, Mom just Googles the magic search word: *Handyman*.

"Adam, the van has all the tools we need," my brother says, then begins to read aloud from the owner's manual: "Step one: Remove the jack from under the spare tire."

At first, even hearing the rustling of instruction pages flip in Brian's hands doesn't calm my nerves or Mom's. She's back in a trance-like gaze, just staring at the destroyed tire.

Brian is steady as he goes, though. He keeps reading to us, his voice soft and even in tone. Soon enough, the words wrap around me like a comforting hug, and I start to follow his commands.

Rolling back the carpet in the van cargo area, I begin to unscrew the bracket around the spare tire. It turns out Brian's directions are pretty simple. Without a hitch I get the bolt off and lift the tire out. Underneath, I find He-man tools, too: a tire jack and a crowbar. They're like a mechanical knight in shining armor that has come to help save the day and get us out of the middle of nowhere.

Within minutes I'm lying on the ground half under the front end of the van and getting grass stains on my clothes. I like this job already.

Next, as Brian instructs, I wedge the mighty jack into a special slot on the bottom of the van. I wiggle out from my spot on the ground and start pumping the crowbar up and down in its slot in the jack. In no time I have the sorry-looking, blown-out tire off and the new spare in place. My hands are full of grease. Changing a tire is fun!

I hear my brother read further from the owner's manual.

"The compact spare tire is made to perform well at speeds less than thirty-five miles per hour," he recites.

Looking at the miles of endless rolling hills, I think about the van poking along at a snail's pace. When I fell asleep, we were weaving along a curvy road next to the Red River of South Dakota. This lush green carpet of foothills is so different from the flat brown prairie north of here around Bismarck.

"It will take forever to get to the ranch," I say, wishing I was already riding high in the saddle of a horse.

"And this is only a three-day vacation," Mom mutters, matching my thoughts.

Mom makes her living as an artist, and missing work for her is like a doughnut junkie trying to go without sugar. She says she likes to work the creative side of her brain. Right now, though, out here in Nowhere, South Dakota, I wonder if she'll ever get back to work.

The sun is higher overhead now, and we have yet to eat lunch. My stomach senses we are miles from a Big Mac or even a gas station with cardboard pizza. And we're miles from the horse-riding ranch. This is turning into a not-so-fun vacation.

Then, in the distance, a vehicle draws near, but it is still too far away to tell make or model. I know cars like my brother knows baseball stats. Then we hear it: *hee-haw, hee-haw.* I sure don't know any car horn like that. "It sounds like a donkey," I say.

"I think the horn is supposed to be a steer," Brian says, pointing to the huge rack of cattle horns mounted on the front grill of the approaching car.

A 1965 Cadillac convertible rolls up, humming low and throaty, the purr of a powerful engine. A classic. That is, if you don't look at the steer horns plastered to the front hood, winging off to each side like they're in flight. They remind me of the University of Texas Longhorns mascot. But I think we're a long way from Texas.

"It must be Big Jim, the horseman," Mom says.

There is no mistaking Jim. He has "rancher" written all over him – the ten-gallon hat, studded shirt, and freshly polished cowboy boots. Any boy would trade his *Star Wars* action figure collection for this real-deal cowboy get-up.

"Howdy partners," he says. "Name's Jim, but everyone calls me Big Jim." A smile flashes across his weather-beaten face. Big Jim takes one step forward, traveling three feet in the giant stride. He stretches out his big hand for each of us to shake. I gladly give him mine. His skin is dry and rough, and the bear-tight grip swallows up my hand. I bet he's strong enough to bench press the Cadillac.

"I headed out here as soon as I got your call," Big Jim says. Mom must have dialed the ranch on her cell phone while I was under the van being Adam the Mechanic.

Big Jim quickly scans the whole scene of our blowout mishap, his gray eyes missing nothing. Then he offers his opinion.

"It looks like you did the job yourself," he says, approvingly.

"That's my boys," Mom says. "They can tackle any project!"

"How far is the ranch?" I ask quickly, before Mom starts going on and on about what great kids we are or how smart we are – stuff that makes me feel like slinking under the Cadillac instead of riding high in the saddle.

"We can only travel slowly on this spare tire," Brian adds to my question.

"Not a problem," Big Jim says. "Why don't you ranch hands ride with me in the convertible and enjoy the open air? Your mom can follow in the van. The ranch is just over yonder," he adds, stretching out his big arm to sweep it across the rolling hills.

Excitedly, Brian and I pile into the Cadillac, sliding across the front seat covered in black and white Holstein cowhide. I only know about the cowhide because of our recent trip to New Salem, home of the world's largest cow, Huge Sue.

The big bench seat swallows us up. My feet barely touch the floor, and I can hardly see over the dash. Even with Big Jim behind the wheel, there is room for two more kids.

He fires up the Caddy and pays it a quick compliment for us: "I love this old car; it's the first one I ever bought and it's still full of pep!"

The boat-size Caddy slowly weaves its way through the green hillside. There is no problem with Mom keeping up with us on the skinny spare tire. Motoring the Wild West convertible around the curvy road is like steering a super-size John Deere tractor.

Soon, miles of white fence appear and horses are here and there, heads down as they graze the green grass. Turning onto a dirt road, the Cadillac spits up dust into Mom's path behind us. At the end of the road, we spot a log house so big it's like a log castle.

"That's the main lodge," Big Jim explains. "That rack of antlers above the front door is from an elk. I shot the big guy myself!"

Behind the lodge, we soon learn, is the massive main barn, and scattered all around the ranch are other small sheds and outbuildings. The pretty white fences from along the road continue here as they weave around the buildings. Only a handful of horses are near the barn right now, and they are all nose-deep into a barrel of water for a drink on this hot Dakota day.

"Over there is the riding ring," Big Jim says, waving his dinosaur-size arm. "The holding pens are along the north side of the barn."

When I hear Big Jim talk about riding, my ears perk up like a dog hearing the word "treat." I've been counting the days until I can be on a horse and feel the thundering hooves rumble beneath me while a wind-blown mane tickles my face.

Big Jim parks the Cadillac in front of a small log cabin with a chunky stone chimney that shoots out puffs of smoke.

"Sophie, the riding instructor, has the place all fired up for you. She thought the evening might get chilly. If it's too warm, though, just let the embers die out," Big Jim explains.

Chilly? I don't think it's been below eighty degrees during our entire North Dakota vacation. If it's going to cool off tonight ... well, I already like South Dakota!

Brian and I slide out of the big car. Through the trees, I see a couple of similar cabins, but no one else seems to be around right now.

"You folks settle in a bit, and then come on down to the lodge for a good supper," Big Jim says as he unloads our suitcases for us.

I nip at Big Jim's heels as he hoofs it to the log cabin while carrying our bags. The cabin is the color of honey and has a long front porch with two rocking chairs that look so comfy they'd put a baby to sleep, no problem.

The screen door creaks a homey little sound when Brian opens it for Big Jim. Mom and I step inside, too. The cabin has a wide-open layout inside and is all wood, all over. The floors are wood planks, and the walls are the same logs as outside. Looking up, I see great big wooden beams stretching to the ceiling. A small kitchen is arranged along one side and, just as Jim said earlier, a nice blaze glows in the stone fireplace. A couch and a pair of armchairs are grouped on a bear-skin rug. The black bear's head points off to one side while its arms and legs are spread flat into the remainder of the rug. It feels rough and shaggy under my shoes.

"The boys can sleep upstairs in the bunks," Big Jim says.

As soon as we notice the open staircase, Brian and I race our way up, following the stairs into a small room. Two log beds are stacked, one on top of the other. They each have wagon wheels for headboards, and the dressers have horseshoes for handles. It's like a real bunkhouse!

"Ma'am," I hear Big Jim say to Mom from down below, "you should sleep in the master bedroom. There's a hot tub on the lower deck."

Hot tub? No wonder Mom picked this ranch.

Brian and I gallop back down the stairs and follow Big Jim out the screen door as he struts back to the Cadillac.

"We can eat supper whenever you want," Big Jim says. "The last guests left this morning, and no one is due in till the weekend. You'll have the ranch to yourself so we can also ride whenever you want."

"Can we ride now?" Brian asks.

Is my brother crazy? My stomach hasn't eaten since sun-up. How can I ride in the saddle without food? "Can we eat first?" I blurt out.

"There's enough daylight for a short ride after supper," Big Jim says. "Just hurry along. I'll tell Sophie to put the chow on."

*   *   *

As we walk toward the lodge, food scents float up my nose. Thank goodness it smells nothing like the school hot lunch "mystery meatloaf." Instead, it smells yummy, like Grandma Schroeder's German cooking. Maybe they'll serve homemade bread with whipped butter. And gravy to pour over a mountain of mashed potatoes. I bet we have a sizzling steak, freshly butchered from the same herd of cattle I saw grazing on the range.

When we arrive for the meal, Big Jim is there, sitting at the head of the table. The rest of the lodge is empty, but it still feels cozy with log furniture and a fresh bakery aroma. Maybe we'll have apple pie with three scoops of ice cream for dessert.

Brian, Mom, and I gather round Big Jim. "I ordered my favorite meal for supper," Big Jim says.

The ranch owner is three times my size, but I'm so hungry I bet I can eat as much as him tonight. I wonder how he likes his steak cooked.

At the table Mom delivers her famous "good manners glare," so Brian and I promptly unfold the red-and-white checked cloth napkins onto our laps. My foot taps; I shift in my seat. Mom gets mad when I use the dining room chair as a jungle gym. I force myself to sit still. Where is dinner?

Through swinging doors, a round-faced, apron-wearing lady brings out big plates of ... pancakes. What kind of chow is this?

"We have our hearty meal at noon time on the ranch," Big Jim says. "No lunch for us ranch hands; it's breakfast, dinner, and supper. Hope you like flapjacks!" Big Jim stabs his fork and scoops five pancakes onto his plate in one swoop.

I stare at the breakfast food. How can a cowboy ride high in the saddle with only flour and water in his gut? I'm really sorry now I missed their "dinner" at our "lunchtime."

Big Jim smears a heap of jam across his pancakes. "Now have some of this chokecherry jam. Don't tickle it with a touch here and there. Slap it on." Big Jim practically swallows a whole pancake in one bite.

No other choice is coming through the kitchen swinging door. Mom doesn't say a word about the pancakes. Nothing can be done, anyhow. She knows it. I know it. So we dive into the stack of flapjacks.

Between mouthfuls, Big Jim says, "Sophie is saddling the horses. She'll signal us when they're ready to ride."

Signal? After a *hee-haw* donkey horn on the Cadillac, I wonder what signal the riding instructor will use. I steam-shovel my pancakes so I'm sure to be ready to ride.

With my belly full of flapjacks, I follow Big Jim across the ranch toward the big barn. It stands tall and broad against the sinking western sun.

"Bloody ready?" a voice calls out as she walks up to us.

"That's Sophie," Big Jim says. "Let's saddle up and ride."

At the barn I see a lady with long, soft yellow hair that almost floats in the air, and she has freckles like gold dust scattered across her nose. Her face looks like she could be a fairy princess who flutters around, waving a wand and granting wishes. But she isn't wearing a crown like a princess or even wearing a cowgirl hat. Instead, her head is covered in a black sturdy hat, like a bike helmet.

Nor does she have fringe on her blouse like a cowgirl would wear. Instead, her coat is black with two tails at the back. And her blouse – it's not satin with beads like pictures of Annie Oakley, but a plain cotton turtleneck. As for cowgirl boots – no spurs that jingle-jangle or tassels that shimmy. Instead, they are tall and black, sleek and slender. Lastly, in her hand, is a cane-like stick, also in black, with a cord attached to it.

"Sophie learned to ride in England," Big Jim says, answering the mystery of the way she is dressed, which is called English riding, not Wild West-style cowboy riding.

"Righty-o, chaps," Sophie says, my eyes glued to her cane.

She must notice my gaze. "It's called a riding crop," Sophie says as she gives it a quick flick of her wrist. The whip cracks like leather lightning. She snaps the whip once more across the dust. It snatches a stick and spins it back to her feet.

Sophie may have the face of a fairy princess, but watching her crack that whip and call out commands, like "halt" and "trot," makes me think she takes no back-talk from anyone. Not even Big Jim. I take two paces away from her. Luckily, she turns and marches into the barn.

Jim leads me near the watering barrels to a golden brown horse he calls Cherokee. I have to look way up, skyward, to see into her big black eyes. Standing on tiptoes, I manage to pet the stubby coarse hair on Cherokee's wide nose. The horse lets out a sudden snort and I jump a little, brushing against the scratchy wool blanket that pokes out from under the saddle.

"Let's get you mounted," Big Jim says, holding out his cupped hands for me to slip my foot inside. With one foot in Jim's hand, I hop three times on the other foot to get enough speed to push myself high into the air to plop in the saddle. My legs hang free now, with the stirrups dangling far below. Jim adjusts the straps to shorten the stirrups so my feet are snug inside the leather bands.

Sitting up atop Cherokee, I can see way across the rolling green meadows of the ranch. It's like being up on a Ferris wheel. Then I look down. The ground is so far away I almost get dizzy. But I love the thrill of carnival rides so I clutch the saddle horn tightly and decide not to look down again for a while.

While Big Jim is boosting Brian onto Lady, his black-and-white-spotted ride, I decide it's a good time to share Mom's secret.

"Ah ... ahem," I say, clearing my throat and stammering a little. Everyone looks at me. "I hate to say this, but ... Mom's afraid of horses."

"What?" Big Jim's jaw drops and his gaze turns quickly toward Mom.

"Only Snowflake, actually," Mom says, talking about a horse in Michigan that lives near a blueberry farm we visit in picking season.

"Snowflake's a toothless old mare," Brian adds with a tease.

"Yeah, but Mom doesn't like his slobber," I say. "Once she tried to feed him a carrot and Snowflake took a little chomp, slobbering all over her arm. Now Mom thinks every time she gets close to Snowflake, the horse wants to swallow her up." Brian and I chuckle at the idea.

"Horse drool can be pretty slimy," Big Jim says. "We'll make sure she won't have to feed her horse, Bullet, any carrots."

"Her name is *Bullet?*" Mom asks, her voice rising with concern.

With a soft chuckle Big Jim adds that, "Bullet is twenty years old, ma'am. She moves like a great-grandmother these days!"

A little smile plays across Mom's lips as his assuring words melt her fear away.

Next, from the barn, Sophie brings out a sleek black horse. "Take Lightning for your ride," she commands Big Jim. "Warm him up for my barrel race practice this evening."

In one smooth motion Big Jim is sitting high in the saddle on Lightning.

"Cheerio, mates," Sophie says with a snap in her voice as she waves us good-bye.

That sharp bite in her British accent is the same bitter tone Dad uses when our neighbor's dog pees on his prize rosebush. Silently, I wish Sophie will be inside that barrel when we get back from horseback riding. Then we could roll her round and round.

"Single file," Jim calls out, leading us down a trail barely wider than the horses. Tall grass from both sides tickles my legs as we mosey along. Cherokee's hooves hammer behind Jim's ride, Lightning. With each clomp I rock gently back and forth in the saddle.

"Go, Lady, Go," I hear Brian say, coaching his horse, but it sounds kind of far away. Twisting in the saddle once to glance backward, I see Brian's horse is still at the gate, grazing on grass. "Giddy-up, giddy-up," Brian says, jingling the reins, but Lady doesn't budge.

"I'll be right there, Brian," Big Jim says as he yanks Lightning's reins and trots the horse back to help my brother.

Suddenly, as soon as Big Jim is out of sight, my Cherokee bolts for it! The rush forward jerks my head back and my feet slip out of the stirrups. Instantly, I'm doing the splits while the horse sprints. With Cherokee galloping at bullet speed, I bounce wildly in the saddle, my butt smacking a hundred slaps a minute. I pull on the reins, but Cherokee knows she's got a beginner on her back.

Cherokee wickedly runs through a row of thick trees. Low hanging branches whip across my face, stinging my cheeks, so I crouch forward and bury my head into her wind-whipped mane. Through the horse hair, I see we're flying fast and the ground is a blur. And I hear Cherokee snorting and puffing.

Next, the horse dives into a steep ditch. I jerk forward, but my death grip on Cherokee's mane keeps me from flying through the air. Cherokee suddenly stops at the muddy creek bank, but clutching her mane again keeps me in the saddle. While I'm out of breath and my head is spinning, get this: Cherokee calmly drops her head to take a sip from the stream. Cripes. This was scarier than the steepest chute on a water slide! And it was just for a slurp of water.

It takes Big Jim about ten minutes to get Brian's horse, Lady, to trot up next to us, but I can still feel the heat in my cheeks when they approach. I feel like a real "city boy."

"Okay partner. You did good," Big Jim says to me.

"Partner?" I mutter to Big Jim, thinking maybe he didn't see me almost getting bucked off Cherokee.

Big Jim nods and smiles wide, all the way from one side of his tanned face to the other. "Cherokee loves to tease a rider," Big Jim says to me. "Now, start the lead, partner, and I'll be right behind."

I think Cherokee hears Big Jim's command because Cherokee simply moseys from the ditch and slowly clomps along the trail. No wonder Big Jim is the ranch master.

We're riding in single file again. I'm in the front and Cherokee is back to calmly clippity-clopping at a gentle pace. Mom's horse, Bullet, lazily pads along, just as Big Jim said she would. Mom wears a peaceful smile.

Behind Mom, Brian's horse still starts and stops whenever it chooses. I imagine Big Jim is using a sugar cube or two to charm Brian's horse back to the ranch so Brian doesn't end up having to sleep in the saddle somewhere out on the trail!

The hilliness of this part of South Dakota has us climbing up muddy slopes and thumping down shallow ravines, all the while weaving around fallen rotting oak trees and pines. Even though it is a slower pace than my racetrack run, my butt bounces in the seat with each step Cherokee takes.

Big Jim had called it the short trail before we started; yet once we are back at the barn, I feel worn out and ease my way out of the saddle. My butt prickles with needle-like pokes as I waddle bow-legged. I spot the hot tub on the deck of our cabin and head straight for it.

"Hey, partner," Big Jim calls to me. "Come down to the riding ring at eight. We'll watch Sophie ride the barrels and then we'll have a campfire."

Big Jim has been calling me "partner" all day. It's nice, 'cause it makes me feel like I've outgrown "city boy" a little. If only I could get my butt to believe it!

*   *   *

I limp my way to the cabin and change into my swim trunks. My stiff butt is glad the hot tub is only a few steps away.

"Brian and I will meet you ring-side to watch Sophie," Mom says, giggling, as she gives me a nice side hug to avoid my butt. That's Mom for you: bright eyes and a laugh that comes easily.

At the hot tub I roll back the cover. Steam swirls from the whirling bath. I gently glide into the waist-high water and sit so the water comes up to my neck. Bubbles tickle my chin as the water swishes about. I put my bruised butt directly in front of a high-powered jet of spraying water. After a short while the hot water does wonders for my stiffness. I climb out, get dressed, and hardly limp now on my way to the riding ring.

Brian and Mom are already ring-side; and inside the circle, Sophie is riding Lightning. Dressed in her trim, dressy, all-black English riding outfit, she races around the big drum barrels set up in the shape of a cloverleaf. The riding crop is tucked under her arm. If I get any closer, I wonder if she'll snap it at me. This is not the barrel race I was hoping for, but I know better, so I keep my distance.

"Barrel racing is one of the five events at Buffalo Ridge Rodeo. Sophie is a five-time winner," Big Jim says.

"Does she use that whip," I ask, more concerned about her weapon than her winnings.

"Nah, it's just for show, like her British costume. It's her way to stand out at the rodeo contests," Big Jim says with a smile. I can tell he's trying hard not to grin too wide at my "city-boy" question.

We watch Sophie perform all her barrel runs, and then Big Jim announces that it's time to toast some marshmallows. "Go on now, partners, and fetch a green stick for roasting over the campfire."

"Why do the boys need a green stick?" Mom asks.

For the first time today I don't feel like the person from the city. Almost in a bragging tone, I explain to Mom that, "A green stick is one that's still growing and fresh. Dead and dried up sticks will just catch fire while we're roasting."

"That's right, partner," Big Jim agrees. "So skedaddle now and rustle up some sticks."

When Brian and I come back with roasting tools in hand, Sophie is stacking wood into the fire pit. Her black whip is nowhere around, but a wooden matchstick hovers from her mouth. It makes her face wrinkle into a deep frown.

She moves the match to one side of her mouth. "You mates ready?" she asks, the matchstick bobs in her mouth as she barks out the question. I take a step back, concerned that she might take a poke at me with the matchstick rather than use it to strike a flame.

"We're ready as soon as the fire is lit," Brian says, holding out his green stick. Not something Einstein would say, but since I'm standing speechless, I'm happy.

"Righty-o, chaps," Sophie says.

Then with one hand Sophie whips the matchstick out of her mouth and strikes its tip with her thumbnail, sparking it on fire.

My jaw drops watching the one-handed, thumb-nail matchstick magic.

Sophie lowers the flaming matchstick to the fire pit and flames begin to lick the logs.

Within a few minutes the fire pit is burning red-hot.

"Start toasting, boys," Big Jim says. "Because once they're golden, Sophie has a special treat for us."

I look at Sophie. She gives me a squinty eye.

Too worried to cross Sophie's path, I follow Big Jim's directions, poking a marshmallow on my stick and hovering it over the flames.

While I slowly twirl the bubbly sugar on the stick, Big Jim shakes out a tablecloth from a picnic basket and covers a nearby table. On a plate he puts cookies that are about as big as Frisbees. "Sophie likes to bake," Big Jim explains.

"Right mate," Sophie says with a cold edge to her voice.

"She made chocolate chip," Big Jim brags.

"You chaps have a favorite?" Sophie asks. Her freckles dance an ugly two-step as her lips turn downward. I wonder if that frown will ever go away.

"What kind is your favorite?" she repeats with a stern, straight-on look.

"Uh ... you know, like that," Brian says, not completely able to give her an answer.

Under Sophie's watchful eye I can't mutter a word, so like a city fool, I simply point at the cookies.

"Jolly good," Sophie says. "Now, put your marshmallow between two biscuits."

"Biscuit?" I ask.

"Sorry, mate," Sophie says, "I meant cookies."

I think it was Sophie saying the word "cookies" that finally made her mouth curl into a small smile. Or maybe it was the warm, fire-roasted marshmallow melting the chocolate chips into a yummy, gooey treat. Either way, Sophie starts telling funny riddles.

"How can a man ride into town on Friday, stay three days, and leave on Friday?" she asks. Her eyes twinkle with excitement since this is her third riddle, and we've yet to have a correct answer.

"How can a man ride into town on Friday, stay three days and leave on Friday?" she repeats the riddle. Then she raises one eyebrow and turns her gaze at me. Her warm smile waits for my reply.

I feel a stupid grin form on my face.

Sophie can tell that, once again, we don't know the answer! She keeps her eyes fixed on me. After a beat, she leans forward and flashes a full force, all teeth smile. "He was riding a bloody horse named Friday."

Everyone roars.

Then, between chuckles I abruptly feel something furry stroke my leg. My mouth freezes. I can't see under the table. My mind runs wild, thinking about the critters and longhorn steer and elk antlers around the ranch. Then, I remember the creek from the horseback ride. It's probably full of muskrats or possum or, worse yet, bobcats! Bears!

Then I hear it. "Arf, arf, arf!" The happy woofing of dogs.

"Meet Pepper and Sly," Big Jim says. "The bigger mutt is Sly and the pint-size puff ball is Pepper."

"Pepper?" I ask, looking at the smaller white and tan fluff ball that looks like a dust mop without the pole.

"Yeah, a ranch hand named him Salt 'n Pepper, but he's known 'round these parts as Pepper," Big Jim says.

The ranch dogs stop barking and now are running in circles around us. I bend over and hold out my hand. "Come here, boys," I say, wiggling my sugary-sticky fingers.

The dogs stop spinning, and their heads turn toward me. Pip-squeak Pepper quickly scampers over. He gives my fingers a quick sniff, and then I feel his small wet nose nuzzle my open palm. Suddenly he leaps into my arms. I giggle with surprise.

By now Brian is clapping his hands and chanting Sly's name. The King-size mutt prances over with a spring in his step, and his long pink tongue hangs out the side of his mouth. With an elephant-size slurp, the mutt wets Brian's arm up to his elbow. "That tickles," Brian tee-hees. Sly sits on his haunches and then lifts a gigantic brown paw, planting it on Brian's chest.

"Sly likes you, Brian," Big Jim says. "He wants to be scratched between his ears."

Instantly, Brian and I have two new friends.

"Can they spend the night at our cabin?" I ask, not wanting to let go of this cuddly fluff ball.

"Sure thing, partner," Big Jim says. "If it's okay with your Mom."

All eyes fix on Mom. She holds up her hands in surrender. "It's Big Jim's cabin. If it's okay with him, it's okay with me."

We hike the short path to the cabin as the dogs bounce along, yapping at our heels. I fill a dish with water. Pepper laps gently while Sly guzzles, sloshing most of the water onto the floor.

Suddenly the room smells like rotten taco meat, or worse yet, a porta-john that has been sitting out in the hot sun.

"Pee-yew. Did you fart, Adam?" Brian asks, wrinkling his nose.

"Not me," I say as my eyes drill to my brother.

"Me, neither," he says now holding his nose tightly with pinched fingers.

A low rumble gurgles from Sly's stomach. Immediately the foul smell worsens.

"It's Sly. He has gas," I say, choking on the words. The horrible odor in the room hangs heavy like a thick fog. Rotten eggs couldn't smell worse. "His name should be Stinky."

"I don't know about that. Farts are pretty *sly*," Brian says.

"Come on, Stinky," I say to Sly. "Let's go outside."

The dogs follow me out the door. Brian slides into a rocker on the front porch. My butt is still a little tender from the wild horse ride so I choose to stand up for a while. "Do you think they'll play fetch?" I ask.

"Don't know; let's try," Brian says.

I grab a baseball out of the van. "Go get it, boy," I yell, tossing the ball.

Instantly Pepper chases his tail, spinning in circles, instead of chasing the ball. But Stinky barks and then dashes after the ball with his mouth wide open, pink tongue flapping and sending spit sailing through the air. He scarfs up the ball with his teeth and gallops back to me. The biggest threat is his body weight coming right at me, not the slobber-soaked ball in his mouth. He stops short and then drops the slimy ball. It rolls to my feet. The big guy wags his tail so hard the whole back half of his body whips side to side.

"He wants more!" I say, scooping up the soggy ball.

I toss the ball again and then wipe my hands on my shorts. Stinky is off like a racehorse while Pepper curls up for a nap nearby. Brian and I play fetch with Stinky until it's so dark we can't see the ball. Luckily there are no more "Stinky"-bombs of bad gas.

Walking back to the cabin I say, "Hey Brian, did you notice we've got better luck with dogs than the horses?"

"That's right, partner," he says.

Once inside the cabin, Mom lays down the law: "After such a full day, it's time for lights out."

Brian snatches the upper bunk, and that's fine by me. I like sleeping closer to the pups, which are nestled on the rug next to the beds.

Before I can even snuggle under the covers, Stinky and Pepper scurry in with me. As we nuzzle together, I feel certain my good luck with the dogs will happen with my horse Cherokee, too. I decide I won't be a "city boy" for the next two ranch days, after all.

Chapter 15

Solving the Mysteries

It started out as a great idea. Mom's plan sounded like the best game ever: a Murder Mystery Dinner Party. Inside one box are clues for eight people to solve a scary crime ... and one of us will be the murderer! This part is kept secret while all the other players try to solve the crime. All we have to do is invite friends to dinner and dress up like a character from the game box. Simple and fun!

"Can I go next door to invite Zach and Joey?" I ask Mom, ready to race away.

"Have your friends invite their parents, too," Mom says. "It will make the party neighborly."

Moments later, I'm darting back into our apartment. "Everyone can come! They all can come!"

"Great; that makes the eight people we need to play the game," Mom says.

"I count seven," I say, thinking about Zach and Joey, Captain Mike, their mom, Brian, Mom and me. "Who's number eight?"

Uh-oh. Suddenly my throat catches, as if someone is pressing a thumb on it. Mom said the party would include neighbors. What if the eighth person is Mad Witch, Mom's landlord who lives upstairs? She's tall enough to loom over me and her voice snaps at me like a bullwhip. Thinking about her instantly makes the kitchen temperature feel twenty degrees hotter.

"My friend, Larry, will be number eight," Mom says.

Instantly, my throat relaxes and I swallow easily, feeling like a nice, soothing Popsicle just slid down it.

"Larry will be fun," I say. I love Larry's laugh. It goes on and on in a loud, crazy way. Sometimes he ends up coughing and beating his chest. That makes me laugh even more.

I grab the Murder Mystery Dinner game box. "Murder at the Art Museum," I read on the lid. On the cover is a picture of a fancy white building lit up like a Christmas tree. That must be the museum, I think, staring at the drawing. The wide front door of the building in the picture is set back away from four tall columns. Banners that hang between the columns read: "*Art Opening Tonight, Artist, Raphaela I. Palleta.*"

"Can I open the game box, now?" I ask.

"Sure," Mom says. "Let's read the directions to know what food to cook for dinner. An art opening should have fancy food like cocktail appetizers." Her eyes shine with glee and she winks.

Cocktails and fancy food? Ah, luckily Mom is just teasing me about those mini-sandwiches with mushy meat in the middle and cut into tiny triangles. She knows I don't care for those bite-size nibbles.

What I care about is the character I'll play at the party. Maybe I'll be the policeman. He's on the cover of the box, too. I can wear a badge and gun just like the picture. I bet he finds all the secret clues. Or maybe I'll be –

Suddenly, I stop daydreaming because, inside the box, I notice the eight player cards show four men and four ladies. But coming to the party are six guys and two girls. What are we going to do?

I shake the box. Nothing else falls out. I poke my hand inside and jab my fingers into every corner. Nothing. I look down on the table. Only eight cards. I flip the cards over. Maybe the back side gives another choice. No luck. I gulp for a breath.

"What's wrong?" Brian asks as he comes into the kitchen.

Sucking for another breath, I try to speak, but it's only a squeak. I slide the eight invitations toward Brian.

"Four guys and four girls," Brian says as he shuffles through the cards. "So what?"

Wheezing, I point to Zach and Joey's house.

"You already invited our two best friends," Brian says.

I nod, waving four wild fingers, again at the house next door.

"And Mom has their parents coming, too," Brian says as he figures out my frantic signal.

My nod confirms the problem of six boys and two girls coming to the party. Time stands still, like the moment I'm at the top of a skateboard ramp looking down, suspended before blast-off and thinking about the big drop ahead.

This murder mystery dinner party was going to be better than a video game marathon because we would get to dress up in costumes. Plus there will be Mom's three-layer-chocolate pudding cake for dessert. It's a tradition she makes for special occasions. But now the party plans are a mess. A big mess. I hang my head. How do we un-invite our best friends?

Brian takes a step toward me. His eyes take in mine. His hand claps my shoulder. He takes a deep breath and then he lets it out, slow and silent, blowing air in my face. This is his serious side at work.

"How about a walk," Brian says.

A walk? Why does my brother want to walk at a time like this? Then I remember. Brian does his best thinking on a walk.

We head outside and I shuffle along, waiting for Brian's wit to kick in. My best thinking is random. It comes any time, in any place. I am kind of unpredictable that way. And right now, I have nothing, so I'm glad to wait my brother out.

Halfway to the corner, Brian stops and says, "I got it. Larry and Captain Mike can dress up as the girls."

Huh? I stare at Brian, thinking he's crazy. Then on second thought, I realize it could work. Captain Mike is always ready for an adventure. He tackled the mighty Missouri River as skipper of the pontoon boat. And Mom's friend, Larry, well, we've had adventures too. Except the adventures with Larry were more from us kids getting into mischief. Larry wasn't the adventurous one. But he was a good sport, even when we cut a spy-hole in the center of his motor home blanket.

"Do you think Larry will dress up like a girl?" I ask.

"Well, maybe it's not such a great idea. Where would Larry find a dress in his extra-large size? Maybe we should cancel the party," Brian says.

"No, no! Let's walk a little farther," I say. I can't let my brother's need to have a perfect plan mess up our celebration. Brian is always the serious one. Somehow I've got to get him to be more like me – ready for a few laughs and a good time.

"Maybe if we walk slower," I suggest, hoping if Brian takes more time to think, he'll come up with another idea.

I jam my hands in my pockets. My fingers brush against the two arrowheads. Since we got back from the ranch, I started carrying them with me all the time, hoping I might find someone to sell them too. But right now, I decide the heck with making money. Maybe the arrowheads can bring me good luck. I decide to take a chance and talk to Joey's make-believe ghost of Custer. I rub the arrowheads together. "Hello, out there," I whisper under my breath so Brian can't hear. "Get me out of this mess. Let this party happen."

We walk a bit more.

"Well ... maybe there's a way," Brian says and pauses. "What if ..." My brother pauses again, longer this time.

I look up to the sky and silently beg, "I promise to eat more vegetables. I'll sit quietly in church. I'll use a dust pan instead of sweeping the dirt under the rug. Please, just let there be a party."

By this time Brian has stopped walking. This is a good sign. It means his thinking is even more serious. He turns to me. His green eyes lock on mine. "Have you noticed Larry smiles every time he sees Mom?" Brian asks.

I nod yes.

"Let's get Mom to ask him," Brian says with a grin spreading across his face.

"That's the answer!" I shout.

Most times Larry gives Mom a peck on the cheek. But the last time they said good-night, when they thought I wasn't looking, it was a kiss on the lips!

"Larry will do anything for Mom," I say.

We dash back to the apartment and find Mom. Excitedly, we rattle off the story of the character mix-up and how we need two more girls for the Murder Mystery Dinner Party.

"And we four young boys can't be girls. We could never go back to school once we dressed-up pretending to be girls," I say. "So that leaves Captain Mike and Larry."

"Do you think they'll do it?" Brian asks, his worry gene kicking in.

"I'm not sure," Mom says.

"What if we bake them your double chocolate chip oatmeal cookies?" I ask, naming Larry's favorite treats and knowing the big guy loves to eat.

"That should help," Mom says, giving a slight nod. It's just a tiny movement. But that itty-bitty nod is my favorite. It means Mom is okay with this.

"So ... will you ask them?" I cross my fingers behind my back, praying Mom will say "yes."

"You want me to ask the grown-up men to be *girls*," she says, raising an eyebrow.

"They'll take you more seriously than us kids," Brian pipes up, remembering our plan that Larry will do anything for Mom.

"Well okay, I'll ask them. I'm the one who bought the game box, after all. Somehow we'll make this work," Mom says. "Go ahead and assign the characters and deliver an invitation to everyone. Then we'll have to look for costumes."

Costumes. I forgot all about the costumes. This is going to be more fun than Halloween. Except for one thing. Every Halloween Mom sews Brian and me the best costumes. And we come up with the props like a cavemen hunting club and a warrior necklace with real-life bones.

"But, Mom!" I say. "There's no time for you to sew costumes."

"Not a problem," she says. "We'll go to the nearly-new store and get some fancy dress-up clothes. It'll be like we're going to a real art opening at the museum, complete with tuxedos and long ball gowns."

I should have known. Mom will be dripping in a diamond necklace and have sparkly rhinestone shoes like Cinderella. Her passion for a fancy costume is as expected as another ninety-degree day in Bismarck.

Then I remember to mention my idea from earlier. "I'm going to play Jim Hall, the security guard. I can shop for a uniform with a nifty badge," I say, snatching the policeman's invitation. I almost snicker, knowing that I won't have to wear a bow tie or stiff shirt now. Tying shoelaces for church is dressy enough for me.

Then my thinking grinds to a halt. What if the security guard is the murderer? Who is more likely to be the crook than the good guy? Sometimes when I act fast and think later, it comes back to haunt me. I look at the card once more. With the idea of wearing a nifty badge, I decide to take the risk and play the security guard.

Brian chooses to be Mark Chase, the architect. For Zach, we pick Tip Wright, a sports writer. Joey, being the youngest player, is Eddie Grayson, a student at the university. It's a perfect match.

"Captain Mike can be the director of the art museum," Brian says. "A director is like the boss, and since Captain Mike is the boss of the pontoon boat, he's ideal to play Emma Dominick."

"And if he's the boss, maybe he won't mind being a girl boss," I say.

"The character of Michelle Gelato is an artist," Brian says. "That should be Mom."

"Let's have Larry play Jasmine Lipton. She's rich and is paying for this fancy art opening. Larry would like to be rich, don't you think?"

"Yeah, then he can dress up in jewels and maybe wear a crown on his head. Wouldn't that be funny?" Brian says.

"Well, I just read something funnier," I say. "Jasmine is a cat lover."

My brother and I both know Larry is allergic to cats.

"Mom would kill us if we secretly invited Butterscotch," I snicker, mentioning the cat from upstairs.

Brian pretends to sneeze like he's having an allergy attack. Then he snort-laughs and slimy snot gushes from his nose. We laugh so hard tears stream down our cheeks.

Finally we quit fooling around and get the invitations delivered. Then Mom drives us to the second-hand shop. The building looks like it was once a grocery store, complete with the automatic front doors that open when you step on a pad. Inside the store is wide open, with row upon row of clothing racks.

"Is this where you bring the clothes we outgrow?" I ask.

"That's right," Mom says. "Clothes are donated, and the money raised from reselling them helps people in need."

"It's like an indoor garage sale," I say.

Mom nods and, with a bounce in her step, wanders toward the princess-style gowns. I rifle through a rack of shirts, seeking one with shiny buttons or doodads for the security guard costume. A-ha. This dark-blue shirt with flaps at the shoulder looks like a policeman wore it. Next I find a thick belt. It's wide enough to sling a pistol through it at the waist. Now for a cap – something that looks like a security guard would wear.

"Hey, Adam. Over here," my brother calls from across the store. I rush over. "This entire box of hats is five dollars," Brian says.

The box is taller than me. Brian tips the box and I sneak a peek inside. On the top layer is a wool ski hat and what looks like a girl's church hat. I give the box a shake. The brim of a blue hat appears. This could be an excellent hat for me. I get a great idea.

"Hey, Mom," I say, "I see the perfect hat for Larry and one for you, too."

She glances at the giant cardboard carton of hats. "Do you have to buy the whole box?"

"Ah, yeah, but there must be ten hats in here. Larry could get a choice," I say, hoping "Larry" is the magic word.

She cocks her head, and with a stern look on her face, takes in the oversize box again. Then she softens a little and asks, "How much do they cost?"

"It'd be about fifty cents a hat," I say, quickly dividing the number of hats into five dollars, making the price sound like a bargain.

I see her mulling this over, all the while giving me a serious eye. I hold my breath. Sometimes it is best to just wait in silence with Mom and don't ask for more. The wait is over when I catch a little twinkle in her eye.

"Slide it up to the cash register," Mom says. "It'll be more fun with hats for everyone."

Yes! I knew using Brian's trick about including Larry would get us the whole box. I can't wait to show Zach and Joey.

Once home, Brian and I haul the box to the backyard. It stands taller than I am. Together we tip the box and dump out the contents. Zach and Joey rush over.

"I can wear this one," Joey says, slipping on what must have once been a fisherman's hat. Stuck into the hat are fishing hooks with feathery things wrapped around them, and a rubber worm dangles off another spot.

"I thought you were a college student?" I ask Joey.

"Uh, yeah. I'm Eddie. But I can be a student who likes to fish," Joey says, nodding his head making the rubber worm swing like an outdoor paper lantern in a wind storm. Joey likes anything that wiggles and jiggles.

On tiptoes, Brian peers into the tall box we thought was empty. "Something is stuck down in the bottom," he says. "It looks like a hat with a medal on it."

"I'll snag it," I say, quickly wanting first dibs on what could be a security guard cap.

In a flash I'm crawling inside the box, not taking the time to tip the box on its side. Instantly I'm head-first into the box with my feet flying right behind. I hit bottom. Ouch. But I'm on a mission. With barely enough room for me to twist upright, I snatch the cap. It's dark blue with a fancy patch on the front that says: *City Cab*. This is perfect. All I need is a magic marker and it can read *City Cop!*

I tuck the cap into my back pocket and try to lift myself up. The box is too tall and narrow. "Hey, you guys, I need help getting out of here," I say as my voice echoes inside the box.

"Brian will help you, Adam," Zach says, "Joey and I just got called home. We have an eye doctor appointment this afternoon."

"Brian, help me out," I call.

"In a minute," my brother says, "I need to run inside to use the bathroom."

"Hey, wait! Don't leave me! Hold it, if you have to," I shout. Suddenly it's getting hot inside the box.

"I can't hold it. I have to go really badly." I hear the apartment door slam.

I'm left trapped inside a cardboard prison. The hot air rises up my legs and hovers around my face. It feels like I have a paper bag over my head as I breathe in the same hot air I'm breathing out. The heat dries up my tongue and sticks to the roof of my mouth. Sweat trickles down my back now, too. What is taking Brian so long?

I stick my chin up high into the air, hoping to suck in cooler air from outside the box. It works! My nose fills with the sweet scent of flowers. Oh no. It's Mad Witch's rosebush – the one with all the bees around it.

Until now my huffing and puffing was the only sound I'd noticed. Worried about the bees, I hold my breath and listen. In the quiet, I hear it: *Buzz – bzz bzz. Buzz – bzz bzz.* It sounds like a hundred bees zooming around right outside my cardboard cell.

Sweat drips off my nose, my armpits are soggy, and my shirt sticks to my back. If the bees get a whiff of the sweet smell of my stinky sweat, I'll be stung a hundred times. Why did I act so fast to grab a hat? I should have thought before placing the cardboard box next to the rosebush.

Then I hear a low growl, slow and steady, like some kind of wild animal. Maybe it's a bear. But I'm in the city. Maybe it's a big angry dog. Next I think of the nearby shed and Custer's ghost! My cheeks blaze red, and it's not from the hot air inside the box. It's from fear.

The grumbling sound comes closer. My heart beats double time. Now the grunting is right outside the box. It's a rough and scratchy groan. I can tell now it's not an animal, it's a person. And this person doesn't sound very friendly. My beet-red cheeks begin to itch as my hot breath bounces off the box and slams me in the face, again and again. I don't think I can stay in here much longer.

"Help," I squeak out. "Who's out there?" My voice echoes in my ears.

The groaning stops. I hear a gasping, choking sound like someone might be in trouble. The top of the box is inches above my head. I claw at the rim. As if I were on a chin-up bar, I pull up and quickly take a peak outside. It's Mad Witch. Laughing. Not snickering her lawn mower choke of heh-heh-heh. She's roaring-out-loud, laughing. Head back and chest heaving, hands on her stomach and tears in her eyes, all her yellow teeth are showing as she's letting it rip. I have never heard Mad Witch laugh before.

My fingers burn and I can't hold myself up any longer. I drop to the bottom of the box.

The laughter fades, and a minute later I hear a squeaking sound followed by Mad Witch's groan. Suddenly the box is struck by an earthquake, knocking me against the side of the cardboard. What if I tip over? If I do crash, the bees will surely attack and sting me. Is that what Mad Witch is trying to do?

Luckily the movement stops as I'm tipped at an angle and held steady. I'm not leaning far enough over to be able to see out of the top of the box. I can still only see blue sky above my head.

Then the squeaking begins again and I feel the box moving. The buzz of bees grows quieter and the smell of roses fades. I must be rolling along like a moving box on a push-cart.

"Rides over," I hear Mad Witch announce in her husky voice. The box stops moving.

"Need some help?" It's my brother. When did he come back?

The box slowly tips to the ground and I crawl out. Cool, fresh air surrounds me. A two-wheel cart stands next to me. It was this push-cart that took me away from the bees.

"Young man, can you push that cart into the shed," Mad Witch asks of Brian.

He pushes the cart through the open door of the shed that Mad Witch uses for a pottery studio. In seconds he has the door closed and the padlock snapped. I feel my stomach ease. That shed makes me nervous. I'm certain Custer's ghost hides in a corner in there!

With my feet safely on the ground, I take a closer look at Mad Witch. Today her hair is sticking out almost like antennas on a space creature. Perhaps she is an alien, not a witch, after all. But then I realize she went out of her way to help me. She gives me a smile that lights up her entire face, melting her fiery eyes into puddles. Her grumbly lawn mower laugh is more like a purr now. Her softened, friendly glow lights up something warm and comforting in me, too. I am certain I have a new friend and not an alien from Mars.

"Thank you, Mrs. Witt," I say.

"Call me, Marge," she says. "I'm a bit like my cat, Butterscotch. It takes me a while to warm up to strangers."

Just then I feel a tickle on my leg. I look down and the monster-size cat is nuzzling tenderly. In fact, for the first time I hear a gentle murmur.

Brian says good-bye to Marge and then nudges me. "Mom wants us to get ready for the party," he says and heads into the apartment.

First, though, I take a moment to give Butterscotch a playful rub. The not-so-beastly cat purrs. Then I wave good-bye to Marge.

"Good-bye, half-pint," she calls to me as a smile crosses her face.

I stare at the lady who saved me from the bee attack. My pulse races, but I know I finally need an answer. I stammer, "uh, Marge ...?"

"Yes, Adam," she softly says my name for the first time instead of calling me "half-pint."

She is my friend, I think to myself. I take a deep breath and blurt out, "Have you ever seen flickering lights from the shed?"

She doesn't answer. I flinch. What if she's seen Custer's ghost? But I can't quit now. I press on, my voice breaks a little, but I squeak out, "And I heard a strange ping-ping sound."

Her face wrinkles as her lips tip upward. "Oh, half-pint," she purrs. "That old shed has faulty and frayed wiring. When the ceramic oven heats up, it draws so much power that the lights flash."

I lick my dry lips. "And the strange pinging?" I ask, thinking that Custer's swords swishing and clashing in battle would sound just like that high pitch.

"That's the pottery in the hot oven. After the pottery cooks the oven is too hot to touch. It takes three days to slowly cool down from the twenty-two hundred degrees. The pottery inside the oven pings as it cools," Marge explains of the mysterious noise.

"But then I heard a rat-ta-tap-tap, like popping," I say, ready to be done with every ghostly thought.

"Popping?" she asks, looking clueless. Then she repeats it, "Popping from the shed? Why don't you show me?"

Before I can answer, Marge swoops her arm around my shoulder and hustles me up to the shed.

"Go ahead, unlock it," she says, slapping a key in my palm.

My shaking fingers fumble with the lock. Am I having trouble opening the lock or am I stalling? I fiddle some more. I'm definitely hesitating. Finally, my fingers slip the key inside and the lock pops open. I circle my fingers around the door latch. Slowly, oh so slowly, I lift the latch.

"Move along, half-pint," Marge says. "Let's go inside."

Sucking in a deep breath of air, I give the heavy door a two-handed shove. It lets out an eerie groan. From inside dark shadows loom, sending a shiver through me. I am certain any minute Custer's ghost will appear.

Marge flicks on the lights. The entire shed glows from the florescent bulbs. I realize the last time I was inside the shed was during the blackout when we blew a fuse and lost power. Now, with the beaming lights and Marge at my side, it feels just a little less scary.

"Which direction do you think you heard that popping?" Marge asks, marching to the middle of the pottery studio.

"Um, from outside, it sounded far away," I say. "Maybe that corner." I point to a distant edge of the shed where a pile of dusty boxes are stacked.

"Well, that could be my dead husband's home brew," she says. "I'd forgotten all about that stuff. He was always bottling up a batch of beer with secret grains and hops."

Straight away, Marge is off to the boxes, shifting and sorting, kicking up a cloud of dust. I shuffle behind.

"Aha! Looky here, half-pint," she calls.

In each hand she waves a brown bottle, while at the same time she kicks several corks across the rough floor. "This hot weather must have caused this old bottled brew to explode."

Just then, Brian is at the doorway. "Adam, it's time to get ready for the party. Mom doesn't want to have to call you again."

"Go on ahead, half-pint," Marge says to me. "It's about time I clean up this old brew, anyhow."

I look at Marge. All my ghostly questions are answered. I could jump for joy, but Brian is waving me to hurry. With a skip in my step, I'm off to begin the party.

Then my hand brushes my pocket. The arrowheads. Just this morning, in a panic, I was talking to Custer's ghost, pleading for the arrowheads to bring me good luck so we could have this party. Now after Marge's explanations I'm thankful there's no ghost ... but could the arrowheads still be lucky?

"Come on, Adam," Brian calls again.

There's no time to wonder. It's time to solve the murder mystery at the dinner party.

* * *

Inside I dress in the dark blue shirt for the party. There I am, in the snazzy shirt and the mirror. Front view. Side. Back. Still skinny as a pixie stick, for sure, but when I puff out my chest, the shirt buttons sparkle. I put on the City Cab cap that has the magic marker re-do and now boasts: *City Cop.*

I feel just like a security guard.

Mom uses a lacy tablecloth to cover the kitchen table, and then she lights some candles to help set the mood. Even with the mismatched jelly-jar glasses, the place looks fancy now.

The doorbell rings and I dart to answer it. Zach's mom is the first to step inside. Her pink princess-like dress touches the floor and it swishes as she walks. The dress has a fancy lace collar and big puffy sleeves that hug her shoulders. Long gloves cover her hands going way up past her elbows.

"Good evening, Master Adam," she says, giving my cheek a tender touch. Her gloved fingers are cottony soft. Wow! She's a beautiful Rhonda Paletta, the sister of the murder victim.

Zach and Joey come in. Zach has an ink pen stuck in his ear to look like Tip Write, the sports reporter. Joey wears his red cowboy boots and the fishing hat. The rubber worm jiggles with each wiggle of his head. And with Joey, it's almost nonstop. He makes a silly college student. Maybe we should change his name from Eddie Grayson, to Giddy Eddie!

I poke my head outside the door. No one else is there. "Where's Captain Mike?" I ask.

"My dad decided to come with Larry," Zach says.

"Do you think they'll come dressed as girls?" I ask, almost dizzy from anticipation.

"He wouldn't tell us," Zach says. "But I can't wait to see."

My eyes dart to Mom, hoping I can spot a clue. Mom's eyebrows go up. Her eyebrows speak a language of their own. Right now, they're saying: I don't know. Guessing which one of us is the murderer at the museum won't be the only mystery tonight. Captain Mike and Larry have us puzzled.

Ding-dong, the doorbell rings.

No one moves. We stare at the door with Spaghetti-O mouths – wide open.

Ding-dong.

Before we can take a step forward, the door slowly creaks open. Two tall strangers are standing there. I rub my eyes and look again. All I see are two heads of crazy yellow hair, so big it's wilder than a rock singer when she whips her head singing. Then I notice the taller one has on a skirt. Dark hairy legs poke out from under the skirt and big feet are squeezed into clunky high heel shoes. This must be Larry.

As for the other "girl," his hairy legs are sticking out of a shiny blue dress, and his shoes match the exact color and shine as the dress. His size tells me he's Captain Mike.

I press my lips tightly together so I won't howl out loud.

"We're here for the mystery dinner," Larry says as a wad of out-of-control curly yellow hair flies around his face. He blows at it to try to get it out of his eyes. Spit flies. When he tries to cover his mouth with his big hand, he loses his balance, stumbling in the high heels. The gorilla-size "girl" falls forward.

"Steady, Jazz-min," Captain Mike says, using Larry's game name.

Captain Mike grabs Larry's arm trying to help his friend from tumbling. The two of them sway. Their curly yellow wigs bounce all about.

I can't take it any longer. I bust out laughing along with everyone else.

Somehow Larry and Captain Mike shuffle into the pretend Ral Museum for an evening of trying to solve the murder mystery.

As we play the game, we collect clues and learn secrets about each other. At first, I think I'm the murderer because we learn the security guard knows the ins and outs of every hidden tunnel under the museum. Then we uncover more clues. It turns out we all have a reason to be the murderer and kill the artist, Raphaela I. Palleta.

Brian leans back in his chair and taps his lower lip with the end of a pencil. It's like he's tapping a coded message to himself, thinking. Finally, Brian says, "I'm guessing the murderer is Mom. The dead artist was Mom's arch enemy, and Mom couldn't face the idea the girl was a better artist than herself, so she killed her."

"Yeah, I think so, too," I say. "Mom stabbed her with Brian's architectural ruler to put the suspicion on him and not her."

"I agree!" Zach says, pointing to the notes he's made in his Tip Write notebook.

"Should we check the answer?" Mom asks. "There are more clues left on the game board."

"Yes, there are clues left, and it's early in the game to be guessing," Captain Mike says. "Remember, I'm the boss of this entire art opening. Think about all the publicity and fame a murder will bring the Museum. I could have killed her."

"Captain Mike is trying to trick us," I say to Brian. "Let's guess!"

My brother taps his pencil one more round of his silent code. Finally he nods. "We're certain we're right," he says.

"Yeah, the kids against the grown-ups," Joey speaks up. His rubber worm wiggles on his hat. All night long, Joey has been squirming in his seat like a three-year-old forced to pose for a painting.

Captain Mike slowly slides the secret envelope from the middle of the game board to Mom. She slips a bright red fingernail under the lip of the envelope and slices it open. A folded card falls out. Brian flips the card over. "Mom's the murderer. Kids win!"

"Hooray! Hooray!" we shout, jumping up and down. I feel the arrowheads bouncing around in my pocket. Was it luck or skill that won the game? After making friends with Marge Witt and learning there's no ghost of Custer living in the shed and now ... this victory!

I have to stop and wonder: Maybe these arrowheads really are lucky charms.

Chapter 16

A Plan Hatched

In my entire life, I have never seen anything this big ... or this green. Out in the field a tank-size machine with monster teeth up front is chomping away. It's like a huge mechanical shark, in a sea of brown wheat, eating everything in its path. And it's rolling right toward us!

Unexpectedly, the roaring green giant rumbles to a stop. Luckily it's a safe distance away. Then a familiar face steps down from the driver's compartment; the big man steps onto a high platform on the big, mean, John Deere machine.

"Howdy, little fellows," Grandpa Joe calls out to us while waving his cap in a huge arc of hello in our direction.

The green farmer's cap catches my eye, of course, because Grandpa Joe gave Brian and me the same kind at the birthday party. Now my brother and I stand beaming, as we're proudly wearing John Deere hats, too.

Grandpa Joe lumbers down from the mighty wheat harvester, and we notice up close that his hat-hair stands on end like a bundle of straw. While he is wiping sweat off his sun-baked face with a handy bandana handkerchief, he takes big, burly steps and is quickly at our side.

"You young bucks ready for a farm tour?"

"You betcha," we say, chuckling a little as we use our best North Dakota slang. The new farm kid in me is itching to let loose. What could possibly be waiting on a farm that would make me feel like a city boy again? Only Cherokee – the race horse – at the ranch could do that, I thought.

"Ms. Moynihan, would you like to join us?" Grandpa Joe says to Mom, who is standing at our side.

"Absolutely," Mom replies.

With pep in my step, I snatch Grandpa Joe's hand. "Give us the tour," I say, giving his sweaty and dirt-crusted hand a tug. This is my favorite kind of hand – one that would never get clean no matter how hard it's scrubbed.

"I reckon I will," he says, his grin widening. "This here is Olsen Farm," Grandpa explains while sweeping his arm in a dramatic gesture across the wide open space around us.

Squinting into the blazing sun, I see miles of wheat dancing in the wind. And where it's not wheat, it's a brown dust bowl. While New York City has the Statue of Liberty and Florida has Disney World, North Dakota proudly has dirt clods as far as the eye can see.

"Is that machine of yours called a combine, Grandpa?" Brian asks.

"That's right. This rig will reap, thrash, and winnow wheat in a single sweep of the field," Grandpa Joe says with a nip of roughness and grit in his voice. While launching proudly into details about his monster of a machine, he stands rocking back on the heels of his worn cowboy boots, thick thumbs hooked into his jean belt loops. With a smile almost as broad as his chest, he boasts, "Yep. This here's my Big Green Machine."

I'm smart enough to know he isn't talking about the Michigan State Spartans football team when he uses the nickname Big Green Machine. He's talking about this house-size combine – this army tank of the prairie.

Taking a closer look now, I notice the combine has a yellow deer logo like the one on the farm caps. After seeing this beast in action, I feel like I'll wear this cap as proudly as Batman standing in front of his Batmobile.

"Let's mosey over yonder," Grandpa Joe says, pointing down a dusty road we're on. "The rest of the farm equipment is in those outbuildings."

My eyes follow his gaze toward several huge, windowless metal buildings with gigantic garage doors at each end. Some of the outbuildings, as they're called, seem bigger than a soccer field. We wander over and peer inside the closest of the gigantic tin boxes. Inside are more monster farm machines with spikes, claws, and metal teeth for chomping crops and digging in the dirt.

"This baby has 205 horsepower," Grandpa says, giving a slap on a tire that towers well over my head. "In tractor talk, horsepower describes how much work is done in a given amount of time. For example, if you lift a 110-pound bale of hay five feet into the air in one second, it equals one horsepower."

Brian is very impressed, of course. "Gosh. I weigh 77 pounds so that tractor could lift me in less than seven-tenths of a second," Brian says, computing math faster than dirt flies in a North Dakota wind storm.

"Darn toot'in, it can!" Grandpa bellows while snatching Brian's cap off his head to rough up his hair. After a good threshing from Grandpa Joe's husky hand, Brian's hair sticks every which way, like he just went through the wheat harvester himself.

Getting back to the tour, Grandpa describes in loving detail the all-important farm equipment packed and stored in the buildings. "Farming is all about the tractor attachments, like this here rig," he says. "It's a field cultivator used to turn over soil while killing weeds. Then we attach that-there grain drill to plant our special seed," Grandpa says, pointing to two pieces of machinery that are three times wider than the tractor.

Seeing up close the monster size of these rigs, I understand why these buildings are as big as soccer fields.

"Let's step outside now; I'll show you a farmer's worst enemy," Grandpa Joe says.

Enemies? Earlier I didn't see any wild animals. I picture mountain lions on attack, or maybe a buffalo stampede. Thoughts of creatures and dangers swirl through my mind like a dust-filled twister.

We step outside. No action, though ... just a meadowlark singing. Maybe the enemy is the overgrown grasshoppers that were big as my fist at the diving-board swimming pool. I swear they had fangs. A swarm of those beasts could chomp and destroy every grain of Grandpa Joe's wheat.

"Grandpa Joe, does the enemy have anything to do with North Dakota's 'oldest rock' joke?" Brian asks.

"Rocks are an enemy?" I ask, sticking a finger in my ear and giving it a wiggle to make sure I heard correctly.

"Sure enough," Grandpa Joe snickers. "See those rock piles?" he asks, pointing toward mounds here and there in the field in front of us. For the first time I notice them, scattered among the rows of wheat. The mounds of fist to skull-size rocks look like gravesites of long lost souls.

Do ya wanna tell the joke, Brian?" Grandpa Joe asks. "Hear-tell, it's a whopper of a story."

Brian nods with a grin and recites the joke: "We don't have to pick rocks. The wind just blows them all away." Then he cracks up with laughter. Even Mom lets out a tee-hee-hee.

I scratch my head. Did I miss the punch line? Mom often calls my brother's sense of humor "dry." She says it's quiet and clever, slowly building up and then unexpected at the punch line. It's unlike my humor, which favors a fast remark or a wild comeback. But what do they mean about picking rocks? Maybe it's all too scientific to be funny to me ...

Grandpa Joe notices I'm not laughing. "Hey, young fellow," he says between howls. "This-here land is riddled with rocks, you see. Nasty buggers. One of those rocks left in the ground will wreck a farmer's plow blade faster than a jackrabbit on moonshine. Those rocks you see? Over here ... over there, over there? My great-grandpappy started pickin' and pilin' here when he was a wee-tyke."

Now I understand the joke! The rocks really are an enemy, but Dakota farmers have been picking them for so long they like to tease one another and credit all the rock piles to the fierce wind, which at times is a wicked enemy, too. Sometimes when things go so wrong, you can only laugh at them to endure the struggles. That's what the joke is all about.

"How'd you young bucks like to gather fresh eggs for dinner from the chicken coop?" Grandpa Joe asks, calling the midday meal "dinner" rather than lunch. I learned this tradition at Big Jim's ranch: In the Dakotas the later meal is supper and the noontime meal is dinner.

"Sure, we can pick eggs," I say. I've never gathered eggs before but figure it can't be too tough.

"We don't keep many barnyard critters around here, but farm fresh eggs from chickens are the best," Grandpa Joe says.

"Where are the hens?" Brian asks, naming the female bird that does the laying.

"Skedaddle over here," Grandpa Joe says. "First we need to get the feed from the farmhouse." He heads toward a two-story, weathered old clapboard house sitting on a patch of brown lawn. Judging by the many windows on the house, it looks like there are enough nooks and crannies for a long, drawn-out game of hide-and-seek in there.

We follow Grandpa Joe's lead. Brian and I hop up the two wooden porch steps, and they creak from our weight.

"You boys can wait on the porch swing," Grandpa Joe says.

The wicker-woven swing is rope-tied from the porch awning, and it's big enough for two, maybe three people. Brian and I settle in and call out to Mom. "Come on up," I say, inviting her to join us on the whale of a swing.

"It's too hot for three in a swing. I'll sit over here," Mom says, settling into a comfy old porch chair with faded flower cushions.

Just as Brian and I get the swing rocking, Grandpa Joe comes out with an old coffee can in hand. As he moves down the porch steps, I hear him rattle something inside the can.

"Mosey this way," he says, leading us across the dusty yard of dry grass and then along one of the gravel driveways connecting all the outbuildings.

"The chickens are just on the other side of the next building," Grandpa Joe directs. "Chickens will eat anything, at any time, so when I get to feeding them, hustle into the coop and fetch the eggs."

This seems easy enough, especially since Grandpa Joe gives us each a pail for the eggs. Just before we round the corner, Grandpa Joe says, "Chick, chick, chick." Watching a mountain-size man rattle a coffee can and whimper chicky-chicky makes me giggle.

But before I can laugh very long, a flock of chickens comes running toward us, lickety-split with their wings flapping. A trail of dust is in their wake.

Quickly they detour, targeting me. A dozen harebrained birds peck in rapid fire at my shorts. I spin in circles trying to chase the hens away.

"What's in your britches?" Grandpa Joe barks.

"Huh?" I squeak, barely able to get one syllable to leave my tightening throat. The hens wildly peck my butt. Others tug on my shorts. Shooing them with one hand, I frantically try to hold my shorts up with the other.

"Adam, what's inside your pocket?" Brian shouts over the cackle of crazy clucking.

My pocket? Grandpa Joe said chickens eat anything. I feel like I'm in preschool and forgot to put on my listening cap. Visions of the wide-mouth pelican at Garrison Dam come racing back. I should have learned my lesson with snack food and snapping birds on that trip. This time I'm not so lucky. There's nowhere to escape.

Whirling around the nipping beaks, I thrust my hand in my pocket and yank out strawberry fruit snacks. The flock goes cuckoo! Jabs and stabs, pins and pricks attack my hand.

"Throw the food!" Grandpa Joe cries, wildly rattling the coffee can of food. But the sound is squashed by the squawking hens.

I have enough sense to toss the fruit snacks. The hens race after the strawberry scent, finally leaving me in peace.

"Now hightail it to the coop while the hens are eating," Grandpa Joe calls out. "But put on the muck boots before you go inside."

"Muck boots?" I ask, knowing my head is a bit dazed from the attack of hens. But boots for mud? The prairie is bone dry; it would take a downpour to make mud.

"Over here, Adam," Brian says, handing me a pair of large rubber boots. "Slip them over your shoes."

I decide not listening once today was enough, so I tug on the boots. Brian and I stomp our way into the chicken coop in the oversize boots. Instantly, a foul smell slaps us in the face.

Pee-yew!

I recognize this rotten odor. Bird poop. I thought the seagulls of Michigan were stinky, but here in close quarters and this heat, it's really, really bad. Worse yet, a fan blows the sour smell right up my nose. "Can we kill the fan?" I choke out.

"No way, Adam; the hens need it. The fan helps cool the coop so they can roost and lay their eggs," he says.

With every step the muck boot squishes in chicken poop. Even the scattered straw on the floor that spills from the hen nests doesn't cover up the vast stink or the vast quantity of bird doo-doo. No wonder Grandpa Joe had us put on the boots. Mom would have our hide if we had chicken poop-coated shoes in the van on the ride home.

Moving forward, my left boot gets swallowed up in a pile of poop. Uh-oh ... the boot sticks – and I stumble. Then my shoe slips out of the boot! I wobble, arms waving wildly as I try to keep my balance. I fly forward, and nose-dive toward the poop. My life flashes before my eyes; I'm going to be spread eagle in stink! Hating to see this happen, I squeeze my eyes shut.

Suddenly I feel myself rising straight up again. Brian has me by the shirt and is yanking me upright. Leaning on my brother for support, I slip my shoe back into the mammoth boot. I'm so grateful to Brian for saving me that I could kiss him. But that thought only lasts a second. Instead, I mumble a meek "thank you."

I set the pail on top of a nesting box for a moment so I can yank on my left boot and free it from the pile of poop.

324

Collecting the pail, I notice the hen nesting boxes line one wall and come chest-high to me. Each nest is brimful with straw, spilling out and blowing in the air from the powerful fan. I cough a little, choking on the dust and dirt. No need to worry about making a mess in this pig pen ... er ... chicken coop.

I reach under the closest nest and the straw inside pricks at my tender, recently chicken-pecked hand. Slowly I rummage through the straw, feeling for an egg.

"You'd better go faster, Adam," Brian says. "We need to be done before the chickens finish eating outside."

Oh, yeah! Visions of charging chickens storming the coop push me to gather the eggs at warp speed now. In less than five minutes, I exit the coop with a pail full of eggs.

Outside the yucky coop I gratefully suck in some fresh air. I'm mighty happy about two things: not to be wearing a coat of bird poop, and breathing without gagging on the stench.

But now in the yard, something is different. Very different. It is no longer a frantic scene like during the fight for fruit snacks. Looking around, I watch several chickens casually peck the ground while others simply enjoy strutting, bobbing their heads back and forth, cooing softly. If they were kittens, I'd swear they were purring.

Brian pokes me in the ribs with his elbow. "Look at them now, Adam. It sure makes a big difference when there's no food around."

I look at him cross-eyed, 'cause I can tell he's laughing at me on the inside for the fruit-snack attack.

"We got the eggs," Brian sings out to Grandpa Joe while showing off his full pail.

"Great. I'll cook us dinner," he says. "My family is away on vacation. That's why I'm working the farm alone for a couple days." He takes my bucket of bounty. "Eggs sunny-side up all the way around?"

I nod yes, not knowing what kind of egg that is, but I figure I've caused enough farm trouble for one day. I don't look for trouble, yet somehow it seems to find me.

Grandpa Joe swings the pails and strolls into the farmhouse.

We're still in the yard, and from the corner of my eye, I see a hen cock its head at me so one eye is looking right at me. The dark, beady eye drills at me. Not trusting my brother's claim that no food means no hassle, a new sense of unease creeps up my spine. Quickly, I pull the lining out of a front pocket to show the beast that I don't have any snacks. I swear its eye winks at me. Just then its head begins to bob, rhythmically. Next its feet start to shuffle, almost tap dancing. Grandpa Joe says chickens have a mind of their own. Right now I'm glad this one seems to like me and is doing a square dance a safe distance away.

What I don't pull out to show are the two arrowheads from my back pocket. I shoved them in there before we left Bismarck. Chickens probably don't go hog-wild over rocks anyway. I brought these arrowheads with the fake certificate so I could trick Grandpa Joe into buying them. After winning at the Murder Mystery Dinner Party, I thought the arrowheads might really be lucky charms for me. Then I remembered last summer and the time I thought a seashell from Grandma Barb was magical good luck. It turned out I didn't need a seashell to be lucky.

So now I figure I could take a chance on the arrowheads not being lucky because I'd rather sell them. I could buy some pretty neat things if I had a little cash. In fact, on the entire ride to the farm, I daydreamed about the new videogame I'd purchase with the money. Or maybe I'd buy a Transformer remote-control car. Lucas has a snazzy one. He hits one simple button, and the car goes from street cruiser to assault mode with five darts ready to launch.

"Chow's on," Grandpa Joe eventually calls to us from the farmhouse, snapping me out of my wishful thinking.

We hustle inside to the homey kitchen, where old-fashioned floral wallpaper is everywhere. On a woven rug in the middle of the old wood floor scuffed from years of wear sits a big round table with eight wooden chairs. Four places are set at the table.

"Go wash up," Grandpa Joe says, waving from the kitchen toward a room off to the side.

Brian goes first. As I wait, Grandpa Joe catches my eye. The rough and tough, strong-as-an-ox farmer is draped in an apron with lace around the edges. I have to look away before I break out in laughter.

My eyes zero in on a spot on the tile floor just inches from Grandpa Joe's feet. At first glance I think it's a man-eating spider. But the thing isn't moving. I give a little sigh of relief when I realize it's simply unidentified farm slime.

"I'll pick it up," I say to Grandpa Joe, stepping across and bending down. With my hand inches away, I stop. A yellow eyeball is staring up at me!

"It's an egg," Grandpa Joe says. "Sunny-side up."

"It's perfect," Brian says, coming from the bathroom.

"Except ... it's on the floor!" I say, stating the obvious.

"Smart young fellow," Grandpa Joe says, grinning while waving a spatula in the air. "The little devil slid right out of the pan."

It's no wonder I like this big guy. Trouble mysteriously finds him – just like it does me.

Grandpa Joe scoops up the egg and tosses it in the trash with a king-size laugh. "'Round here we like to play the game forward. What's done is done. It does no good to worry about the past. Just work hard to make it right on the next round."

There are plenty of other hot-from-the-pan eggs for lunch – I mean, dinner. Grandpa Joe serves the eggs with a hearty piece of ham for each of us.

After helping with the dishes, I'm alone with Grandpa in the kitchen. The arrowheads feel heavy in my pocket, but not as heavy as my chest because my heart is hammering. I wrap sweaty fingers around the arrowheads and rub the fake certificate.

"Have you ever seen a real-deal arrowhead?" I blurt out, afraid if I hesitate I can kiss the snazzy remote controlled car good-bye. I yank the two stones out of my pocket.

"Hmm," Grandpa Joe says, staring at the smooth rocks.

I drop the arrowheads into his big hands. The jagged-edged stones look as rough and worn as Grandpa Joe's hard working hands.

"What's the piece of paper?" His crystal-clear blue eyes shine on me like glass marbles.

"Oh, this," I say, starting to unfold the make-believe certificate.

I look up. Suddenly the twinkle in his eye sharply shoots in my direction, like an arrowhead stabbing at me. Trouble surrounds me. Only this time I'm the one who brought it on.

My mouth is dry as chicken coop dust, but I manage to spit out a few words. "This is just scrap paper," I say, noticing the sunny-side-up, floor-model egg on top of the trash. I quickly wad up the fake certificate and shove it in my pocket.

Mom calls from outside, "It's time to say good-bye."

I look at the egg and decide right then and there I want to be like Grandpa Joe. I'm going to play the game forward. When we get back to the apartment, I'll give back to Joey the beloved arrowheads.

Chapter 17

Packing Bags

The shrill of the Spider-Man alarm clock wails through the Bat Cave. I growl as I roll out of bed to shut off the blaring alarm. It's six-forty-five in the morning and it's still summer vacation so why am I forcing my eyes to open? Oh, yeah, the Business Bobcat is back! Mom is worried about making a big art deadline she has this week. In fact, she is so concerned about no Family Time with Brian and me that she went on-line and signed us up for a week of YMCA summer camp. That way she can concentrate during the day and have free time with us in the evening. The schedule is great for Mom, but I'm not sure about me. Summer vacation is all about sleeping in.

Shuffling to the bathroom, I squint in the mirror. With my hair standing in tufts here and there, I look like one of Grandpa Joe's scarecrows. Yes, the flypaper lop-sided hair cut has grown enough that I should be using a comb – but I just slap on a ball cap and call it good.

While brushing my teeth, I remember that the only good thing about this horrid time of day is I'll be meeting my best friend Zach in twenty minutes. Zach's Mom said he could go to Y-camp with Brian and me. I'm filled with pride as a wide-mouth grin spreads across my face. We three older boys will march into Y-camp ready to conquer any sport they throw at us. As a team, we're unstoppable especially in baseball or basketball or soccer or –

"Adam, breakfast is ready," Mom calls from the kitchen.

Two pieces of French toast under my belt, I'm riding co-pilot while Brian and Zach are in the minivan middle row. Shortly, Mom drops us off at Y-Camp.

"Do you want me to go in with you?" Mom asks.

I cringe – worried that Mom will do that hugs-and-kisses thing like when I was little, on the first day of school. "No, I've got the attendance form you printed off. We're good to go," I say, quickly hopping out of the van and shutting the door. I blow her a kiss because I know Mom still likes the mushy stuff.

Mom flashes a full-face smile. Brian and Zach are at my side, and we hike up the steps to the YMCA as Mom drives off.

"Welcome, boys," a teenage camp worker says to us. She is wearing an orange T-shirt with "Healthy Fun – Summer Learning" printed on it, along with nine small Y-Camp symbols and pictures. My eyes zero in on three of them: a soccer ball, a racing boat, a campfire. I pretty much ignore the chef's hat, the art palette, some building blocks, and some other things.

The other symbols should have been a warning sign, but my morning brain is still too sluggish to catch on.

"My name is Isabell," the girl says in a voice that is sweet like sugar-frosted flakes. "The first thing we're going to do is put each of you on different teams."

Different teams?

We can't be split up!

We're like the Three Musketeers. We're inseparable.

Suddenly I'm wide awake. A buzzing begins in my ears and spreads like wildfire through my brain. I vibrate with terror or panic or something.

Before I can blink, Brian and Zach are swooshed away and I'm left with Isabell.

"We have an opening with the water-activity group today," Isabell says, sounding all sugar-frosted-flaky again. "It's a small group taking a bus down to the river. It says on your form, Adam, that you've passed advanced swimming."

Isabell's voice rattles around in my brain, but I can barely make out what she's talking about. I'm still shocked at being separated from my brother and best friend. Conquering Y-Camp was our goal, yes, but together was how we were going to do it. Not separated like this!

"The bus is over here," Isabell explains while moving toward a mini-van with the nine-symbol Y-Camp logo on the side.

My legs won't move, though. Not forward, not backward.

Isabell notices I'm stuck in place. "You can swim ... can't you?" she asks.

I try to answer, but only some strange sound chokes out of my throat.

It must have sounded like a yes because Isabell is opening the door of the van and pointing for me to get in. "Don't forget your backpack with your lunch and swim gear," she adds.

I force myself to step into the middle section of the van, whimpering.

That's when it happens.

"Ah-da-um Moynihan." My name echoes around me. Only one person can make the name Adam into a three syllable word. Yep. It's Glitzy Georgia, the girl three houses down from Zach's. She has a flair for drama and is snooty as all get-out.

"How wonderful! You already know someone at camp," Isabell says, riding co-pilot up front. "Georgia can be your swim buddy."

Wonderful? I'm forced to wake up before seven, I get kidnapped from my brother and best friend, and now I'm harnessed with this girl. Trouble just seems to find me. Like yesterday, I stepped in some dog poop taking the shortcut that I'm not supposed to use across Marge's lawn. It squished in between the grooves of my shoes so tightly that the stink followed me around for hours. That was bad; today is much worse!

From my slumped position in the van, I raise my head enough to see there are four other kids riding along. I don't know any of them. It makes me realize if Hannah is at Y-Camp, she is separated from her sister, too.

The van heads west and stops at the Missouri River. We climb out and Isabell hands us each a booklet on boating and water sports.

"We're jet skiing, today," Isabell says.

Instantly my mood changes! I sit up straight, feeling punchy and tingly all over. I attempt to smother the silly grin that threatens to split my face in two. I've never been on a jet ski, but the roar and power are something I will surely love. Driving a jet ski will be ten times better than riding on a motorcycle.

We gather 'round a picnic table, and Isabell reviews the booklet with us. Sadly, I learn I need to be fourteen years old and have a boating safety certificate before I can operate a jet ski ... which means I'll just be the kid riding behind.

Unfortunately most of the day is spent learning about water safety. Glitzy Georgia is latched to my side, reciting water safety rules at rapid-fire.

"Never ride a jet ski in a designated swim area," she spouts off. "Keep a safe distance from other water users ..."

Isabell thinks Georgia's got gumption, which I think is a fancy word for "teacher's pet."

The actual riding on a jet ski doesn't even happen until way past lunch. This is when I finally dump Georgia.

I take my place at the river bank with a life jacket strapped on. I watch as the jet-ski bobs nearby in the water.

"Adam, you're first," Isabell says, padding the seat behind her as she straddles the machine.

I don't know if I get to ride first because I'm the new kid, but I don't want to jinx my chances so I step right up. Isabell turns the key, and the motor roars to life! With one twist of the accelerator, the jet-ski bucks forward and skates across the water. The wind whips her ponytail in my face. Isabell loops the jet-ski in a circle, and cold, wet spray shoots up, tickling my skin. Life is good again.

At the end of the awesome ride, my legs are still vibrating when I hop off. I'm beginning to like Y-Camp. That is until we get back to the building at the end of the day.

"I had a cooking class," Brian gripes.

"And I had bead-making," Zach snips.

"You've got to kidding!" I whine, feeling my day sinking fast again.

"Well, just wait. You'll have to do them tomorrow, little brother," Brian says.

I moan and bury my head in my hands. Then I hear it. A snicker. I open my eyes and see Brian and Zach struggling to keep a straight face.

"Adam! It's a joke! We had karate and robotic Legos," Brian says with a big smile.

"Yeah, look at the list," Zach says, showing me pages of Y-Camp activities. "We can pick our own things to do."

The rest of the week I rock out with Frisbee golf, dodge ball, archery, and soccer – lots of cool stuff. I continue to be separated from Brian and Zach each day, but at least I don't see Glitzy Georgia again.

*   *   *

Now it's Saturday, our last night in Bismarck. A pup tent glows in the dusky light like a giant Halloween jack-o-lantern. I've waited all day for this special evening – to sleep out under the stars. To pretend I am General Custer. To pretend the backyard at Mom's place is the battlefield at Little Big Horn.

"Look how dark it's getting back here," Brian says. "I forgot the streetlights are only in the front of the house. Did you think it would be this dark?"

"It crossed my mind," I say, knowing I've pictured this campout a hundred times. I've been dreaming about sleeping outside, nightly, without grown-ups.

Then from behind we hear a clickity-clack of footsteps, followed by a big grunt. We turn and see Joey hauling a jam-packed suitcase across the cement steps.

"I'm ready to be a real cowboy and sleep in a tent," he says, dressed in his Davy Crocket coonskin cap and his red cowboy boots, of course.

This little guy is one proud cowboy.

"So why the big suitcase?" I ask.

"I wanted to pack my most important treasures," Joey says, giving the heavy suitcase one more tug. It pops open, exploding all the things Joey thinks he needs for one night of camping: superhero action figures, baseball cards, yo-yos, a spin top, a Nerf football.

Joey hunts through his overflowing suitcase for something in particular. "This is my favorite. A real cowboy never goes anywhere without a harmonica," Joey says as he presses it to his lips and wheezes in and out.

I cover my ears. Joey doesn't sound anything like Papa, who loves country Western music and plays the harmonica very well. "Can you play Sneaky Snake?" I ask, naming a favorite song.

Joey puffs on the harmonica, but the tune doesn't improve. We won't be singing along to this cowboy.

Suddenly Joey stops screeching on the harmonica. Instead, his eyes lock onto us. It's the first time he's stopped fiddling with his gear to take a look at us.

"Hey, I thought this was a cattle-drive campout. But you guys don't look like cowboys," he says.

Brian and I are dressed like soldiers.

"It's camouflage," Brian says.

"Yeah, Mom gave us the outfits as a going-away gift to take back to Michigan." I explain to Joey. "We picked spy wear so we can hide among all the trees back home."

Tomorrow we fly back to Dad's house. Thinking about leaving turns my inside to jelly. Saying good-bye is never easy. It helps knowing Mom will be coming to visit us fairly soon. She never misses our first soccer game. And now, with Joey's silliness, it's like he's helping to candy-coat this tough time.

"Gee, Adam, I'd like some army clothes, too," Joey says. "Do you think I could come to Michigan?"

This kid is young enough to think anything is possible.

"Hey, little guy," I say, putting my arm on his shoulder. "Michigan is a long ways away. Besides, you wouldn't like it much there."

"Why not?" Joey asks. His head drops, and his big blue eyes fill with water.

"Because you couldn't cheer for the Minnesota Vikings," I say, naming Joey's favorite football team.

"Why not?"

"When you live in Michigan, you cheer for the Detroit Lions," I say.

"Oh, I'd never cheer for the Lions. Not even for cool soldier gear," Joey says, his teary eyes disappearing as he dives back into his suitcase, shifting and sorting through the heap of treasures. His fun-loving spirit takes away the punch-in-the-gut feeling I have from talking about leaving. Besides, how can I feel sad when Joey pulls out a jar with a fat, slimy critter squirming inside of it?

"It's a baby snake," Joey tells us with glee as he opens the lid and digs his hand inside. He pulls out the brown, wiggly thing, letting it crawl across his palm. What a kid! This is a worm, not a baby snake.

Since this little guy believes a worm is a baby snake, I think he'll believe eerie ghost stories, too. I can't decide which scary story to tell first when it's "lights out" in the pup tent. I'm full of confidence now that Marge had all the answers to the ghostly happenings in the shed.

"Where's your brother?" I ask.

"Zach should be here any minute. He's bringing our sleeping gear. I couldn't carry it all in my suitcase," Joey says.

Seconds later, it's not Zach who comes around the corner. No such luck. It's Hannah and Glitzy Georgia.

I stare at them open-mouthed, wondering who invited them.

"Oh, hey girls," Joey says all yippy-skippy. "It's swell you could come."

"Where's Zach?" Glitzy Georgia asks, making the "z" in Zach's name sound like a series of "s" sounds like the hiss of a snake. And not a baby snake like Joey's worm.

339

Just then, Annie comes bounding around the corner and starts barking at Hannah and Georgia.

"Hey, sweet pup," Hannah coos as she drops to her knees and reaches out to pet Annie. The dog licks her fingers and then rolls over, waiting for belly rubs from this new human. Hannah giggles and pets Annie's tummy.

Next, Zach comes around the corner, carrying two pillows and some lightweight blankets.

"Everyone's here, so let the party begin!" Joey exclaims.

I suck in air and take two giant steps backwards. "What party?" I ask, doubting I can squeeze any more ugliness into my response. "I thought this was a cow-BOYS campout," I say, making sure the word "boys" is loud and clear.

"Oh, Adam, this campout is for you boys. We're just here because we told Joey how you won the arrowheads back," Hannah says. "He thought we should celebrate by watching you do more magic. We love magic!" She sparkles with a big smile as excitement takes over her face.

"Well, um, I don't know a lot of tricks," I say, suddenly feeling a bit shy.

"Then show us the disappearing-dime trick again," Georgia says. "It was awesome."

Responding to her enthusiasm, an unfamiliar feeling of lightness rises in my chest. Could this be pride? I cock my head. Did Glitzy Georgia just pay me a compliment? The girl who blasted out the boat safety answers before I could get a chance to utter a sound.

I reach in my pocket to check for coins, but all I pull out is the fake arrowhead certificate and a piece of beef jerky left over from Y-Camp. The paper falls to the ground. Annie is quick to snatch it up and whisk it away. In seconds the pup has the paper gobbled up. It must have had jerky juice on it.

"What was that?" Georgia asks.

"I hope it wasn't important," Brian says.

"Nah. It was something I don't need anymore," I say, remembering I want to play the game forward and make things right. To do this, I should skip fooling others, which means I don't need the fake arrowhead certificate. "It looks like I don't have any coins to do the disappearing trick," I say.

"That's too bad, Ah-da-um," Glitzy Georgia says, but this time when she turns my name into a three-syllable word, it sings like a sweet song instead of an irritating one. Then she adds, "I know a lot about rules and regulations but not much about fun magic stuff. Maybe you could teach me some other time."

I can't believe Glitzy Georgia is admitting she can be a smarty-pants and now wants to play nice. Maybe she's like Marge and Butterscotch and it takes her a while to warm up to new kids. Perhaps I should give her a chance. Besides, it's how to play the game forward. What's done is done, after all.

"Sure, maybe we can do some stuff when Brian and I come back for winter break," I say.

Just then Annie yaps. But it becomes more of a cough. Then the dog gags and spits.

"Oh no! Annie's barfing!" Joey cries.

Annie throws up near Joey's cowboy boots. Brian crouches down to inspect the mess.

"There's your note, Adam" he says, pointing.

"Roger that," Zach agrees as he hunches over the slimy heap.

The black ink is blurry on the mushy slobber-soaked paper wad.

"You sure you don't need this note?" Zach asks, poking his nose closer to the soggy mess and adjusting his eyeglasses. "We might be able to save some of it. We could de-code Operation Slime."

"Nah, I'm, good," I say. The blurry ink tells me I'm doing the right thing.

Just then the porch light flicks on and Mom comes out the door. "It's nine o'clock and time to call it a night," she says.

"Oh, hi, Mrs. Moynihan," the girls say. "We need to be heading home, anyway. We'll see you Michigan boys for winter break. Goodnight, Zach. Toodle-oo, Joey."

Glitzy Georgia and Hannah round the corner and are out of sight. It feels good to have two more North Dakota friends to visit.

"Okay, boys, I'll take the lantern inside now," Mom says. Then she scoops Brian and me into a quick goodnight hug, minus the kisses, thank goodness. Next she heads into the apartment and turns off the porch light.

"At last, the campout can begin!" I cheer.

We snuggle into the pup tent, bumping into one another in the pitch darkness. Annie yips and bounces about, tickling us.

"I can't see my hand," Joey says, his voice a little shaky.

Without wasting a minute, I'm ready to blurt out an eerie story. "Listen," I pause. "I hear the ghost of General Custer." I hesitate again. Since the boys can't see my face, I make a hissing sound. "It's coming from inside Mad Witch's shed," I say, using a hoarse voice.

I nudge Brian to get him to play along with the ghost story.

"The shed has … sharp … pointed … pitch forks," he says, snarling out the sounds.

Silence.

"Joey?" I ask into the blackness. No sound from the little guy. "Hey, Joey. Are you awake?" I jiggle Joey's shoulder. Then a full-blown snore rattles the tent around us.

"He's sound asleep!" Brian says, amazed at how quickly the little guy "gave up the ghost."

"Hey, Zach. Can you wake up your brother?" I ask.

He doesn't answer. The only sound is Joey's wheeze and heavy breathing.

"Wow. Zach's asleep, too, Adam!" Brian says. "So much for your spooky ghost stories. I'm going to sleep, too, I guess." And with that, I hear Brian roll over. In minutes his snoring fills the tent.

Annie's still awake for now, and she licks my face. At least one cowpoke is around to enjoy the campout, even though she happens to be a dog. But soon, I'm falling asleep, too.

*　*　*

The next morning I see Zach next door, dragging a big box.

"What are you doing?" I ask.

"We packed old clothes for charity," Zach says. "I have to load it in the van."

"Let me help," I say.

"Roger that," Zach says, squatting down. We shove our hands under the bottom and struggle to wrap our arms around the sides of the huge box.

"Ready, set … lift," Zach says. The box tips sideways. The lid pops open, and a puff of red fabric rolls out. "What's this?" I ask, holding up what looks like a heavy-duty sleeping bag with arms.

"A down jacket," Zach says.

I slide the jacket on and zip up the front. The sleeves stick straight out. There is so much fluff; my arms won't hang at my side.

"You look like you're ready to be Santa's helper at the North Pole," Brian says, coming up the driveway from the apartment.

"Who would wear this?" I ask Zach, trying to walk in the wad of puff. I stumble and then tumble down the driveway.

344

Zach chases after me. "It's my old winter jacket," he says.

Looking up from the ground, I ask, "Why do you wear such a thick jacket?"

Zach gives me a blank stare. He doesn't say anything. He scratches his head and then he reaches his hand out to help me off the ground.

But I stay put, distracted by the fact that I'm roasting in this heavy-duty jacket. I pat the sides of the jacket, thinking there might be solar panels built in and sunbeams are heating me up. "I'm so hot I feel like a kernel of corn ready to pop," I say.

"You wouldn't feel that hot if you were wearing that jacket in December," Zach says.

"What happens in December?" I ask.

"It's winter."

"I know it's winter. We have winter in Michigan. But I don't have a coat like this," I say.

"How do you stay warm?" Zach asks, like he can't believe I've never seen a puff-ball coat that makes you look like the Abominable Snowman and roasts you like a marshmallow at a campfire.

"I stay warm in a ski jacket," I say, not believing Zach doesn't wear a normal winter jacket.

Mom comes up the drive and is carrying our backpacks for the trip to the airport. "Getting ready for your Christmas visit, Adam?" she asks.

Now I stare at Mom. Is she as crazy as Zach? "Do people really wear a jacket like this?" I ask her.

"Sure do. North Dakota winters are bitterly cold. Maybe Zach has an extra jacket you'll be able to borrow," Mom says as she casually tosses the backpacks into the van. "We need to get your suitcases loaded now."

I'm still lying on the ground in the Artic sweat suit as I watch Brian and Mom head back to the apartment. If I don't get up off the driveway, I will be left for the snowplow to scrape away next winter. Then Brian will be traveling alone and telling the tales. I can handle Brian being a storyteller, but I don't want to miss out on the thrill of an adventure so I start to scoop myself up off the ground.

As I struggle to sit forward, Joey wanders over and gazes down into my face, nose to nose.

"I'm ready to play army," the little guy says.

Joey is dressed in green shorts and a T-shirt. What's different, for once, is that he's not wearing his famous red cowboy boots! Instead, I notice oversize gym shoes are tugged onto the wrong feet. They're laced up tight and have been scribbled on with brown and green markers. In fact, on closer look, I see Joey has colored his arms and legs with marker too. I guess Joey found camouflage one way or another.

With Joey's help, I get up off the ground and slip off Zach's beastly jacket. I guess I'll find out in December if I need a funny, fluffy sleeping bag for a winter jacket.

"Hey, Joey, I don't have much time before we leave for Michigan, but I want to give you something," I say, reaching into my pocket for the arrowheads, having decided to play the game forward and make things right. "Joey ..." my voice trails off, then drops to a whisper, "there really isn't a ghost of Cus–"

The little tyke wrinkles his nose and his freckles begin to dance, but out of nowhere, as I am saying the name "Custer," his smile collapses and a serious pout begins. His lower lip curls and begins to quiver.

Then I remember another lesson I learned from Grandpa Joe about the rocks in the fields. The rocks that are everywhere in the fields are so difficult for the farmers that after years of struggles, they decide to laugh and joke about them. They learn to make the best of a tough situation.

"What, Adam? Did you hear Custer's ghost again?" Joey asks me, his worried eyes searching mine.

"I sure did hear Custer's ghost," I say, deciding to make the best of a tough situation. "And he told me to give you the arrowheads for safe keeping!" I take the two stones from my pocket and place them in Joey's hand.

I see Joey's smile go so wide and toothy that it seems like he might split his cheeks. The top of the little guy's head only comes to the tip of my chin, but I realize friendship doesn't have much to do with inches, or age, or anything else. I give Joey's brown mop-top hair a muss.

From the back yard we hear a loud squeak. It's the sound of the rusty wheels of Marge Witt's push-cart, onto which

Brian has loaded The Beast – my jam-packed black travel bag. The combination lock holding the latch from busting open clangs as it scrapes the ground.

"The Beast is just too heavy to carry," Brian says as he steers the cart toward the van. "Mom's right behind, Adam. It's time to leave for the airport."

My stomach feels like I've been slammed with a dodge ball. It feels like this every time Brian and I say good-bye when a visit ends. But like the farmers and their field stones, I can fight this challenge – and even make it fun. It helps knowing I'll be back soon enough to joke around with my friends again. Besides, next time I'll be smarter about what to pack and maybe only need a regular-size suitcase.

Beached in a Camper: Three Weeks Surviving an Older Brother, Bug Bites, Water Bombs and a Girl.

If you enjoyed <u>Trouble Out West,</u> then you will be delighted with <u>Beached in a Camper.</u> The story revolves around family fun at the lake in the summer. You'll laugh at two brothers as they stumble throughout a campground into quicksand, seagull poop and a handful of sticky situations. Solving a riddle from Grandma brings younger brother, Adam, the luck he needs – sometimes. Of course, older brother, Brian, with friends Red, Freckles, and Hulk, manage to land smack dab in the middle of things, too. From tree forts to frog warts, the kids are in for mayhem and mishaps along the shores of Lake Michigan.

Purchase Kate's first book at www.amazon.com or www. moynihangallery.com.

Author Kate Moynihan –

Kate juggles her creative juices, a retail shop, and her eighty-eight year old mom, all the while, writing family stories, adding a twist or two ... maybe three.

You can visit her art gallery in downtown Holland, Michigan and watch her toss vivid bits of paint onto oil canvases and watercolor paintings. She's been hanging her hat in her shop for twenty-two years. Find out more about Kate at www.moynihangallery.com and visit her blog: The Artsy Shopkeeper.